Shad Hadid

AND THE ALCHEMISTS OF ALEXANDRIA

Praise for

SHAD HADID AND THE ALCHEMISTS OF ALEXANDRIA

"*Shad Hadid and the Alchemists of Alexandria* is a heartwarming,
mouthwatering tale packed to the brim with humor, action,
and culinary delights. Alchemizing the magic school trope with
traditional Lebanese culture, author George Jreije creates a rich,
one-of-a-kind world that readers won't want to leave."

—**SOMAN CHAINANI**, *New York Times* bestselling author
of the School for Good and Evil series

"A heartfelt adventure rooted deeply in culture,
Shad Hadid tugged at my heartstrings, made me laugh,
and dazzled me with the ultracool magic-science of alchemy!"

—**XIRAN JAY ZHAO**, #1 *New York Times* bestselling author of
Iron Widow and the Zachary Ying series

"Shad Hadid is a hero unlike any other. His journey of friendship
and self-discovery satisfied me as much as a good dessert."

—**SARAH KAPIT**, author of *Get a Grip, Vivy Cohen!*

"Shad pulls readers in with his sharp wit and delicious baked goods,
taking them on an action-packed adventure filled with intrigue
and hijinks. Get ready to dive into the immersive world of alchemy!"

—**ADRIANNA CUEVAS**, author of the Pura Belpré
Honor Book *The Total Eclipse of Nestor Lopez*

"A magical and enthralling adventure, George Jreije conjures a truly
magnificent tale of intrigue, loss, humor, and, most importantly, the courage
of a young boy to fully recognize his potential as a powerful alchemist.
I can't WAIT for Arab boys to get the representation they deserve!"

—**JAMAR J. PERRY**, author of *Cameron Battle and the Hidden Kingdoms*

"In this action-packed, funny, heartfelt story, Shad stands up
to everyone from middle school bullies to necromancers.
Here comes a brave new hero that kids will adore!"

—**KATIE ZHAO**, author of *The Dragon Warrior* and the Winnie Zeng series

GEORGE JREIJE

Shad Hadid

AND THE ALCHEMISTS OF ALEXANDRIA

HARPER
An Imprint of HarperCollinsPublishers

Library of Congress Cataloging-in-Publication Data
Names: Jreije, George, author.
Title: Shad Hadid and the alchemists of Alexandria / by George Jreije.
Description: First edition. | New York : Harper, an imprint of
HarperCollins Publishers, [2022] | Audience: Ages 8-12. | Audience:
Grades 4-6. | Summary: After twelve-year-old Lebanese-American
Shad Hadid discovers he is an Alchemist, he receives an invitation to
the Alexandria Academy where he discovers not everything is as it
seems and shadowy figures are lurking around every corner.
Identifiers: LCCN 2022001907 | ISBN 9780063094819 (hardcover)
Subjects: CYAC: Alchemy–Fiction. | Schools–Fiction. | Friendship–
Fiction. | Lebanese Americans–Fiction. | LCGFT: Novels.
Classification: LCC PZ7.1.J825 Sh 2022 | DDC [Fic]–dc23
LC record available at https://lccn.loc.gov/2022001907

Typography by Molly Fehr
22 23 24 25 26   PC/LSCH   10 9 8 7 6 5 4 3 2 1
❖

First Edition

For Mom and Dad,
who sacrificed everything so that I might dream.

Chapter 1

There was no such thing as magic.

But if there was, it would be the cakes on display through the bakery window. Freshly baked namoura cakes, to be exact. Soft on the inside, crisp on the outside, and sugary sweet all over.

A rosewater scent wafted from an open window and I sidestepped over to ogle a tray of baklava. Lucky for me, the only Arabic bakery in Maine, Halwa Heaven, was just a block from Portland Middle School. My last class had finally gotten out, and holy cannoli, was I glad to be done with pre-algebra.

I leaned in closer, licking my lips. Inside, rows and rows of pastries were stacked on top of each other, all fresh and ready to be eaten. I *needed* a taste. Something brushed against my shoulder and I sprang around, suddenly aware of the drool rolling down my chin. I quickly wiped my mouth with the back of my hand.

It was an old lady holding a cane. "Sorry, young man," she said, offering a wrinkly smile and reaching for the door handle.

I hurried forward to help her. I held the door open long enough for her to get inside and, just when I was ready to close it behind her, the baker appeared.

Clad in a white jacket with his belly falling over an apron, he shot me a disapproving stare. I was jealous of that belly. Sure, I had some pudge, but nothing like his. One day, I'd eat enough sweets to earn a sumo stomach too.

"How many times must I tell you *not* to stand outside my bakery?" he asked, emphasizing his *k*'s in a thick accent. My teta did the same thing. Unlike her, though, the baker curled his lips into a deep frown and said, "You are bad for business."

I ignored him like I always did and stepped back over to the open window, continuing to stare inside. The baker's assistants hurried back and forth, helping the woman and the other customers with their orders of mouthwatering baklava, crispy knafeh, and everything in between. I remembered my family shop in Lebanon, all the customers asking for help in Arabic, and my baba's hospitality. How he would welcome all types of people, if only for a sip of tea to warm the belly. It sure used to warm mine.

Watching the happenings in the bakery felt like stepping into a time machine, except with loads of sugar. But just as the heavenly smell of pies began to drift out, the baker slammed the window shut in my face.

I stuck my tongue out. One day, my bakery would be right next to his, only bigger and with ten times the sweets. Closing my eyes, I pictured the baker's white hat atop my curly black hair, his spotless jacket buttoned up to my neck.

The only problem with my plan was that I had no money and still lived with my grandmother. She only spoke a little English and liked it when I called her Teta instead of Grandma. Teta was too old to teach me about recipes and ingredients from Baba's shop. She was too old for a lot of things.

"Figs, I need to cook dinner!" I said, realizing that Teta would be waiting on me. "Oh, I'm such a bahle."

I'd turned to head home when, out of nowhere, a wet blob smacked the back of my neck. It stung as I reached around, wondering if a pigeon had just used my head for its toilet seat. My fingers ran across something gooey. A closer look revealed a yellowish slime.

"An egg?" My stomach felt woozy as I flicked away the goo.

Laughter came from across the street. My throat burned at the sight of Sarah Decker, our middle school's nastiest bully. Two boys and a girl, each as tall and imposing as her, stood there too. All of them were in my sixth-grade class, and they were laughing.

Laughing at me.

Teta had always told me that demons were real, and Sarah was definitely one of them, or at least a distant cousin. Exhibit A: a carton in her hand with a single egg missing, the one that she'd just launched at me. Exhibit B: her signature devilish gap-toothed grin, pasted on her face right now.

Maybe that was why I hadn't felt guilty about yesterday, when I stuffed her backpack with used paper towels from the bathroom trash. Since she'd come with three of the biggest, most frightening twelve-year-olds at Portland Middle School, she'd probably taken my prank the wrong way. Well, since I'd meant to annoy her, I guess she took it the *right* way.

In my defense, she started it . . . two years ago. We were friends before then, but her parents didn't like that I wasn't born in America. When she told me, I said her parents were a couple of moldy eggplants. Then she shoved me into a locker. But I, Shad Hadid, never do two things: rely on anyone else, *or* let a bully mess with me and get away with it. Thus, our rivalry was born.

Sarah pulled another egg from the carton and turned to her friends. "Did everyone see that throw? Perfect angle, just the right velocity . . . and score!"

Sarah is a science and math whiz, which makes her different from the other bullies, especially since she is smart enough to turn basically anything into a lean-mean-wedgie-machine. Her friends, on the other hand, aren't so smart.

"What's a velo-city?" asked Anthony Clarke, captain of the wrestling team.

Meanwhile, Catherine Lee reached for an egg only to have her hand slapped away by Sarah. "Let me have a try," said Catherine. "It's not like he can run–he's slower than a camel! They have those where you're from, right, Shad?"

Camel? The insult made my skin crawl. "You fig-heads have it all geographically wrong," I shouted. "There aren't any camels in Lebanon. I don't pay attention in school, and even I know that!"

Sarah and her friends laughed even harder. "Fig-head?" she asked. "Who says that?"

"Someone who can actually read," I shot back. "Unlike *you.*"

All of them quieted and Sarah's face went red, and she picked up another egg. Not good.

"You think you're so funny, huh?" she shouted, rushing to the other side of the street. *My* side. "Since you love food, how about I make an omelet out of your head!"

She brought her arm back to throw, but I dashed down the street. Behind me, I heard the *thwack* of an egg breaking against the bakery glass and then the door swinging open. One of the baker's assistants stepped outside and shouted at Sarah and her friends. She called Sarah something in Arabic that, had it come out of my mouth, would have made Teta slap me into another dimension.

My Sultan of Slam wrestling backpack thudded against my butt as I raced down the block. Sarah had already crossed the street with her friends, only twenty feet away and gaining on me with each stride. I hadn't thought past calling her a fig-head, but what was I supposed to do? They were picking on me. Saying nothing was worse than saying the wrong thing, right?

Egg after egg started raining down. Some soared by while others painted the wall in yellow. One egg hit the sidewalk right next to me and bits of yolk splattered onto my sneakers.

"You can't outrun us!" said Sarah.

She was right. While I could barely even run, Sarah could both run *and* throw. But I was darn good at hide-and-seek. While eggs smashed all over the pavement, I rounded the building that connected several stores to the bakery. An alley I could hide in was up ahead. Now, I hadn't outgrown what Teta called my *baby fat*, and the alley was pretty narrow. Still, I sucked in my stomach and squeezed inside.

My fear of Sarah totally outweighed my fear of tight spaces. Although my hands were trembling, legs getting noodly, I snaked out through the long alley and ...

"Holy cannoli," I whispered.

Directly ahead, where the back of the bakery should be, was a large, colorful garden. Well, more like a mini-jungle. I approached a few fruit trees: oranges, bananas, and even figs. Purple and brown and other weird-colored flowers sprang up in the corners, while moss climbed up the building's walls.

I used the short lead I had on Sarah to catch my breath. Between the scent of sweat and the rotting egg on my neck, the aroma of the flowers was hard to notice. I was still wobbly on my feet, and when I reached back to flick off the yolk, the alley darkened.

I glanced up at a large black figure hovering over me as if descending from the sky. A shadow.

I'd once convinced myself that the scarf hanging from my closet door was a ghost. I'd refused to leave my bed until Baba put it around his neck and started dancing the dabke. I wiped my eyes, sure this was some kind of similar mistake.

Nope. The shadow was real, and it had no face or shape.

I jerked away from what looked like a large batch of chocolate pudding that had learned to walk. It drew closer. I kicked it, but my foot passed right through.

"You are trespassing where you do not belong," it said with a raspy voice that sounded hollow and lifeless.

I tried to scream, but could only muster a faint croak.

"Who's trespassing?" I asked, looking around, my hands

shaking, knees wobbling. "Not me, I was just... just leaving!"

I didn't believe in magic, or monsters, or any of the things from the stories Teta told me growing up. But there was no denying this thing—whatever it was—was real, and terror gripped me. Breathing became harder. Each step back felt like lifting a shoe full of bricks. All I could do was keep moving away until I thudded against a wall and crumpled to the ground.

The shadow hovered closer and closer. Sitting there, shaking, I held my legs and watched it grow as tall as a basketball hoop and wider than a billboard. It blocked out all daylight. I was done. Finished. Pooped. It raised a shadowy tentacle and I shoved my head between my knees, unable to look.

But as the shadow brushed my cheek, a shrill cry pierced my ears.

"Begone, necromancer!" shouted a new voice.

Boom!

An explosion shook the ground beneath my feet. I looked up and the shadow vanished. Sunlight poured back into the alley, onto my face, and lit up the lush, colorful garden.

Just a second ago, that *thing* had cornered me. Now there was a man who wore a faded navy coat that ran down to the ankles, too-big glasses, and had wild hair that shot out in every direction. His skin was tanned like mine, giving him the look of an Arab Albert Einstein. He also wore an unusual belt beneath his coat, pouches hanging from all around it. And one veiny hand held a leash for his pet . . . salamander?

He furrowed an eyebrow and asked, "Who in the elements are you, and what are you doing in my alley?"

Chapter 2

"**Answer my question**," he said sharply. He adjusted his thick-rimmed glasses, the space between his bushy eyebrows creasing. "How did you find this alley? It should be hidden."

"Well, it's not," I said, my voice still shaky.

"Don't you lie to me," he said. "I have Truth Dust and I am not afraid to use it."

Truth Dust? I had to admit I was curious, but not enough that I didn't want to rush home after encountering a walking, talking shadow. And I could hear the video from our last school assembly repeating the words *stranger danger* in my head.

"This is not a public alley," he said. "Besides, children should not be wandering into alleys alone. You ought to stay close to your friends."

I'm *not* a child. And I hate when people tell me I should be with friends. Always, they say *friends this* or *friends that*.

"I do perfectly fine on my own," I snapped.

"Clearly you had that necromancer handled." He rolled his eyes and stuck a hand into one of the several pouches hanging around his belt. He fed whatever he pulled out to the salamander.

"That's what you call the shadowy thing that attacked me?" I asked. "A necromancer?"

The old man ignored me. "Go back the way you came, boy. Parents shouldn't let their kids wander around like this."

The mention of my parents lit an angry fire in me. This man didn't know that right after Baba closed our family shop and brought us to America five years ago, he and his father, my jiduh, died in a car accident. He also didn't know that my mama had left Baba seven years ago, back when I was just four years old. Now she lived in Lebanon with my evil stepfamily and I was sure she'd forgotten I even existed. Sometimes, I tried calling her old number, but not once had she ever picked up.

Yet all my anger simmered to fear at the thought of the monster. *Necromancer.* Just the name of it gave me goose bumps. And I might have demanded to know more about it if the guy didn't have a salamander the size of my arm.

"I'll be out of here in a second, Gramps."

"Gramps? Are you calling me old?"

"You bet your tush I am. And you better believe that—"

A scraping sound came from the alley. I twisted around and almost screamed. It was Sarah, her mischievous grin stretched from ear to ear. She and her friends had found me, and they were squeezing their way through.

"Hey, you've gotta help me with these . . . oh figs!"

The old man and his salamander were gone. So much for adult intervention.

"I *do* know how to read," said Sarah. "You're going to wish you'd stayed home today!"

I couldn't decide what was more terrifying: being cornered by that shadow monster or Sarah Decker. I needed to think fast if I didn't want to get covered in sticky eggs. A sudden memory crossed my mind, a trick my jiduh would use to keep cats away from our shop in Lebanon.

I reached down and grabbed a clump of dirt beneath my sneakers. From inside my backpack, I reached into my Persian Punisher wrestling lunch box for a salt packet. My fingers were shaking from the pressure. I ripped open the packet, mixed in the salt with the dirt, and spat into them both to create a mushy, stinky clump. It was disgusting and perfect and missing just one more key ingredient . . .

Leaning in like Jiduh would when making his stink bombs, I imagined the most disgusting smell: my used school gym clothes. I whispered the words into my hand, following Jiduh's instructions. He'd always said that thoughts were just as real as any other ingredient.

Sarah was nearly out of the alley, her grin now devilish. But her expression changed to surprise when she saw me smiling back.

"I'm not the one who's cornered," I said, aiming. "You are!"

I chucked my stink bomb as hard as I could into the alley and it hit one of the walls right in front of Sarah. She was only a few steps away, a full foot taller than me and much scarier up close. But then the clump began to work its magic, because all the kids in the alley stopped.

"What's that smell?" asked the girl behind Sarah, scrunching up her nose.

Her friends turned and ran back the way they'd come. Sarah gagged, but she held out the longest, giving me a frown that said we weren't finished. Then she hurried down the other end of the alley and disappeared.

I looked at the stinky clump, more than a little proud of myself. When I told other students that my baba once owned a shop in Lebanon, I never mentioned what *kind* of shop. We sold unusual ingredients. Not spices and vegetables but ground-up flowers, animal intestines, stuff like that. We also sold charms. Knickknacks that Baba said would keep away demons or help a person run faster. Of course, those were for the gullible. The only exception was the stink bombs. Those, like the bakery sweets, were as real as it got.

Ding!

My watch chimed. It was 4:00 p.m.–I really needed to hurry home. Teta would be waiting on me for dinner. But I couldn't go back through the alley or I'd die from the stink. I glanced around the garden and stiffened up like a statue.

"By the elements," said the strange old man. He'd reappeared, standing with his giant salamander. "I saw what you did to those children. Who taught you that?"

Scrambling back, I asked, "Where did you come from? You . . . you vanished like a ghost earlier!"

He bent over and laughed, sounding younger now, his navy-blue coat drifting with his movements. He reached into a pouch and flung a green powder into my face. I stumbled away and sneezed. The powder went up my nose and into my mouth, tasting and smelling foul. It burned my eyes, and everything went blurry.

Things transformed all around me. The brick wall beyond this mini-jungle wasn't a brick wall, but the bakery. A back door hung wide open behind one of the orange trees. And the old man . . . he wasn't so old anymore. His hair darkened from gray to black, he still wore the same coat and belt, and his belly began to grow. The salamander wasn't a salamander anymore either, but a cat licking its butt.

The man's changing face was the weirdest part of it. I wiped my eyes just to be sure I was seeing clearly, but he looked exactly like . . .

"You're the baker!" I said.

My breath got quicker and quicker until I was hyper-ventilating. This was just a dream, right? People can't change the size of their bellies. I'd been trying to make mine bigger for years.

The baker snickered, lifting the cat into his arms. "What has gotten you so wound up, boy? I simply used a decanter that undid my Illusion Alchemy."

"You used a what? De-cant-or?" I didn't understand. "A . . . alchemy?"

I'd read stories about magic and fairies. Alchemy kind of fell into that category–the one for, you know, *stories*. Maybe he'd read one too many of those. I couldn't think of any other explanation for what was going on.

"Ah, now I see how you were able to walk right through," he said, bending to pick up a palm-sized metal block. Beside it lay a broken line of string. "My Walling Charm fell off the alley entrance. By the elements, just wait until I get my hands on those squirrels. . . ."

The alley around me blurred while he held the strange block in his hands. When I leaned closer to see what made it so special, the baker raised it high up above my head.

"I'll fix this later," he said, pocketing the cube. "Now

tell me what you know of alchemy."

"Alchemy?" I asked. "You mean the stink bomb?"

"By the elements, of course that's what I mean. Only, alchemists call it an Odor Charm rather than a *stink bomb*, and you got the key ingredients wrong. Count yourself lucky the alchemy still worked." He picked up my Persian Punisher lunch box, and when I reached for it, he drew it back. "Tell me, what is your name?"

I puffed my chest and said, "My name is Roger McLardface."

"McLardface?"

He narrowed his eyes but held out his hand for me to shake. His cat made a noise that sounded like a growl. Hesitantly, I reached out and he gripped my fingers tight. Even after a couple shakes, he didn't let go.

Then, before I could jerk free, he threw another powder from one of his pouches into my face. I swallowed some and breathed in the rest through my nose.

"I warned you I would use my Truth Dust, didn't I?" he said, letting go of my hand. "Now, what is your real name?"

"It's Shad," I said, coughing and sneezing. "Shad Hadid."

"And I am Kahem," he said, handing me back my lunch box once I'd stopped coughing. "That Truth Dust scrambles your brain cells so you can tell no lies. It shall last for the next thirty minutes."

I took a step back toward the alley. Truth Dust, shape-shifting, necromancers, secret gardens . . . talk about creepy.

"Where did you get Truth Dust?" I asked, my throat as dry as the Sahara Desert. "That stuff tastes like burnt falafel."

A cloud passed overhead as the baker took a step closer, the alley darkening around us. "Anything is possible for an alchemist," he said. "I am one of the last in the world. And young Shad, you are an alchemist too."

Chapter 3

I couldn't believe what Kahem was saying. Apparently, I had this strange ability, one that allowed me to take random ingredients like dirt and turn them into amazing things.

"So, you're saying alchemists can do magic," I said. "And that I am one of them because I made a stink bomb?"

Kahem sighed. "Not magic, *alchemy*. Listen, I will be gone on private business for a day or two, but if you were to come by this Saturday . . . well, I may have time to explain in more detail."

I didn't know if that old majnoon had expected me to believe his nonsense, but I was eleven. I wasn't born yesterday.

The "necromancer" was likely some kind of projection, a trick to scare normal people like me out of our lunch money. And his transformation from an old man . . . well, anyone can do that with a bit of makeup, right? I wasn't about to trust a person I hardly knew after all that had just happened.

"Hey, I think you dropped some of that Truth Debris," I said, pointing behind Kahem.

"Truth *Dust*," he said, shaking his head and turning around. "The first thing I will teach you is–"

I ran around the orange trees and through the bakery's back door. Once in the kitchen, I squeezed between the two assistants as they angrily shouted at me.

While I had so many questions, none of them were as important as getting home and checking on Teta. I hurried through Portland, arriving back in my neighborhood before the sun started to set. The other middle schoolers who walked home were gone now. The sidewalk was about as empty as it got . . .

. . . until I turned a street corner and skidded to a stop right behind Sarah Decker. She knelt on the ground with a can of tuna in one hand, back facing me, and she was talking to someone.

"*Meow!*" screamed a cat, which darted into a tight crack behind one of the apartments.

"You scared her away," said Sarah with a snarl. She stood up, towering over me like the shadow from earlier. "I knew you'd be easy to ambush if I just stuck around. You might be the most brainless kid in our class."

None of her friends were with her, and it was obvious

why. She smelled like a skunk farted on another skunk. I was surprised that the stray cat could stand it.

"Well, I'm actually the second. The first would be Peter Gamble," I said.

Wait. That wasn't what I'd meant to say. Trying again, I shouted, "I could probably be an average student, even if I am a few leaves short of a fig tree when it comes to pre-algebra. Cut me a break. I have a lot going on!"

Oh no . . . it was the Truth Dust. That stuff was real. How could I insult Sarah with the truth?

She looked as confused as I was, but still angry. She made a fist with her hand and pounded it into her other palm. "Now it's time for payback."

I tried to say sorry, but what came out instead was, "Hey, look, you're about two steps from watching me pee in my pants, but if anyone deserves payback, it's you. You were the one chasing me, and *you* are the school bully. People are only nice to you because they're scared of you!"

Sarah stopped coming toward me and tilted her head. "Everyone at school likes me because I'm popular," she said. "What would you know? You're so irrelevant, you're basically a ghost. No one wants to be *your* friend."

"I'd rather have no friends than fake friends," I said, wishing the Truth Dust would stop making me say silly things. "And it's *your* fault we aren't friends anymore, remember? Your parents told you to stop hanging out with me, which was totally rude!"

"Why are you bringing that up?" she asked. "Aren't you scared of what I'll do?"

I shrugged. "After my mama met my stepfather, she left my baba and made me move into her new husband's fancy house. Only, my stepsiblings didn't like sharing. They put bugs in my pillow and hid my underwear. It lasted for two years until my stepfather, who was *always* away for work, came home one day and blamed me for coloring in the white spaces of his favorite painting. He demanded I leave, despite Mama's protests, and Baba happily took me back. Both of us, along with my grandparents, moved to America then. Mama hasn't answered a single one of my calls since. So, not to be rude, but my stepfamily is way higher than you on the bully scale."

Sarah hesitated and her lip quivered like she was going to cry. "This is *so* weird. Why are you telling me this?"

I wanted to say that she was the weird one, and that even the trash in her backpack smelled better than she did right then. What came out of me was a series of guilty admissions. "It's this Truth Dust. And I'm sorry about putting the trash in your backpack, and for starting that rumor about you eating mustard straight from the packet. It's just . . . sometimes I get scared, and I cope by fighting fire with fire."

I didn't even know I felt some of the things I was saying until I said them. I was pretty sure that I'd lost my marbles, every single one of them. Maybe Sarah would knock them back into place with her fist. Or she would squeeze me into Shad juice and serve me to her friends at lunch.

Instead, she rolled her eyes before saying, "Ugh, this is so not cool, dude. Just get out of my way."

She knocked me aside with her shoulder and ran down the sidewalk. I nervously turned and watched her disappear around the corner. The air still smelled like all the rotten things in the world mushed into a perfume. If only Jiduh were alive to smell how good a job I did.

It suddenly dawned on me how lucky I was that our grade's most terrible bully just let me walk away without even a noogie.

But I didn't have time to dwell on that or the effects of the Truth Dirt–or debris, or whatever it was called. Without wasting another second, I hurried down the sidewalk. Teta had some explaining to do.

I arrived home with my hair sticking to my face in sweaty clumps.

It was 4:30 p.m., an hour past when I usually got back. Thankfully, Teta was asleep and I slipped into the shower without her noticing. If she'd been awake, I doubted that I could've given an answer for why I was so late without sounding like a complete majnoon.

Hi, Teta, sorry, I had to find a way around our school's biggest bully, a humongous shadow monster, but also the baker . . . yeah, that *one*. He can change how poofy his hair is, and he gave me *Truth Dust* that helped me deal with the bully. Oh, and the baker has a pet that can shape-shift from a salamander to a cat.

That probably would've given her a heart attack. At seventy-eight, she spends her days in her bed, sleeping, or on the couch watching Arabic soap operas.

After a quick shower, I tiptoed across our apartment to her room. She breathed through tubes in her nose that helped get the oxygen into her body. To keep warm, she'd buried herself under a mountain of sheets. Back in Lebanon, we never had heat, but we had closets full of sheets. I guess Teta hadn't gotten the memo that things were different in America.

Leaning in, I whispered, "I failed another science lab today. They wanted us to dissect these frogs, but I felt bad for mine, so I gave it a proper burial in the baseball field. That earned me a one-way ticket to the principal's office."

She heard none of that, of course. I just felt less guilty about messing up if I told her, even if she was sleeping. And now that I'd gotten the confession out of the way, it was time for Shad the boring student to become Shad the totally butt-kicking chef. I carefully shut her bedroom door on my way out.

Calling my kitchen a disaster would have been an understatement. In the sink, I faced a stack of dishes that would probably come down on me like a Jenga puzzle if I wasn't careful. Beneath my feet, each step I took made a crunching sound from all the crumbs. The fridge had even been left open. I'd need to see if anything spoiled while I was at school. The first two were probably my fault for slacking on chores, but the third was definitely Teta. She'd grab the milk to make Turkish coffee and almost always forget to shut the fridge.

I sighed and got to cleaning. Teta couldn't do much around the apartment. Cleaning and cooking always fell on me, and after all that, there was still homework. Well, sometimes I ignored the homework part.

Messy or not, this was still my happy place. Rosemary, basil, and the other herbs with their unique scents, the shelves and shelves of spoons, scales, pots, and pans. The Sultan of Slam had his muscles, and I had my wooden spatula. No Arab chef can work without one. And when I closed my eyes, I saw myself as a chef, puffy white hat and all.

I bent to open one of the bottom cabinets. The one with all *my* stuff—wooden spoons, rollers, and other baking supplies.

The doctors said Teta couldn't have sugar, so I kept my baking to myself. Saving up the leftover change from the grocery money she gave me, I bought utensils and ingredients, everything I needed to satisfy my sweet tooth.

I laid out a bag of rice, crushed pistachios, rose water, and sugar, then yanked a carton of coconut milk from the fridge. Picturing the rice pudding the ingredients would make, I licked my lips while I set the rice to boil in a small pot. As it finished cooking, I pictured the measurements in my head, not relying on any tools or recipes, trying to *feel* what seemed right as I eased in the milk, sugar, and rose water. Baba had once told me that true Arabic cooking relied on the imagination. And while steam rose from the pot, the pudding thickened. A scent of rosy sweetness filled the kitchen.

"Heaven," I whispered, enjoying that smell for a few minutes until the pudding was ready. "Now for the final step . . ."

I poured the thick pudding into a container before adding a coat of ground pistachios along the surface. If only Baba could see me now. Mama too. She used to love when I watched her baking. Sighing, I considered the pudding. All that was left was to let the mixture cool.

With my baking done for the day, I eased my rice pudding in the fridge, shoving it into a compartment too far back for Teta to reach.

That would make a tasty dessert for later, but now the time had come for part two of my chores for the night– preparing dinner.

Chapter 4

Teta's shuffling footsteps came as I finished making a large bowl of tabbouleh: one cup of onions, one cup of tomatoes, and two cups of parsley, all mixed with freshly squeezed lemon juice.

"You've been sleeping for a long time," I said, taking her arm and helping her into the kitchen. "Are your headaches better?"

I helped her into a chair at the kitchen table, which was shaped in a semicircle against the wall and faced the only window in the kitchen. The sun had set by the time I'd finished preparing our meal, which was perfect because every night since we'd moved in, we'd eaten dinner in front of the twinkling stars. Being on the second floor meant we couldn't see the cars passing below, only hear them as they rumbled through our busy street.

Teta groaned, bending slowly to adjust one of her slippers. She leaned back, holding her belly in her arms as she said, "Shaddo, Shaddo." It was the nickname she'd used for me for as long as I could remember.

Mixing the tabbouleh, I turned and looked over my shoulder. "What is it, Teta? The food's ready, I'm going to bring you a plate."

"Habibi, when did you become my caretaker?" she asked. "Am I not supposed to be the one taking care of you?" Her accent was thick since she'd never fully learned English, but I liked that. Her voice reminded me of our old life in Lebanon.

"Just focus on getting comfy," I said, not mentioning that she hadn't cooked in years. "Where's your breathing machine?"

She chuckled and placed her hand over mine. "Do not worry about that."

I *did* worry. Her fingers were shaking, her breath becoming heavy. If alchemy was real, I'd invent a charm to make Teta twenty years younger.

She broke into a coughing fit, using her arms to cover her mouth. I handed her the half-filled brik and she lifted the drinking jug to her lips. Water flowed out from the spout and she gulped down every last drop. Even as the coughing stopped, it hurt knowing that she was sick and that, one day, she'd be gone just like Baba and Jiduh.

Tears threatening my eyes, I brought the bowls full of tabbouleh and set them on the table. Teta's shaky fingers picked up a knife sitting on the table and she used it to dig out the insides of a squash. Stuffing it with rice, she smiled up at me, hands working without her even paying attention.

"Tell me, what is this I am making?" she asked.

I rolled my eyes. "Duh, it's kousa."

"Good. Good." She set down a final stuffed squash, one of my favorite meals, and wiped her fingers with a cloth. "Now it is your turn. Make some stuffing and help your grandmother with her kousa. What am I missing?"

I groaned. With our dinner waiting, she sure picked a weird time to prepare food, but the proper ingredients were laid out around the table. Rice, pepper, chopped onions . . .

"You're missing the ground beef," I said. "That's the most important ingredient!"

Teta slowly lifted her shoulders. "Perhaps you should try something new?"

Memories of Teta's cooking lessons flooded my mind, times when she *accidentally* left out ingredients or forgot the right measurements. It had taken me a few years to realize it was all on purpose. She had been trying to teach me to create new recipes for the same foods. To make my own measurements.

And I was pretty darn good at it. For whatever reason, my brain connected the dots with food. Teta would clap or take me to the Arabic bakery each time I passed one of her tests, so I kept doing it. Even now, I could see the solution since we had no beef.

"Pass me that can," I said.

Combining everything with one hand while accepting a can of chickpeas with the other, I smushed the new ingredients with the old. Everything fit nicely into the squash. Meanwhile, Teta's wrinkly smile widened, stretching from ear to ear. Her smile was the reason I fell in love with food. Why I dreamed of being a baker.

But as soon as I finished, glancing over at all the medicines organized at one end of the table, worry clouded my mind. My fear of one day losing Teta. She was the last living person on my baba's side of the family, and Mama's side had probably forgotten I even existed, the way she had.

"My Shaddo," Teta said, running a hand through my thick, curly hair. "I see the sadness in your eyes. You cannot feel this way, not when you make me so very proud."

"But why can't Mama be proud of me too?" I asked, my lower lip trembling. "Do you think she'll at least call on my birthday this year?"

Teta's expression hardened. Gray eyebrows furrowing, she shook her head. "We do not talk of your mama. I told you this, Shaddo. Not in this house."

"But *why*?"

"Because she abandoned you," she snapped. "That is that."

Listening to Teta, my heart sank. She was right. Mama had been there for the early years, so why'd she decide to leave? I still couldn't understand what made her new family so special. More special than me.

Teta nudged the spoon into my hand. As she began to eat, I replayed the events of the afternoon in my head. The memory still felt hazy, like one of those bad dreams after gorging on an entire chocolate cake. Alchemists weren't real. Yet when I thought back to our family shop in Lebanon, I couldn't remember any ordinary ingredients like the ones I used for cooking. I remembered Jiduh holding up a plastic bag full of strange purple-colored plants.

"This will heal any burn, no matter how bad," he had told me.

Or on another occasion, Baba had taken me to the shop and was speaking to a customer: "Oh, you sink whenever you try to swim? I have just the thing!"

The memory was so vivid, so odd, and I recalled how Baba had walked over to a shelf and pulled out a strangely wrapped box.

"Shaddo," said Teta. "Why do you not eat?"

I opened wide and began to shovel spoonful after spoonful into my mouth, but my grandmother saw through the act. She was basically a mind reader.

And I couldn't hold in my questions any longer. If the Truth Dust had really worked, maybe the baker was right about other things. Maybe Teta hadn't told me the *whole* truth about our family.

The truth about alchemy.

After swallowing the food in my mouth, I asked, "What kind of shop did we have in Lebanon?"

"Shop?" Teta gazed out the window. She smiled, the tiny gray hairs on her chin moving. "Ah, we had such a beautiful shop. . . ."

I leaned in closer, ready to hear her say we sold vegetables, plants, or something boring. Something that would prove I was just remembering my childhood wrong.

Instead, switching to Arabic, she said, "We sold Voice-Change Juice, Baby-Sleeping Sniffers, Cow Dung Lotion for Rashes, Herbal Teas for Happiness, and our most popular item was our trademark Mold Milk for Memories."

I set down the soup and asked, "M . . . moldy milk?"

Teta was still looking out the window, as if seeing the night sky helped her remember. I was beginning to wonder if something had gotten into her oxygen machine.

Thinking about Kahem, his shape-shifting cat, and the shadow monster, I asked, "So all those things we sold, did we use alchemy to make them?"

Teta smiled. "Alchemy? Yes, of course."

My stomach began to ache. Had I heard her right? If

I had, then Jiduh's stink bomb trick really was alchemy. I was the son and grandson of alchemists.

"Why did no one ever tell me?" I asked.

She said, "Oh, you did not know, habibi? I thought it was . . . what is the word?"

"Obvious?"

"Yes, *obvi-oos*."

The food I'd just eaten felt like rocks in my belly. My whole childhood was a lie. My best memories from Lebanon were in our family shop, and I hadn't even known what we were selling.

"So . . . it was an alchemy shop?" I asked. "Alchemy like the bedtime stories you'd tell me?"

"Yes," she said, "those stories were passed down from your ancestors."

My head began to spin. Had my family's history been kept from me, or was it my fault for not believing the stories?

I opened my mouth to ask about alchemy, Baba, or one of the million other things crossing my mind, but then stopped. Teta was gazing up at the stars, her lower lip trembling, catching silent tears as they rolled down her wrinkly cheeks. I'd never seen her cry before. Not even at Baba's and Jiduh's funerals, when she'd held me tight.

I reached over and grasped her hand, asking, "Did I say something wrong? Teta, I'd never mean to hurt you. . . ."

A long silence stretched between us. Slowly, she slid off her chair. Her feet shuffled out of the kitchen faster than she'd moved in years.

"Stay in your seat," she ordered before disappearing through the kitchen door.

I finished my tabbouleh while anxiously waiting. Grabbing my plate and Teta's, I got up and stacked them on top of the mountain of dishes in the sink. Arabic music filtered in from the living room television as I returned to my seat until, finally, the door reopened and Teta shuffled in, her breathing heavy.

I helped her into the chair, noticing the green, pocket-sized book in her hands. She lifted it to her face, blowing a thick layer of dust right into my nostrils.

I scrunched my nose and sneezed. "Talk about allergies, Teta!"

She set the book down, its pages old and yellowing, and pushed it toward me with trembling fingers. Her expression fixed on me with seriousness. "There is much to apologize for," she said. "To you, and to my son."

"You mean Baba?"

"I do," she said, placing her hand on top of mine. "This alchemy book was his. Passed down from parent to child since long before your teta was born. Since before *my* teta was born. It reveals the secrets of the ancient craft, and your baba wished to teach you. But . . . I stopped him."

Now tears threatened my eyes. Baba hadn't just been an alchemist; he had planned to teach me too. I was meant to carry on our family tradition. "You stopped him? Teta, I don't understand."

She squeezed my hand. "We had just left our country after your stepfather bought our shop's building and raised the rent to drive us out of business. Without any money, I was scared. We needed a new start, a safe life for *you*."

"And what about Mama? Wouldn't she have wanted to protect me too?"

Teta sighed, her leathery hand brushing my shoulder. "She and that new husband of hers would have taken everything. Even that book you hold now. I am lucky to have kept it—and you—away from them, my Shaddo."

Picking up Baba's book, I flipped through pages full of recipes just like a cookbook, only they contained strange ingredients. Things like sulfur, zinc, and even something called galena.

Meanwhile, Teta's gaze had shifted to the stars, her eyes avoiding mine. I didn't want her to hurt. To feel guilty. Setting a hand over hers, I said, "You're the best teta I could ever ask for. Do you know that?"

She laughed, bringing me into a tight hug. When we pulled away, she was sitting up straighter. As if a big weight had just rolled off her shoulders.

Yet now that she'd explained the truth about our family, there was someone else I needed answers from. Someone who'd claimed they might be able to tell me more about my family as well as this strange book. . . .

The *alchemist*.

Chapter 5

I rounded the street corner and headed toward Halwa Heaven's hidden alleyway.

Rays of sunlight brightened the sky this Saturday morning, the very first day of summer break. The day Kahem said to meet him here if I wanted to learn more. After what Teta had told me about our family, there was so much I needed to know. Hopefully, she would be all right back home. She usually sleeps until the afternoon on weekends, but in case I was late, I left a lamb and potato stew she could quickly heat in the microwave.

All thoughts of Teta and her next meal vanished as I heard something that stopped me in my tracks. . . .

"Coach is the *worst*. It's summer, can't she give us a break?"

"Tell me about it. My dad was going to make us pancakes for breakfast, but instead we'll be practicing our batting all morning. I barely had time to eat a bagel!"

The voices coming around the side of the bakery

sounded familiar, sending a chill down my back. I hurried into the alley and peeked out, careful not to be seen, when Sarah Decker appeared on the crosswalk down the street. Dressed in Portland Middle's softball team uniform, two friends walked on either side of her. One I recognized as Catherine from our last run-in, and the other was Eliana, a girl from my gym class.

"Maybe we can stop and get some desserts here after practice," said Eliana, pointing as they passed the bakery's side entrance.

Sarah shook her head. "I can't. My parents want me to get a head start on summer reading."

"Oh, *come on*," complained Catherine. "Aren't your parents on vacation or something? You have the whole summer to read!"

"Hold on," said Eliana. "Your parents went on vacation without you *again*. What's their deal?"

Sarah stomped her foot, quieting them. "The *deal* is that both of you should mind your own business. Got it?"

Catherine held up her hands. "Loud and clear."

"Yeah, we didn't mean to hurt your feelings," said Eliana. "Do you know the boy who always stands in front of the window, Shad? I heard nobody wanted to sign his yearbook."

Sarah put up a hand. "First off, neither of you hurt my feelings. Second, let's not talk about Shad. Besides, I heard this bakery's pastries are stale."

I didn't realize how tightly I gripped the brick wall until my fingers started to ache. It stank that Sarah's parents hadn't taken her on vacation, but her friends really did need to mind their business. Who cared if nobody signed my yearbook? I didn't want a bunch of people scribbling all over the pages anyways.

"The nerve of those girls," said a new voice above me. "Whose pastries are they calling stale?"

My heart nearly leapt out of my chest when I turned and Kahem was standing right behind me. Wearing the same navy-blue coat as last time, the alchemist held a croissant in his hands, chocolate covering his lips. He offered me half and I shook my head. Luckily, Sarah and her friends had disappeared.

I couldn't contain my excitement. "You said you'd tell me more if I came, right? I asked my teta if we were really alchemists. She–"

Kahem shushed me. "Do not just shout the word *alchemist* around the neighborhood! We must be careful. Or did you forget a necromancer attacked you in this very spot?"

"Sorry," I said, "I just want to hear more about my family. There's so much I don't know, and there isn't really anyone left who could tell me."

Kahem's wrinkles softened. "Listen, I know nothing about your family, but I *did* offer to educate you, so follow me and I will explain the basics of alchemy."

He turned and headed into the dark alley, forcing me to hurry after so I could keep up with his long strides. As I squeezed through the alley, I reached into the back pocket of my shorts for Baba's old book. Yanking it out as I stepped into the garden, I saw the title was written in both Arabic and English. *The Alchemist's Hand.*

"The basics?" I asked. "Like the stuff in this book?"

Kahem's jaw dropped. He snatched it out of my hands, flipping through the old pages. I reached to get it back, but Kahem shoved me away with his belly.

"Where in the elements did you find this?" he asked, closing the book.

I stepped back, caught off guard by the serious look in Kahem's eyes. "Well . . . it belonged to my baba. My teta gave it to me."

Kahem flipped the book sideways, upside down. "Unbelievable," he muttered, shoving the pages in my face. "Can you read this, my boy? What does it say?"

I shrugged, glancing at the page in front of me. "Just some alchemy recipes. You know, like a cookbook, except for other stuff. Like, this one is for something called a Disappearing Dust."

"As I live and breathe," he gasped. "You can truly read it!"

Scrunching my face, I said, "Dude, I may have failed

English class, but not because I can't read."

"No, Shad, you do not understand," he said. "I cannot see the words. This is no ordinary book, but *The Alchemist's Hand*. It is the oldest alchemy guidebook in existence. Your parents had to have your eyes charmed at birth so that you could one day read it."

I staggered back. A knot forming in my throat, I said, "Ch-charmed?"

Kahem nodded and lifted the book, light reflecting off the dark green cover. Baba really had been an alchemist, and he'd wanted me to grow up and become one too. He trusted me with our family secrets. The truth sent a jolt of excitement through me.

Shoving it back into my hands, Kahem said, "Protect this book and let no one know of its existence. There may not be another like it. But before you trouble yourself with that text, I must teach you the ingredients."

Kahem gestured all around us. A morning glow cast light over the small but packed collection of flowers, trees, and bushes. How was it even possible to grow all these things in a city?

"You are seeing all of this because I have removed the Illusion Charm," Kahem explained. "Otherwise, I would never dare reveal my garden to outsiders, especially non-alchemists like that girl and her friends who were chasing you."

I nodded, a strange sense of pride welling within.

Kahem clearly didn't trust just anyone to come here, but he trusted *me*. Studying the view, I asked, "So, these are alchemy ingredients? But they're plants."

Kahem stopped to pick some blueberries from a small patch and offered me one, saying, "The list of what can be used to make alchemy is endless, but we are limited to the ingredients we possess. That is why my belt and coat are loaded with pockets. If we run out of ingredients, we risk running out of alchemy."

"But if ingredients can be found anywhere," I said, scooping up some dirt in my hand, "then why worry about carrying all that stuff around?"

"Can you bake a pistachio maamoul pastry without pistachios?" he asked, answering my question with another. "Alchemy is like baking in this way. It requires very precise ingredients and a careful process. And, like anything we create, the result will come in the form of either a liquid, a gas, or a solid. That brings me to your first lesson—alchemy is a science."

I nearly choked on the berry. Science was literally my *worst* subject in school. Cells and molecules and earthquakes, all of it made as much sense to me as a cake without frosting. Not to mention, lab assignments and Shad Hadid were a recipe for disaster.

My alchemy teacher must have noticed, because he shook his head. "Lesson two is that science, *true science*, does not disregard the power of the mind. Of the imagination.

The first alchemists realized that by combining scientific principles with their imaginations, they could make the impossible happen."

"Jiduh's trick!" I said, suddenly understanding. "After I mixed the ingredients for my stink bomb, Jiduh always taught me to close my eyes and imagine the worst smell in the world. That was his special trick."

Kahem placed a hand on my shoulder. "Precisely, my boy. Some alchemists pray, some meditate, but they *all* combine natural science with the power of the mind."

He led me in between two palm trees, the tallest in his collection. A third, smaller tree had sprouted out from a patch of dirt, rising to be nearly as high as my waist. Kahem bent down and motioned me closer.

"Do you know what this is?" he asked. When I ran a finger along its rough surface, shaking my head, he continued, "The green cover of your father's guidebook tells me you come from Lebanese alchemists, which makes the cedar tree special."

My mind flashed back to Lebanon. Mountains of cedars stretching to the sky, snow covering their branches in the wintertime, and how they always carried a refreshing earthy smell. I couldn't hold back my smile.

"Last thing," said Kahem. "Every alchemist has an ancestral root. A plant that is native to the land from which their ancestors–the first alchemists–came. Just as science reminds us that we are atoms and molecules, an ancestral root reminds us that alchemy is a part of us too. It is in our history."

"Wait a second. Cedar trees, my ancestors…" I recalled a wooden tree Jiduh had nailed to our doorway once I moved back home with Baba years ago, and it all made sense. "Do people normally hang their ancestral root in their houses?"

Kahem stroked his chin. "Only families who hold a deep connection to their alchemy tradition. That charm must have helped disguise your location from the necromancers."

Meow.

We both turned around, to where a fluffy orange cat pawed at the blueberry bushes, knocking as many down as she could eat. Kahem grabbed the cat in his big hands, turning her over and tickling her belly.

"Who is a good kitty-alchemist?" he said. "Yolla is a capable sniffer."

I scratched my head. "*Sniffer?*"

"I've trained her to smell alchemy," he explained. "Many such pets exist. It was she who alerted me to the necromancer attacking you."

While he fed Yolla a treat, I ran my finger along the tiny spindles blossoming forth from the cedar's branches. "So, now that you've explained everything, maybe you can teach me?"

Kahem folded his arms over his belly. Even under

the shade of the alley, I could see his face going red. I'd annoyed him. It was the same look that my teachers gave me when I didn't pass in my homework, probably Mama's look whenever she decided not to answer my calls. I took a step back, getting ready for the inevitable *no, of course I don't want you.*

Instead, he let out a long sigh and adjusted his belt. "When I was a boy, I had no family, nothing. Yet a kind teacher gave me a chance I did not deserve, and maybe it is my turn to repay that favor by training you. Besides, I find myself needing an apprentice since my last one . . . well, don't worry about that. I just need a new apprentice."

"Since your last one what?" I asked, several words finishing the sentence in my mind.

Exploded.

Melted.

Turned into a bug that got squashed.

"Left," he said. "She was in college, and she decided to leave me for a big medical company. No loyalty, that girl. Now, do you wish to learn the ancient art of alchemy or not?"

"Holy cannoli, yes!" I shouted without hesitation.

This was my chance to become like Baba, and who knew if I'd get another.

"And could you also show me how to make some of Halwa Heaven's famous baklava?" I asked.

Kahem's sudden, boisterous laugh echoed across the garden. He came to stand over me, casting a long shadow, and drew a folded piece of paper from one of his pockets. "My boy, you remind me too much of myself, and not in the right ways. Now, take this list. I wrote down all the tasks you must complete today."

The paper fell onto the ground beside me and I picked it up, scanning through the tasks. *Sweep the alley, pick the weeds, trim the bushes.*

"These are chores!" I complained.

Kahem shrugged. "Training, chores, there's no difference."

I swallowed and cast my gaze back toward the alley, where Kahem and I had first met. I still couldn't wrap my mind around why he'd offered to train me. He was an expert on this stuff, not to mention an expert baker. Meanwhile, I was barely passing middle school.

"Do you really believe *I* can be an alchemist?"

Kahem chuckled, bending down so we were eye to eye. He smelled like sweat and grass, his wild hair drifting in a light breeze. "Indeed I do," he said, "but alchemy is a dying craft. Due to war and greed and human messiness, we have ruined what was once a thriving art. Many of the remaining masters, few that they are, have gone into hiding, or worse, chosen the dark path of Shadow Alchemy."

"Like the shadow in the alley!"

"A necromancer," Kahem corrected me. "And it was here for me. They're getting too close to my hideout. Necromancers are persistent when it comes to dealing with their enemies."

"Are you going to leave?" I asked, suddenly worried I'd lose Kahem just as fast as I'd met him.

"Not yet," he said, reaching into his pocket and pressing a sticky glob to the wall. "This new Illusion Charm should throw them off for a short while longer, but we must be cautious in these dark times. You know, legend holds that Shadow Alchemy began with the first necromancer. They were a powerful elder who, upon seeing their friends refusing to teach the outside world, created a new form of alchemy in secret. They began spreading this alchemy to all who would listen, but never stopped to ask if those receiving the training had pure intentions. Over time, their order grew to chase a new goal . . . the key to immortality."

I suddenly thought of Teta, and how much I'd love for her to always be by my side. "Why does it matter if they want a longer life?" I asked. "Getting to live a few extra years doesn't seem like such a bad thing. Besides, there's a section in the guidebook all about that kind of alchemy."

I brought out *The Alchemist's Hand* and flipped to the back. Several pages were missing, but several had survived and I read through the names of the mixtures.

"It says right here," I said, holding it up before

remembering Kahem couldn't read it. "Uh, this one is called Revival Elixir."

"By the elements," Kahem gasped. He snatched the book from my hands and slammed it shut, pressing it into my chest. "Listen to me, boy. That elixir is one of the reasons the alchemist elders decided to stop making those guidebooks ages ago. Because of it, they ordered all copies of *The Alchemist's Hand* to be destroyed, and that is why few survive today. You must *never* consider crafting such a mixture."

"Why not?" I asked.

He grabbed my shirt and yanked me in close. "All that separates us from the necromancers is balance. Just as there is life, there must be death. Immortality would change the very foundation of our world. The necromancers are already capable of great evil. Can you imagine what would happen if they lived forever? I once had many alchemist friends, some I loved dearly. At least until they were . . ."

Kahem shook his head.

"Necromancers will not stop until every alchemist either joins their cause or is eliminated. They have come close to achieving their goal on a handful of occasions across the centuries. Every time, the mightiest of us have managed to beat them back, for only alchemy can overcome alchemy. Yet if they were to succeed, they would use immortality not to give to others, but to *take* from them. To become rich and powerful and force every single person you love to their will. After all, who can fight an army that can never die?"

The thought of anyone hurting Teta had my stomach doing backflips. Slowly, I shoved the alchemy book back in my pocket. "I–I don't know."

"Neither do I," he said, rising to tower over me once more. "Now, before you do start your chores, remind me . . . what three lessons did you learn today?"

"A pop quiz?" I asked, freezing up. "But the school year just ended!"

"Indeed it has," he said, rubbing his belly. "And your training, young Shad, has only just begun."

Chapter 6

A pinch of zinc, but only a pinch. Kahem's instructions echoed in my head as I dipped two fingers into the worn leather pouch and let the contents fall into the boiling flask. Every ingredient had been perfectly measured, every flame carefully set, as I plugged my ears and braced for the huge puff of smoke in three, two . . .

"One?" I whispered, watching the zinc mix into the flask and fizzle away.

I stood in the center of an abandoned boat factory the size of our school. Soon after Kahem began my training, he had brought me to this warehouse, which he'd turned into an alchemy lab. The stairs and machines had rotted away, leaving only a handful of tables that he'd dragged to the middle of the space. Huge dust-coated windows allowed just enough sunlight through. I would have preferred a few lamps, maybe a disco ball, but I guessed Kahem wanted to keep it old-school.

I picked up the paper where Kahem had scribbled a practice recipe. Like, *really* scribbled. I'd seen first graders with better handwriting, but I tried my best to decipher the note he'd given me just before taking Yolla for a walk. Ingredient by ingredient, I scanned through the recipe. Four drops of vinegar, two pinches of mercury, a pinch of zinc . . .

"Lavender ether," I muttered, smacking my head. "Wow, I'm such a fig."

I stuck a hand inside my green alchemist's coat, searching for the right vial. After two weeks of training, I'd learned just one thing, and it was that being an alchemist required brains. More than I had. I mean, how could anyone learn the hundreds of ingredients Kahem used each day? I *still* hadn't gotten a single recipe to go right. Not one.

When I yanked out the vial of lavender ether, it appeared as clear as water and lighter than a feather. I unscrewed the top and, slowly, ever so carefully, I let a drop fall, holding my breath so I didn't move and miss the flask.

Whoosh!

I jerked back as blue-green smoke rose. Even though I hurried away, some of the fumes hit my face, and the mixture was about as pungent as an unflushed toilet on a hot day. I'd forgotten *my* first rule of alchemy—always block your nose. Still, at least this time the chemicals hadn't singed the curls hanging down my forehead. That was progress.

I turned off the fire to let the mixture cool. It was gooey, smelly, and thick. I reached for the flask, but a hand slapped mine away.

"What in the elements are you doing?"

I startled. My heartbeat surged from zero to riding-in-an-Arab-taxi. Kahem stood right behind me. Yolla licked my sneakers while I stiffened, frozen as though he'd used a Stilling Elixir.

"I've been observing long enough to see you nearly put yourself in a coma!" he said. "Never hold a freshly mixed elixir close to your face. They take time to settle. Sometimes just a few moments, but some of the more advanced mixtures might take hours or even days."

I carefully placed a cover over the flask. "Uh . . . yeah, I knew that!"

"But you didn't know the recipe called for hibiscus extract rather than lavender ether," he said, jabbing a finger at the empty vial I'd just used. And when I shrugged, he leaned over me and said, "Remind me, what is alchemy first and foremost?"

Oh no, not *this* again. It was only my fifth lesson, but I was already sick of having to answer this question.

"Alchemy is science," I grumbled.

"Precisely!" said Kahem, his alchemist's coat swinging wildly.

Hurrying to the table next to mine with Yolla in tow, he placed an empty jar at the center. No fire. No measurements. He simply reached out and sprinkled in one ingredient after another, almost without looking. I'd never seen him put together a mixture so quick. He slid a pouch back into his coat, reached into his belt for a vial, and paused.

"Alchemy is indeed a science," he said, grabbing the jar and rushing back to my workstation. With the vial still in hand, he set the jar down, continuing, "And science requires caution. Each day, I begin to think you have learned that, and then I remember I cannot simply tell you. I must *show* you."

I winced at his cold words, but then he raised the vial. Tipping it slightly, he allowed just a drop to fall before leaping away and whisking me back with him.

Boom!

An explosion rocked the entire workstation, clouds of purples and reds and blues all rising through the air. Sparks flew, exploding like fireworks. Who needed algebra when Kahem could teach me *that*?

"Impressed?" he asked. "You should know, the first time I attempted that particular dust, someone had to call the fire department."

"No way. You messed up?"

He nodded. "Royally. More than once."

In that moment, my doubts disappeared. If Kahem had ever made a mistake while training, that meant Baba had to have too. And the same with his baba before him. I couldn't give up. Each failure was a chance to learn, to get closer to becoming a real alchemist like they had been.

Once the fireworks settled and the multicolored smoke vanished, I returned to my workstation—a table with two Bunsen burners and a shelf of different-sized flasks—and I studied another practice recipe Kahem had written down. The light in the warehouse was dimming. I'd narrowed my eyes and tried focusing on the words when a hairy hand snatched away the paper.

"It's been three hours, that's enough practice for today."

Kahem nudged me toward the warehouse exit, where the sunset peeked through the giant door. We walked out together. I smiled, wondering just what this summer would look like. Hoping beyond hope that every Sunday could end this way.

Once we stepped outside, the wind whipping our coats around, Kahem took his hand off my shoulder. For a second, I expected him to say that he'd changed his mind. That I wasn't cut out for alchemy. My gut told me that things were going well as we stood at the edge of the Portland pier. But good things like this didn't usually last.

Not for me, at least.

Kahem picked up Yolla, stroking her orange fur. Shockingly, he didn't say not to return. Instead, his lips twitched into something of a grin.

Sometimes, it still occurred to me that most people go their whole lives never knowing about alchemy, or that their own baker could practice it. "Are there any *good* alchemists left in the world?" I asked. "You're the only one I've met. Besides my baba, that is."

"There were once thousands upon thousands of us, schools with too many students to count." Kahem set Yolla down and closed his eyes. I wondered if he was imagining how nice things might have been back when he was a young alchemist like me. He sighed and said, "Now, only perhaps a few hundred alchemists remain. The merchants of alchemical ingredients, historians who knew of all our ancient books, anyone who did not join the necromancers has been forced into hiding. I know of but *one* alchemy school left, and I was banned from there long ago for . . . reasons I do not need to share."

At the sound of merchants, my ears perked up. After all, Baba and Jiduh and Teta had owned a shop that sold alchemy stuff back in Lebanon. They were merchants too. Maybe Teta hadn't told me the truth of why we came to America. Maybe Baba brought us to be safe from the necromancers. To protect *me*.

I bunched my hands into fists, angry that the necromancers might've caused people like my family so much trouble. What if Baba and Jiduh didn't die in a car accident? What if...

Closing my eyes, I tried to forget the thought. It hurt worse than a belly cramp, and besides, Kahem had mentioned a school for alchemy. I could only imagine how amazing that sounded. Maybe I'd be able to pass *those* classes.

Kahem snapped his fingers in front of my face. "Forget about everything except your training for now," he said. "We will meet here at the same time tomorrow, and don't be a moment late. Got it?"

"Got it."

Yet as I headed home, the necromancers were still in my thoughts, swirling across the back of my mind like the shadowy tendrils they formed.

Chapter 7

oday was the day. The BIGGEST day. After an entire summer, a whole three months since I'd first been saved by Kahem, August 30 was here—my twelfth birthday.

It was also the second day back at school after summer break, though none of my classmates cared about my birthday. If only Mama would call. Teta would hate to hear me say that, but I couldn't fight the disappointment. This happened every year on this day, and I wasn't sure why I bothered holding out hope.

On the other hand, Sarah had thankfully ignored me all the times we ran into each other this summer, and that hadn't changed today. When we crossed paths in the cafeteria, she didn't shove french fries up my nose, which felt like ten birthday presents in one.

This day could only get better now that I was headed to meet Kahem. All but skipping to the bakery, I struggled to hold in my excitement.

"Ahlan, Shad!" said the baker's assistants, Rumi and Miriam, as I arrived at Halwa Heaven.

They were full-fledged bakers now. Kahem had placed them in charge while he trained me in alchemy.

Still, it was rare that they would smile, let alone invite me in. They must have known the Arab philosophy on birthdays. It was the one day each year that, no matter who you were, enemies became friends, and everyone got along. Miriam was putting the finishing touches on my cake. She glazed the chocolate with blue frosting, which reminded me of the beaches in Lebanon.

Unwittingly, I reached for a taste of the frosting, but she swatted my hand away. I couldn't help it. The cake, it was perfect.

Miriam put down her tools and, as if holding a baby, lifted the cake off the baking table and placed it into an empty box. "I must admit," she said, "you make me a jealous woman with all these sweets. How old will you be turning?"

"Twelve."

"Kna'ish?" repeated Rumi in Arabic. "Well, you are no boy. Being twelve means you have grown up, and that calls for a gift!"

Rumi counted twelve pieces of baklava from the refrigerator, my favorite ones with the pistachio centers. He took the baklava and placed them in a separate box from the cake and wrapped both boxes in thick red ribbons. I could hardly lift the bag that held them, which meant lots of sweets for Teta and me. Even if her doctor warned her against having any, we would make an exception today.

"Oh, and before I forget," said Miriam, digging into the pouch in her apron. "Here. This is from Kahem. He said something about a last-minute trip, and is sorry about not being here himself, but he will see you later tonight."

She held out a small brown box. A red ribbon was wrapped around it, but apart from that, it had no markings or notes. Did it hold some kind of alchemy, a charm perhaps? Mysterious, but that was probably exactly what Kahem intended.

Holding the gift to my chest, I asked, "Why didn't he tell me where he was going?"

"I don't ask," she said, shrugging. "He's always disappearing, that one."

I stuffed it into the bag with the cake and baklava. "Shukran!" I shouted gratefully, going out the door. It was cloudy, but rays of sunlight broke through the gray sky, shining down in patches across the street. I made a game of running through them.

Normally, I might've first looked left and right: the Sarah Decker Protocol. Yet for the first time since I could remember, I didn't need it.

When I arrived home, the patches of sun were

becoming harder and harder to spot under the clouds, and rain dotted my face. The umbrella in my backpack was useless with my arms full of cake. I rushed inside and climbed the stairs into our apartment, where, after setting the bag down on the couch, I tiptoed toward Teta's bedroom. Not only would there be cake waiting for her, but baklava too. She'd *love* that.

"Is someone asleep?" I asked, peering through the door.

It was dinnertime, which meant she'd be hungry. But in my excitement, I missed the door frame, stumbling over it and falling flat on the floor beside Teta.

"Oh crud!" I said, rising to my feet and rubbing my forehead.

If she hadn't heard me call her name, Teta would certainly be startled awake from that. I only hoped she hadn't freaked out.

I got back up, wobbly, but Teta hadn't woken up. Her eyes were still closed, and she was lying in the bed, unmoving. Part of me was confused, but also annoyed. Didn't she know it was my birthday?

I placed a hand gently on her shoulder. "Yalla," I whispered, telling her to hurry. "Teta, you should wake up or you won't sleep well tonight. Also, it's my birthday, remember?"

She still didn't wake up. She didn't move at all, and I couldn't hear her breathing. I put my hand in hers and shook her arm. Still nothing. Her hands felt cold, despite the heater in the room.

"Teta?" I asked again. "Do you not want cake? It's my birthday, Teta. Wake up!"

I shouted and shook her harder. I couldn't hear her heartbeat or feel her warm breath. Nothing was working. I shouted louder and louder until I was tasting my tears, trying not to panic, unable to accept she was really gone.

I bent over to listen for a heartbeat again when *The Alchemist's Hand* fell out of my back pocket. It wasn't a coincidence. Teta was dead. And there was only one thing I could do, something that Kahem had refused to teach me—Revival Alchemy.

Chapter 8

I rushed into my bedroom, digging through my closet and slipping on my alchemy belt. Frantically, I flipped through the pages of *The Alchemist's Hand,* knowing each passing second was a second wasted.

Healing Elixirs were near the last section. I scanned through until I saw the one that I wanted, Revival Elixir. The name gave me shivers, but I forced myself to read the ingredients once, twice, and then I repeated them again and again aloud.

"Salt, mercury, zaffer, sulfur, and flakes of gold," I said, rushing into the kitchen to place a pot to boil.

Kahem had warned me never to practice alchemy away from the warehouse. I'd obeyed. Like all the other silly rules he'd made me follow, I never dared question it. But Teta was worth breaking the rules. I had no one else. She was my friend, my family, and so much more. The thought of being without her, of being alone . . .

Forcing tears back, I focused on the measurements listed in the guidebook as the water in the pot boiled. A pinch of this, a handful of that. I was reaching from side to side, fumbling to get to each stinkin' pouch as quick as my hands allowed.

Soon it came time for the last of the ingredients . . . three flakes of gold.

Improvising, I hurried into my room, grabbed a small plastic bag from my sock drawer, and rushed back to the kitchen. Pulling a golden bracelet out of the plastic bag, I held it over the boiling water, although I knew it was a long shot. Kahem was always going on about the first rule of alchemy being the most important. He'd have said that I needed to have the *exact* ingredients to work, but I didn't. This bracelet likely wasn't pure gold. It could just be half, or even none at all. And yet . . .

"Sorry for this, Jiduh. I know you'd understand." I dropped the bracelet my grandfather had left me into the mixture.

Whoosh!

The entire kitchen filled with a strong red smoke that tickled my throat and had me hunched over, coughing. I waved the smoke away from my face and peered into the pot. There was nothing. Only a small bloodred pebble.

Without thinking, I snatched it up and rushed to Teta. My hand was wet, and I looked down, hoping the pebble was dissolving so that I could feed it to her, or sprinkle it over her like Sleeping Dust. Nope. It was only my tears streaming down my cheeks.

There were four types of alchemy. Dusts, to be breathed in or swallowed (or thrown at the face, which Kahem liked to do). Elixirs, to be self-consumed. Charms, which were physical, needing to be worn and held. And mists, which could only be breathed in, though they were the quickest to work. But the more advanced recipes didn't say which type they were. That was left to the more experienced alchemists to know, and I was just a beginner. I'd have to try each one.

I held the pebble up to Teta's face and, after that, I put it on her neck to wear. Those didn't work, so I opened Teta's mouth and eased it inside, closing her lips shut and holding my hand over her chest. I waited and waited. Tears streamed down my face like a waterfall.

Then I heard the faint whisperings of air moving in and out—a breath. Teta was breathing again.

Her eyes opened and she tilted her head slightly toward me. "Shad?" Her voice was barely a whisper. "What is happening?"

I nestled my face against her and listened to her heartbeat, making her shirt wet from my cheeks. I didn't know what to say or do, other than wrap my arms around her tight. There was no telling how long the elixir would last.

But what if its effects were permanent? Maybe the elixir had revived her for good.

Teta ran a hand through my hair. "You brought me back, didn't you? Habibi, some things in this world are not meant for us to change."

My heart nearly stopped at the sight of her face. She was pale and sweaty. Just when I was ready to tell her what I'd done, she broke into a sudden coughing fit. I steadied her back up against the bedpost and waited for the coughing to pass.

My head was shaking. "You can't go. Not yet."

"Nothing in this life lasts forever, Shaddo. But never fear; only look up and you will find me among the stars."

"Not today," I said, choking up. "Not on my birthday!"

Teta whispered, "Do not allow your dreams to die. Do as your father wished: become an alchemist and follow your heart, wherever it takes you."

"I will, Teta, I promise. And you'll help because I'm going to save you!"

Her eyes shone glossy in the light. I wondered if she was holding back tears. Hoping to be strong for me. "You will let me go in peace," she said. "And I want you to . . ."

Her eyes closed, lips doing the same.

"What is it?" My hands clasped together, begging for her to finish. "Please, tell me."

"How nice to end my journey with this gift, a few moments longer with my greatest joy," she said, her voice barely audible. "Promise me you will find others who care about you. When you do, protect them like you have protected me, my beautiful boy. We cannot face this world alone, Shaddo."

I shook my head, squeezing the sheets. "I don't want anyone else, Teta. Don't leave!"

The room went silent. Teta's eyes remained closed, her lips having curled into a wide grin. I had no one to cook dinner for. No one left to love me despite all my faults. Mama was in Lebanon with another family, and Kahem didn't love me. He was just my alchemy teacher.

Teta hadn't wanted me to be lonely, but sitting in that room, my heart was a failed elixir. A pie left in the oven for too long. It was mush, and I sat by Teta's side, crying. I didn't know how long I was there, only that when I got up, I wasn't hungry. The sight of the cake made me want to vomit.

I called the police two hours later. It was a miracle they understood what I was saying through the sobs. Paramedics carried her into an ambulance and drove away. The cake was sitting on the couch and one of the police officers brought it to me as I hunched over the kitchen table, wondering why the stars had taken Teta from me.

"Young man, is there an adult around, someone you could stay with?" she asked.

My mind raced through lies, excuses that would get them to leave. "Yes, I already told the ambulance lady. A man named Kahem Khatib. He lives here in Portland."

The officer quirked an eyebrow. "Who?"

"K-A-H-E-M," I said, spelling out his name, but the officers insisted there was no Kahem in the database.

"You know, the guy who owns the Arabic bakery, Halwa Heaven?" I motioned a big circle around my stomach to describe his large belly.

The officers looked at each other. One of them searched for the bakery's number on their phone and began to call while the other sat me down and waited. Neither of us said a word until, after a minute, the officer who called walked back in.

"Shad, no one's ever heard of a Kahem at Halwa Heaven."

I wrinkled my forehead in confusion, glancing across the table to the box of baklava. Even those delicious sweets couldn't drum up my appetite, and, after the first police officer gave me the news, she handed me her phone.

"I found a note," she said. "It was on your grandmother's nightstand, with your name and a phone number scribbled on it. Could it be an emergency contact?"

My throat went dry as I read the number. *Mama's* number. Teta wouldn't want me to call, but both she and Kahem were gone, so what choice did I have? Fingers shaking, I grabbed the cell phone that the officer held up and began to dial.

The phone rang thrice before something strange happened. For the first time since I'd moved from Lebanon, in all the countless calls I'd made, someone answered.

Voice quivering, I said, "Mama?"

A few moments of silence, and then, "Shad, is that you?"

"Yeah, it's me," I said, surprised at how different the voice on the other end of the line sounded from what I remembered. "I have some bad news. Something happened to Teta and now I . . . I don't have anywhere to go. Baba, Jiduh, everyone else is gone and there's this baker, Kahem . . ."

My stomach dropped at the sound of two distinct voices snickering, and it became clear Mama wasn't on the line. No, that had to be Yakoub and Layla, my horrible stepsiblings. Memories of their pranks sent a shiver crawling up my back. Swallowing tears, I shook my head at having told them *everything*.

"Who are you both talking to?" snapped a third voice.

I gasped, hearing that deep, terrifying shout. My stepfather. I remembered him with his well-made suits, his thick-rimmed glasses, and his dead eyes. Kahem always wore a frown, but it wasn't angry. My stepfather's frown had been angry, mean, and full of malice—just like my stepsiblings.

I hung up the phone and set it on the table. One officer

was snooping through the apartment, and the other, standing right behind me, had been speaking to someone on their radio. Both were too busy to notice I'd ended the call. Or see me sobbing into my hands. After all these years, I'd thought that just this once, Mama would want to talk to me. That she'd care.

"Guess I'm really alone now," I said, wiping my eyes and gazing out through the kitchen window.

The stars twinkled amid an especially dark night. When we first came to America, I would get nightmares and Teta would wake me and say, *No matter where you are, those stars are the same as they were in Lebanon.*

Was Teta already up there among the stars? Sighing, I shifted in the seat until a glimmer at the end of the table caught my eye. Something I hadn't noticed before.

"My birthday gift from Teta?" I wondered, reaching for a small box adorned in paper wrapping, yellowed like the pages from *The Alchemist's Hand* stuffed in my back pocket.

Ripping it open, I found a note written in Arabic. Time had given it holes and all sorts of stains. I began to read it in my head. . . .

Shaddo, you will carry on our traditions, so my gift is your father's most prized possession: a necklace he made as a young alchemist. Chase your dreams, habibi.

Beneath the note sat a necklace of wooden beads connected by rope. Each time my fingers brushed the necklace, a wave of relief tingled across my body. I lifted it up to the light and blinked away more tears.

"The best gift I've ever gotten," I said, glancing up at the stars. "Wherever you are, Teta, thank you."

Chapter 9

I grabbed a tissue and blew my nose, then grabbed a few more to wipe my teary eyes. Baba had taken over the family shop, an alchemy store, when he was thirty years old, but I hadn't asked Teta about that since the night I met Kahem. Just what kind of an alchemist was Baba? I had so many questions, and now that Teta was gone, there was no one left to answer them. Not even Kahem knew.

"Wait a sec," I said, whispering so neither of the police officers could hear. "I forgot about Kahem's gift."

Putting Baba's necklace around my neck, I rushed into the living room, where my birthday cake still sat on the couch. I dug through the large bakery bag until I found the small red-ribboned brown box. Heading into my room, I prodded the ribbon. As if by magic, it unfurled, the box opening to reveal an envelope. A red seal marked the center, where an alif, the first letter of the Arabic alphabet, had been imprinted.

Pressing a finger to the seal caused it to dissolve until it completely vanished. My eyes darted to the kitchen doorway, then around the living room. Luckily, no one was there to see what had just happened. I could hardly believe it myself.

I reached into the envelope, but the officer who'd been on the phone placed a hand on my shoulder and I jolted, quickly stuffing it into my pocket. "We have someone here to see you," she said. "He is a doctor, and he wants to help you find a more comfortable place to sleep tonight."

I opened my mouth to speak, but my throat burned from crying. Why did I need someone to help me find a place to sleep? My bed was still here, in our apartment.

The man who entered the room was a giant. He had a thick blond mustache that curled at the sides, and his muscles were bulging from beneath his clothes. But what worried me the most was his coat, with its long and draping sleeves, puffy from vial holders and pouch compartments sewn on the inside. Definitely an alchemist's coat.

"Hello, Shad," he said. "I saw a cake—is it your birthday?"

He looked at me with wide green eyes, almost like I was a spectacle, an animal at a zoo exhibit. Behind him, the police officer stood watch by the doorway. It didn't look like I had a choice but to talk to this alchemist, who was seriously giving me chills, especially around my neck, where I'd put on Teta's gift.

"You couldn't tell by my name on the cake?"

"Well, I am sorry for your loss," he said, folding his large arms across his beefy chest. "My name is Dr. Salazar, and I am here to help you find a place to stay tonight, but first, why don't you tell me about this Kahem fellow?"

"I . . . I don't need help. I want to stay *here* tonight."

Dr. Salazar turned to the policewoman and nodded. She walked away, leaving just the two of us. He reached into his coat and pulled out a glass vial. Inside, a milky-colored swirl shook with the man's movements. As he began to unscrew the cover, I stumbled back against the window.

"Come with me," said Dr. Salazar. He stepped forward with the vial in his hand and began to whisper something in Arabic.

A mist rose out of the vial. It floated up near his face and he waved his hand, which directed the mist around the room. Kahem had never shown me you could control the direction of mist.

"Now," said Dr. Salazar. "Let me help you. Otherwise I have to—"

I didn't listen to the rest of what he said because I'd rushed out through my window and onto the fire escape. I could hear stomping as Dr. Salazar chased after me.

From the fire escape to the ladder to the dumpster in my alley, I scrambled down to the street.

When I turned back to my apartment, the place Teta and I'd called home, I saw something terrible drifting out from my bedroom window. Black tendrils curled, contorted, and out of them two bright eyes peered down.

I hurried away from my building, not stopping for a single breath while I made for the bakery. It was dark and wind swept across the empty sidewalks. Shivering, I stumbled my way downtown, but the bakery was closed. Halwa Heaven's lights were shut off, no sweets on display at this late hour.

I didn't know what to do. Where to go. The sounds of an approaching police cruiser gave me no choice but to run, so I hurried down the street, running until I found an abandoned home near the edge of Portland, hidden by a creaky wooden fence. I slipped into the yard while flashes of blue and red lit the sky. The police were searching for me, and so was that scary Dr. Salazar.

I sighed, my hunger suddenly returning. Why didn't people keep fridges in their abandoned backyards? Arabs always had spare food lying around.

Along with the hunger, exhaustion from all the exercise of carrying cakes and running from mustached weirdos had my eyelids feeling like they weighed a hundred pounds each. I closed my eyes and wished for somewhere warm to sleep, something warm to eat.

"Teta, I need you," I said, and remembered her note, which I'd mistakenly left behind at the apartment.

At least I'd kept the last thing she gave me. Running my fingers along the wooden beads, a calm swept through my body. The necklace reminded me why I wanted to be an alchemist. Not because it's like baking, or because nothing felt better than making my own charms, but because Baba was an alchemist. And if Teta had wanted me to grow up to be like someone, it was him. Kind, loving, protective, he was everything my stepfather wasn't.

I reached into my pocket and drew out Kahem's gift, the envelope. It was almost unreadable in the dark. Almost. The yard was lit only by the moon. I ripped open the small envelope, squinting, and forced my eyes to adjust.

Shad,

You are invited to join the 2,223rd class of the Alexandria Academy, a school for gifted young minds. Please let us know of your decision by taking this note and waving it over your head should you accept or burning it should you refuse.

We eagerly await your decision.

Yours in the pursuit of truth,

The Deans

Unsure if this was some sort of joke, I decided to follow the strange instructions, moving toward the sidewalk for better lighting as I raised the note and began to wave it over my head.

I don't know what I expected, but I jolted at what felt like a bus colliding into me. Yelping as I fell back onto the ground, my knees and hands sank into the mushy dirt, and when I got up, I was spitting out clumps of grass. The note had been knocked out of my hands and I searched for it.

"Ouch," said someone from the ground beside me. They were rubbing their cheek. "Is that you, Shad?"

I gulped in fear, recognizing the culprit's voice. Of all the people in Portland, Sarah Decker had just crashed into me.

Her brown hair was all over her face, sticking to the sweat. Her eyes were wide and angry looking. "You live here?" she asked. "Why am I not surprised."

"No, I don't live here!" I argued. "I'm just passing through. Do *you* live here?"

"Do you want me to shove your head into the dirt?"

I raised my hands, starting to remember how scary Sarah could be. But before I could apologize, a tingle overcame me, and my fingers began to tremble. In fact, I began to shake all over.

Sarah was shaking too. She pointed at me and asked,

"W-what d-did y-y-you do to m-me?"

"M-me?" I asked. "It w-was you! D-d-did y-you j-just g-give me lice?"

The trembling passed before I'd finished talking, and then we were just sitting in the dirt.

"Are you, like, five years old?" she asked. "Lice is only in your hair."

"That's what someone with lice would say," I snapped, to which she rolled her eyes. "If you don't live in this house, what are you doing here?"

"Leaving," she said. "I was taking a shortcut after we egged Ms. Maroulis's house."

"Oh."

I pretended it was normal that she'd just admitted to throwing eggs at our English teacher's home. In fairness, Sarah was still kind of a bully, just not to me. But she could get in trouble if I ratted her out, which meant she trusted me. I didn't know if that was a good thing.

"Gotta run," she said.

Like a cat, Sarah rolled onto her stomach, got to her feet, and vaulted over the fence, landing somewhere in the next-door neighbor's yard. I heard her footsteps as they faded into the dark.

Panic set in the moment that Sarah vanished. I'd lost my invitation to the Alexandria Academy. Searching the ground, I spotted only a small scrap. The wind might have blown the rest of it away. I stomped in frustration, annoyed with myself for being so careless.

I'd meant to leave what remained of the note on the ground. It was trash, just a scrap, right? But I held it up in my hand first and my heart stopped. Under the light of the moon, barely visible, a single word shone bright as a star.

Accepted.

Chapter 10

"Consider yourself lucky to have been accepted," said Kahem, studying what remained of the invitation. "You cut it very close to the deadline."

After a night spent in the yard of the abandoned house, waiting until the stars faded and the sun peeked out over the fence, I'd trekked the rest of the way to Kahem's warehouse. Now, sniffling and hungry, I sat by one of the workstation tables and munched on some leftover falafel.

"Geez, I'm so lucky that I have to go to a school without even my mentor...."

"By the elements!" he snapped. "The Academy is the final school preserving the ancient ways of your ancestors, the one location that the necromancers couldn't get to. Back when I was a student, I would run through the halls with my book bag filled to the brim with alchemy ingredients. Older students would be practicing new charms on one another, and you could be learning how to craft a Disguise Mist in one class, then practicing how to duel in the next."

"Okay, I guess you're right," I admitted. "Learning to duel *would* be pretty cool . . . if I could afford it. Forget tuition, I don't even have the money for a plane ticket."

"Tuition?" asked Kahem. "The Alexandria Academy needs no money from you. Admittance is free, just as it has always been thanks to generous donations and an ancient reserve that has lasted through the ages."

I nodded, all while wondering just who could afford to donate to this school. Kahem sure couldn't. Otherwise, I doubt he'd be practicing alchemy in this dusty old warehouse.

"Count yourself lucky," he continued. "A friend checked your father's old mailbox in Lebanon every day until the note arrived. Otherwise, it might have come and gone without our noticing. Now tell me what happened yesterday."

The mention of yesterday clouded all my thoughts; the memory of Teta made my throat go dry. I took a deep, shuddering breath, but managed to hold firm as I explained what happened. He let me talk right up until I told him about the Revival Alchemy, about what Teta told me.

"You did what?" he asked as I winced, expecting a scolding. Yet he only frowned. "A golden necklace in the place of pure gold can never work. It was a miracle the charm lasted even a few moments. Tell me, what of the police? Surely they did not just let you walk away."

I shook my head, not keen on mentioning that I'd run away from home and further worrying my alchemy teacher.

But Kahem stepped forward and placed a firm hand on my shoulder. "Are you *sure* that you don't remember anything else?"

I swallowed. "Nope, nothing at all."

"Very well."

Kahem smiled like he was the bad guy in a Disney movie, then he began to reach back inside his alchemist's coat. My nerves were afire. Yolla purred, coming closer and clearly expecting a treat as Kahem dug around in the coat. Yet the moment I glanced away, dust hit my face, getting into my throat, up my nose.

I coughed. "What the figs was that for?"

"Spit it out," said Kahem. "What are you not telling me?"

When I didn't answer, Kahem stiffened. He reached back into his coat and removed a pouch. I flinched when he dipped a finger inside, raising it back to whiff the mixture.

"Is that Truth Dust?" I asked.

"It is," he admitted. "But it did not work . . . why?"

Suddenly, my alchemy teacher's hands gripped me as

he arched an eyebrow. He patted my pockets, arms, back, and even belly as if I were coming through airport security. The search stopped when he got to my chest, eyes widening, and pointed at my neck.

"What are you wearing?" he demanded.

I gently eased out my necklace. "Teta gave me this for my birthday. It belonged to Baba."

"Interesting," he said. "This appears to be a decanter crafted with cedarwood. A charm able to protect you from danger and yet still allow you to practice alchemy. I can make something like it, but nothing *this* advanced."

I glanced down in awe, tears brimming. Had Baba truly been able to craft something that an alchemist as powerful as Kahem couldn't? Even after he was gone, he still protected me in his own way.

Gripping it tight, I admitted, "There was this one person who also visited me last night. His name was Dr. Sala-something. He wore an alchemist's coat and had a big mustache and . . . and I ran from him!"

His mustache and creepy smile were clear in my head, and I shivered. Even now, a part of me still felt like I was being chased.

"Curse my luck," said Kahem. "His name is *Salazar*, a truly evil and particularly crafty necromancer. He must have had one of his underlings place alchemy-detecting charms in your area."

Hearing that nearly made me faint. "All this time, we were practicing alchemy in your warehouse. How didn't they sense that?"

"Simple," he said. "My protective alchemy, such as the Illusion Charms we practiced this summer, disguise our work from the outside world. Even those necromancer devices cannot detect our presence, and it is a good thing they do not reveal what specific alchemy you performed either. If Salazar and his evil companions learned you were working with a Revival Elixir, we would all be in trouble."

I stiffened, suddenly disappointed that I'd been so careless. But truth be told, seeing Teta smile again, if only for a few moments, was worth it. It now made sense why someone would want such a powerful alchemy, especially if it was meant to save their loved ones.

But then I remembered Teta's warning. *Some things in this world are not meant for us to change.*

"Don't worry," Kahem continued. "As I said, you will be safe from the likes of Salazar at the Academy. It will succeed where I have failed."

"You didn't fail," I said. "Those necromancers are just sneaky."

"Sneaky, yes." Kahem turned, as if a necromancer might be hiding in the shadows this very second. Twisting back to me, he looked at my dirty shirt. "Hold on—is your alchemist's coat still at your apartment?"

"Well, yeah," I said, bowing my head in shame. "I left all my alchemy gear in my closet: the ingredients, the coat, the belt with the pouches . . . all except for *this*."

I reached into my back pocket and drew out *The Alchemist's Hand*. Like the necklace Teta had given me, this had belonged to Baba. My heart swelled with hope that, for now, I'd kept it safe.

Kahem took a step closer and came out of the darkness. Bending down, he said, "I will go back for your belongings, but before that, I need you to understand one thing. You can now name enough ingredients to prepare any novice recipe. You are bright, Shad. By the elements, you are an alchemist. But no matter what, you must never, ever mention my name at the Academy."

"Never mention your name?" I asked. "But you're my teacher!"

"Yes, and I will continue to be," he said. "Remember when I told you how dangerous these times are? We cannot take risks with the necromancers lurking about. You never know who their spies might be."

Kahem rushed toward his workstation and began picking ingredients out of containers and stuffing his pouches. The fact that I could no longer train with him made me feel empty, despite the falafel.

"What will I do about Teta? I can't just leave her. . . ."

Kahem stopped for just a moment, swallowing. "I will see to it that your teta receives the finest of funerals, my boy. You have the promise of a master alchemist."

While still fighting to hold myself together, I mumbled, "Thank you."

"Of course," he said, bending to gaze into my eyes. "But please *never* attempt Revival Alchemy again. Remember, it is the responsibility of us alchemists to keep the necromancers from learning that recipe. That is why *The Alchemist's Hand* must never fall into their possession. Do you understand?"

I nodded, averting my gaze. This was what Teta had warned me about. I'd been so desperate that I did something far worse than breaking the rules of alchemy. Worse than forgetting my stuff in the apartment too.

Pressing *The Alchemist's Hand* into Kahem's chest, I said, "I can't take this. It's too risky and . . . I let you down. Just destroy it like the alchemy elders wanted."

"Enough of that talk," he snapped, shoving it back into my grip. "You learned your lesson. Besides, those books are nearly impossible to destroy. If I knew how, do you think I would have let you keep it all this time? Now, protect your guidebook and become an alchemist worth my time."

"How am I supposed to do that alone?" I asked. "Can't I just live with you?"

"I am afraid that is not an option." He pointed to his fluffy orange cat, which I had learned *was* a cat, and not a salamander at all. "Yolla hates sharing our house. That's why I can't keep a steady girlfriend."

Yolla meowed and, under my breath, I said, "Yeah, I'm sure *that's* the reason why."

By the time Kahem stopped rushing around the warehouse, all his workstations were nearly empty, his coat stuffed. His pockets overflowed with bags of gypsum, acacia roots, and loads of other ingredients.

Approaching me, he said, "I want you at the Academy so you can learn to practice alchemy where it's safe, but I also have a mission."

Suddenly, any doubts about leaving Kahem faded away as I leaned closer, my chest swelling with excitement. Kahem had trusted me with some of his secrets, but never a mission.

"Can you keep your eyes and ears open for me?" he asked. "If you hear anything that I should know, remember it. If you discover anything the necromancers might want, hide it."

"How can I get messages to you?" I asked. "It's not like I have a phone!"

Kahem sighed. "I would *never* leave you, Shad. As my apprentice, trust that I will find a way into the Alexandria Academy so that we can work together. But you must be vigilant while you wait for me, understood?"

I began to nod just as an ear-rattling rumble came from just outside the warehouse. Kahem jolted, one of his vials falling out of a pouch and shattering on the floor. Neither of us were expecting a visitor.

"Shad Hadid of Beirut, Lebanon," said a voice. "My tracker indicates you are here, so come on out and let's get moving. We have a tight schedule to keep."

Kahem stepped to block me from whoever was entering the warehouse. I was ready for that creepy Dr. Shazam, or whatever his name was. Or the police, who didn't believe Kahem existed.

Instead, a woman stepped through the sliding door. Her ruby-red suit, black high heels, and curly white hair distinguished her as someone who, at the very least, knew how to dress like a dried-up tomato.

Kahem reached into his coat and pulled out a small wool pouch. "Guard the book at all costs and never forget the mission," he said. "Your baba's charm will protect you better than anything I could craft, so protect that too. We will meet again once I get into the Academy, inshallah."

"Wait, I have questions!"

I reached to grab his coat, not wanting to be left alone with the tomato lady. Kahem threw down the gross-smelling dust and a blast of red smoke overtook us. I waved it away from my face. When the smoke cleared, I stood at the center of the warehouse, alone.

The lady frowned and asked, "You are Shad, I presume?"

"T-that's me," I said, my voice shaky.

"You may call me Dean Hayek," said the woman, her heels click-clacking along the cement. "I am here to escort you to the Alexandria Academy. I found you through the tracker in your invitation."

My whole body unstiffened. What a relief that she was with the Academy.

"That invitation was *so* cool," I said. "What kind of alchemy was in it?"

"Alchemy?" she asked. "You can play pretend during our ride. For now, please gather your things and meet me outside. We are running on a *tight* schedule."

The woman stepped out, leaving me to stand alone in the warehouse. My *things* were just Baba's charm and *The Alchemist's Hand.* Of course, on my workstation were some empty flasks, jars half-full of mercury, and other common alchemical ingredients, but that stuff was mostly junk. With nothing to carry them in, they would just mix and cross-contaminate, one of alchemy's major no-no's.

It was weird to leave the warehouse for good. Every day I'd spent here over the past few months was like stepping into a dream. Kahem always found a way to amaze me right before repeating the same three words: *It's just science.* Reliving those memories hurt. I couldn't help but feel a connection to this worn-down building, this large heap of scrap and glass.

"Ma'a salama," I said to my old workstation, to the new and old flasks, the spiders crawling in the corners.

I wanted to be sure I got the chance to say goodbye to whatever I could from now on. I'd already missed my chance with Baba, Jiduh, and Teta. The only other goodbye I wished I could've given was to the algebra teacher who gave me an F, but that would've included a stink bomb to the face.

I stepped outside as cool air slapped my cheeks. Dean Hayek led me to the pier. On the way, she asked, "No luggage?"

It suddenly struck me that I was about to go to a school in an unknown location with complete strangers. Even more terrifying, Kahem wouldn't be there to protect me from the necromancers, who I still didn't know much about.

But without a choice, I shrugged and said, "I prefer to travel light."

Dean Hayek arched her eyebrows but didn't say anything. We walked toward the pier. My nerves were making Kahem's falafel bounce around my stomach.

The dean stopped at the edge of the water and dug a remote out of her purse. "Do you get seasick?"

"I don't think so," I said, looking around, wondering why she would ask.

There wasn't a boat to be seen. The approaching autumn in Portland meant all the boats would be docked. Until then, the piers were always empty for vacation season. Always. I'd turned to ask Dean Hayek just what was happening when I heard a noise and felt the rumbling beneath my toes.

The water level rose, starting to splash my ankles. What looked like a turtle shell began to rise out of the dark depths. Except it was bigger than a shell, like a hundred times bigger. I pinched myself. Nope, not dreaming.

"Holy cannoli. . . ."

A massive, perfectly polished orange submarine settled into Portland Harbor. This was like no submarine I'd seen in the movies. It was basically a school bus, coated with bright orange paint and with windows for each seat. I struggled to read the other markings on the submarine but understood the words on the top.

Instant Oasis: Your Guide to the World

When Dean Hayek clicked another button on the remote, the roof slid open like a convertible sports car. I rubbed my eyes to make sure it was real.

"Get in," she said, "we're late."

Now, when I'd imagined what it would be like to climb into a submarine, there were a few things I expected: cup holders, pet hair, and maybe a quarter in between the seats.

What I didn't expect were seats facing each other like a stretch limo. Nor did I expect five other students all staring at me. But most of all, I did *not* expect the familiar face now staring up at me. The *last* person I wanted to see right now.

Chapter 11

"Mother mercury," whispered Sarah Decker. "You better tell me what's going on!"

The others turned to face her, the same confusion in their eyes. It wasn't normal to see Sarah like this; she was worried, maybe even as scared as I was.

"When did you get an invitation to the Academy?" I asked sharply, trying to keep my voice down.

I was angry. She didn't deserve this. I *had* to go to the Academy. My other options were living with the worst stepfamily ever or getting kidnapped by a bunch of evil alchemists who could turn themselves into shadows. Not Sarah. Her family had enough money to buy a lifetime supply of baklava, or a chocolate-milk Jacuzzi. And besides, the other kids all looked a little like me, with their dark hair and olive skin. Sarah was pale, taller than anyone else, and just in the last week had probably dealt out more wedgies than there were people in the submarine.

"Invitation?" She scrunched her forehead. "What invitation? Apparently, the teacher whose house I egged had a pretty good security system. She brought in a video of me right in front of her doorstep, but just as the principal was about to expel me, this lady showed up and told my parents that I'd gotten into this wacky boarding school for science and math. My mom and pops are making me go as punishment. Now I have to leave home, leave my friends, and we were just about to learn about ancient torture methods in history class." She squeezed her hand into a fist. "It's all so unfair!"

Sarah's eyes turned glossy, as if she was going to cry. I cleared my throat and asked, "Did you say you were going to a school for science and math? You . . . you mean alchemy, right?"

Dean Hayek's neck snapped around so fast that I thought her head might spin right off. She looked at me the way the Persian Punisher looked at his wrestling rival, King Crush. Everyone hated King Crush.

"Again with this alchemy?" she said. "Our science program is the best in the world. Do *not* insult the Academy with your silly ideas."

"Insult the Academy? All I said was alch–"

She pointed a finger in warning. "I don't have the patience for jokes right now." Then she turned back around.

Okay, now I was *really* confused. The other students in the submarine were too busy staring out the circular windows. Sarah just shrugged.

When I'd waved the invitation over my head last night, Sarah had crashed into me, so whatever alchemy was in the invitation must have gotten on her. She must have been accepted into the Academy by accident, and she'd only agreed to come because she would've gotten expelled either way.

"Oh figs," I whispered. "I'm about to be stuck in a new school with Sarah Decker, and it's all my fault. . . ."

No matter how hard I tried, I couldn't settle into my rigid seat. Gazing out the window, I didn't see any sharks or whales or sunken ships, only schools of small fish that darted out of the way. Occasionally, a piece of trash would drift by, and I'd try to guess what it was.

A shoulder brushed mine and I leaned away from Sarah, still finding it hard to believe that she was here with me. Her head nearly touched the roof, and her pale arms were crossed. Below our seats were cup holders with water bottles in them, and she'd been sipping one.

Drawing a deep, courageous breath, I asked, "Any idea where we're headed?"

She furrowed her eyebrows. "No, now stop bothering me."

Bothering her? I almost talked back, but she'd probably throw me out the window if I did, so I decided to keep quiet and stay on her good side.

If you hear anything that I should know, remember it. If you discover anything the necromancers might want, hide it.

Kahem's words were echoing in my ears when the submarine took a sudden turn and flung me into Sarah. She shoved me off, but not a moment passed before one of the students pointed and began to laugh.

I turned and saw that the water Sarah had been drinking splashed her shirt. Now her freckled face had gone red in embarrassment. I hadn't ever seen anyone make fun of her. Her eyes welled with tears. Maybe that was why she was a bully in the first place—because she feared being bullied herself.

I reached into my pocket and dug out a napkin to give her.

A voice in my head told me that she deserved to know *why* she got invited to the Academy. That it was completely by coincidence. But that would only make her feel like an outsider, and having known that feeling my entire life, I knew no one deserved that. Not even Sarah Decker.

She snatched the napkin out of my hand. For a second, it looked like she was going to say something like *I don't need your help*, but then she turned to the two students who were still laughing and snapped, "Shut your filthy traps. Both of you are lucky to be sitting on the other side of me and out of reach."

The old Sarah was back, and her threat got them to quiet down real fast.

For a long while, no one seemed to notice when I reached into my back pocket and pulled out *The Alchemist's Hand*. Even gripping it felt weird since I'd never held the last of *anything* before. In the kitchen, I always let Teta have the last grape leaf or the last cup of chicken soup.

While I didn't feel worthy to hold this old-as-bones text, Kahem had given me a mission. Even if the Alexandria Academy was safe from the necromancers, not a soul would lay their hands on the guidebook. In the meantime, I would take Kahem's advice from our training and use it to learn. To honor Teta's wish and carry on the Hadid family tradition.

Bending down over the guidebook, I opened the pages and flipped to the middle: *Beginner to Intermediate Healing Mists*.

Without reading the recipes, I glazed over the names of mists and tried to recite their ingredients from memory. It was my way of dealing with stressful times. I used to read the recipes of my favorite sweets back in Portland Middle during class. While alchemy had replaced baking for the most part, the only real difference was that, instead of mixing cake batter, now I was mixing elixirs.

Looking through the guidebook reminded me of being back in the warehouse, playing with Yolla's fluffy orange fur and listening to Kahem curse at his failed experiments. I closed my eyes and tried not to think about them. The more I did, the more I realized that from Baba to Teta and finally Kahem, I'd always had at least one person to look after me. That wasn't true anymore. Now I was alone.

"Hey," whispered Sarah.

I shut *The Alchemist's Hand* and slid it beneath my jeans, pretending to have been looking at my fingernails when I leaned up. "What's up?" I asked. "That shirt dry yet?"

She gazed down at her shirt and shook her head. "What are you hiding under your butt?"

I swallowed back my surprise and shoved the guidebook further beneath my jeans. "None of your business."

Sarah sighed, turning to look at the sleeping student on her other side. A snot bubble worked its way in and out of his nose as he hugged the pillow that came with his seat. If only I could do the same.

The submarine suddenly jerked again, this time rattling me in the seat and then slowing to a stop. We'd hit some sort of dock. My legs had fallen asleep, and I could tell by the way the students were looking at each other–or by how they were trying not to look at each other–that I wasn't the only nervous one.

"You may now exit," said a robotic voice from the submarine speaker system. "Do not forget your belongings, or they will be destroyed."

I slid *The Alchemist's Hand* into my back pocket and patted my jeans just to be sure. Dean Hayek lifted her remote and jammed a button. The submarine ceiling creaked open and bright, blinding light attacked my eyes. The others gasped too.

"All right, everyone off," she said, making sure we all stayed together as we got out.

I forced myself to breathe. The sunlight burned so strong that I needed to shield my eyes as I stepped onto sand. Warm winds rushed my face and I sucked in a breath of hot air.

"Holy cannoli," I whispered, hardly able to believe my eyes.

Our orange submarine rose out of a small lake. It was the only water around. An oasis, just like the submarine's name.

It wasn't alone. A long queue of submarines lined up along a walkway. One by one, other people of different ages were climbing out of them. I hurried to where Dean Hayek stood with the rest of the students from our submarine.

Did she seriously not believe in alchemy? We were in the middle of nowhere, for fig's sake. How could there be a patch of water this deep?

Whoosh!

A gust of wind nearly blew me into the air. It cleared the sand to reveal a red road, which led up a long, twisty path toward an unimaginably high fortress wall.

The gathering crowd started up the red road, and we fell into line. One of the kids from our submarine crew trudged right up behind me. Herman, that was what he'd said his name was during the ride. He dragged two designer-brand suitcases and smelled like cologne, yuck.

"No bags?" he asked.

"Yeah, you know . . ." I fumbled for an excuse, and came up with, "My parents wanted my suitcases delivered. Can't waste energy dragging them around, right?"

Sarah passed us, one eyebrow raised, with an expression that said, *Your pants must be on fire, because you are one huge liar.*

I ignored her. What was I supposed to do? Baba, Jiduh, and Teta had left me with nothing. It wasn't my fault that I didn't have designer clothes.

"Makes sense," said Herman. "Travel is *such* a pain."

I gulped, fighting back the guilt of the lie.

"What's the deal?" asked Sarah. "Looks like a plain old desert!"

She wasn't wrong. Stretching out on either side of the road was sand. Nothing but millions of tiny grains of sand.

I kept looking around, trying to find clues that could tell me where we were. Instead, I spotted a sign by the red road with one sentence written in shimmering bronze, the same handwriting that had been on the school invitation.

Welcome to Alexandria Town:
Home to the Oldest School in the World.

Chapter 12

W*e followed the caravan of* travelers up the road. With no luggage, I used my hands to protect my eyes from all the blowing sand.

"Ugh, every year I tell them to put up the screens," said Dean Hayek, shouldering her purse with one hand and sliding on sunglasses with her other.

Most of the adults and older-looking students wore sunglasses, while the kids from the submarine and I were left to fend off the sand. All except one girl, who dug her hands into the sand and lifted a giant beetle to use as a shield.

"Look at this!" she shouted. "Desert bugs out here are *so* cool, am I right?"

We all ignored her.

"This sand is terrible for my pores. I wonder if this school has a spa," Herman complained.

Sarah shoved him aside. "I'll dunk your head in a toilet, maybe that'll—"

A noise cut her off and I lifted my head to find the gate opening like a bank vault. Everyone began streaming inside, and when I turned to look back down the trail, the Instant Oasis had vanished.

An entire town lay on the other side of the gate. Neighborhoods of sturdy concrete homes rose across the long, curvy hill, none more than two or three stories high. It reminded me of my village back in Lebanon, each house so close to the next that someone could jump from rooftop to rooftop. But unlike Lebanon, multicolored roads brightened up this town. The smaller roads were yellow, green, and blue, while the main road was raspberry red.

Old men and women sat on benches, talking, feeding birds, and all while wearing loose, colorful robes, dresses, and headscarves.

I couldn't tell if this place was high-tech or old-fashioned. No one was using smartphones, and none of the watches that adults wore were digital. Yet when I caught up to Dean Hayek and my classmates, they were boarding a spotless white bus. Only it wasn't an ordinary bus; it had no wheels. I bent over and saw that there was at least a foot between the bus and the redbrick road where it just floated.

"I don't get it," said Sarah. "The amount of power needed, the mechanics. I keep up on all the latest technology websites and I've never seen anything like this!"

"What if it's not ordinary tech?" I said, scratching my

head. "What if it's alchemy, maybe an Advanced Magnetism Charm?"

Several students turned to me, wrinkling their foreheads in confusion. The girl who'd been eating sand passed us, now with a finger up her nose. She patted my shoulder with her other hand, laughing.

"You've been watching some weird stuff on YouTube," Sarah said, shaking her head.

Why were they pretending like *I* was the weird one? The fact that everyone was acting like alchemy didn't exist was getting me worked up. "I wasn't trying to be funny," I said. "This is what the Alexandria Academy is all about; so what if they used alchemy to—"

"Everyone on the bus. Hurry it up!"

The dean glanced down from the front-most seat, where the bus didn't have a driver. I hurried up a ramp, finding an empty spot by a window. Only after the bus jerked into motion did I notice we weren't the only thing floating around. As we rode uphill, I saw children and adults in floating wheelchairs, parents pushing floating strollers for babies, and floating scooters being ridden by kids who looked to be in elementary school. Behind us, the main gate opened again. Adults, their children, and more students with luggage streamed through.

Even with some air-conditioning, I melted like a Popsicle in the desert heat. My jeans were too hot for this weather and my dirty T-shirt was basically a sweat sponge. Luckily, no one had decided to sit with me. Having not showered for two days, I was too scared to sniff my shirt.

I heard Herman's voice in the seat behind me. It sounded like he was whispering to another student.

"What do you mean?" the other student asked him. "Shad got into the school, that means he's a descendent of one of the founding scholars."

"No," said Herman. "I knew something was off when none of his clothes were designer brand. My cell phone plan doesn't work out here, but there was Wi-Fi in the submarine and I googled the Hadid family. Do you know what I found? Not a thing."

I swallowed, wondering if there was another Shad on the bus. But Herman said *Hadid*, which was my last name. He'd searched me on the internet. The thought made me grab my gut because it felt like someone had just punched it. I mean, holy cannoli, we'd only just met, and they were already spreading rumors.

But what if Herman was right? Was I really a descendent of someone who founded this school? Teta and Jiduh had always said the Hadids only lived in Lebanon. Kahem had told me that no alchemists he knew shared my last name. Maybe Sarah wasn't the only mistake. Maybe I didn't belong here either.

The bus slowed to a full stop. The older passengers

stepped off first. I didn't look at their faces, too busy trying to ignore Herman's eyes burning into the back of my head.

"Wake up, Sleeping Beauty!" Sarah shook the boy with curly brown hair who'd ridden with us on the submarine. He'd slept through that ride too.

After being jerked around like the broken bubble gum dispenser at the Portland Stop n' Buy, the sleeping boy jolted awake. It didn't bother me that Sarah was going to be my classmate, but if I didn't say anything now, she'd be the same bully she was back home.

I tugged on her shirt and said, "You should cut that out."

"Cut what out?"

"That. What you just did to the dude!"

She furrowed her eyebrows. "Mind your business if you know what's good for you, Shad."

The threat got me stone silent, and Sarah followed the others off the bus, lifting her wrist to check something on her smartwatch. Eager to get out of this sauna of a ride, I rushed after her while keeping a safe distance.

"Wasn't that bus cool?" one student asked. "Dean Hayek told me it was scrapped, but some of the older kids at the Academy made it work again."

I didn't know how a student could possibly remodel a bus like that. Building a Lego set was hard enough for me.

Instead of thinking too hard, I gazed around for a bakery, but froze.

Atop the last hill, the Alexandria Academy was unquestionable: a palace with four tall, swirling spires at every corner, brilliant blue flames rising from inside each one. A large clock tower with Arabic numbers rose out of the middle, and a massive bell just below that. The alif that had been in my invitation was carved into a rock only a few feet from where we stood, and an arching walkway led through an open gate. The sight gave me chills, even in this heat.

"This is a school?" asked Sarah. "Looks like a museum."

A man almost as pale as her in a suit and purple-lens sunglasses stepped out from inside the archway. His gray hair, like his beard, was neatly trimmed and short. He walked over to Dean Hayek with several students following. They looked around our age, but they didn't have suitcases, and they wore white, puffy pants and shirts.

"Welcome, Theresa," said the man, with a slightly raspy voice. "You have a way of making your students feel welcome."

Dean Hayek almost didn't frown for once. "Yes, I suppose that I do. If only the same were true for you, Dean Ibrahim."

Watching Dean Ibrahim speak with her, his smile widening, reminded me of someone I knew. But who?

Behind him, several of the students in white puffy uniforms were giving me odd looks. At least, that's what I thought until one of them pointed at Sarah. A student whispered into another student's ear, and they both erupted into laughter. Sarah furrowed her eyebrows right back at them. I wondered if that bothered her as much as it would've bothered me.

We passed under the archway leading into the palace. I squeezed my hands in my pockets and tried to calm my nerves. The first day of any school year always felt like this. No friends, new bullies, and tough classes.

Even if I didn't feel like I belonged here, I needed to give this place a chance. Kahem had asked me to. And more than that, I was carrying on my family's tradition. From Jiduh to Baba and now me, alchemy was a part of the Hadid legacy.

A legacy I intended to carry on.

Chapter 13

After passing through the school's front gates, I stood at the center of a courtyard. About one hundred new students packed in around me, but all I could see were books.

Shelves and shelves of them surrounded the courtyard, protected by the shade of the palace. Where Portland Middle had lockers, the walkways here were neatly arranged sections of paperbound and hardcover books, both thick and thin. More confusing than even that were the students walking by them.

Older-looking kids in loose-fitting white uniforms stared at us as they passed. They carried ordinary school stuff, like pens and textbooks. And then there were things that were . . . well, unordinary.

One student held a laser pointer that projected a dog as if the student were walking it. The dog barked at several of us in the courtyard while its owner said, "Quiet, or I'll reconfigure you to be a poodle!"

They passed a student who, after grabbing one of the books straight off the shelf, turned to reveal a strapless backpack; it looked like the actual pack was floating behind using magnets. Several other students appeared to have those. Still, the weirdest of all the gizmos was the dragonfly drone. Unlike the dog hologram, this drone didn't bother anyone. Its metal wings flapped quietly alongside an older boy, who toggled a remote in one hand.

I tried not to stare, but even the nice malls back home didn't have this kind of tech.

As I wandered around the courtyard, any classmates who weren't gawking at all the gizmos were mumbling about how unfair it was that they had to give up their phones. Apparently, the school had a strict rule against using outside technology. A small part of me enjoyed hearing their complaints, especially the ones from Herman. He struggled in a game of tug-of-war with an adult over his phone. I'd never had a phone, so I didn't mind.

But then again, I never needed one in the first place. No one ever called me. Mama certainly didn't; she hadn't even reached out on my twelfth birthday.

While I explored the multicolored flowers growing along the edge of the courtyard, a boy leaned over to a smaller girl next to me and whispered, "I heard second-years talking about how the Academy built robotic animals with sharp teeth and claws. If you wander out of your room at night, they try and bite your legs off."

The girl whimpered and backed away from the boy, who kept coming closer. I couldn't just stand by and watch. So, as the boy cornered her, I stepped in.

"Why don't you leave her alone?" I asked.

The boy stood up to be a full head taller than me. "And what if I stay, what are *you* going to do?"

He rolled up his sleeves to display golden armbands on one wrist and a fancy-looking watch on the other. A hunch told me this rich fig and Herman would get along just fine. But I hadn't expected him to turn on me. Without my alchemy belt full of ingredients, I was just as helpless as the girl he was picking on.

Still, I never backed down to bullies in Portland, so why start here? I took a step toward the boy and said, "Try me."

His fingers tightened into fists, but luckily, another student grabbed his attention. One I should've expected . . . Sarah Decker.

"Is Shad already annoying you?" she asked, approaching with her hand raised for a fist bump. "I'm his former bully, you know. The name's Sarah Decker."

The boy gave her a once-over, and then grunted snobbily. "Whatever."

Sarah dropped her hand as he walked away, treating her like she didn't even exist. Her eyes did a twitchy thing, appearing glossy in the sunlight. Why did I feel like a hand had grabbed my heart and squeezed? I couldn't stop watching when, finding a group of what must have been friends, the bully turned and pointed at Sarah. They laughed and she stomped off.

Had someone just bullied Sarah Decker?

The smaller girl now stood in the center of the courtyard, her poofy hair swinging as she glanced left and right. I couldn't tell if she was searching for a friend or looking to avoid any other bullies, but I strode toward her all the same.

"Hey, I'm Shad!"

Tilting her head, she waved. "Thanks for helping me out, Shad. I'm—"

But then my foot caught on something or, as I found out while falling, *someone*. I yelped and landed on one knee. Beside me, the napper from the bus jerked awake. He gazed left and right with a befuddled look that said, *Where am I?*

Another student had already begun chatting with the girl, so, turning back to the boy, I asked, "It's the first day of school—are you trying to make a kabees of yourself?"

The boy yawned, stretching out his arms and scratching his bed head. "Did you just call me a pickle? By the way, I'm Donald Tahir, but I prefer Donny."

"I'm glad you speak Arabic, Donny, but you can't just

fall asleep wherever you want."

Donny scratched his head. "Why not?"

Before I could answer, a voice interrupted our conversation, amplified as though with loudspeakers I couldn't see. "Welcome, students of our 2,223rd class!"

I held a hand over my eyes to block the sun and saw a group of seven adults standing at the base of a large podium. Deans Hayek and Ibrahim were among them, but the one who spoke into the microphone looked much older than the rest, a woman with gray hair clipped short. She wore the same baggy top and bottom as the older students in the hallways, except in a sky-blue color.

"How neat is this place?" she asked, pointing to the student with the dragonfly drone, who smiled and waved back. "I'm using voice amplifiers that are invisible to the naked eye, and all of you arrived on one of our trademark Instant Oasis submarines. All of it was designed by our gifted students. Now, what if I told you that, like those other students, you were hand selected to be here? It's true. On this day 2,223 years ago, the world's finest scholars created a school to carry on their love for math and science. We are all descendants of those scholars, both here in the Academy and in Alexandria Town. This is our special bond."

Now, it could have been nerves, but Drowsy Donny turned to me and mumbled, "Not her. She was probably one of those founding scholars herself."

There aren't many things better than a well-timed joke, and that one was spot-on. I nearly doubled over with laughter, raising a thumbs-up to Donny, who froze. His eyes began to widen. The girl in front of me turned and frowned. I stopped laughing and noticed many of the other students were staring, some of them with their jaws dropped.

Oh figs. Everyone had heard Donny's joke—the voice amplifiers didn't just work for the podium.

The only adult smiling in the courtyard was the old woman. The adults who stood on either side of her all shook their heads. Suddenly, the sun outside felt a hundred times warmer.

"May I ask, first-years, who among you said that?"

The crowd of students parted for Donny, whose eyes bulged, tears brimming. He was genuinely scared.

I couldn't stand to watch, even though it wasn't my problem. Sometimes, the right thing was the right thing, even if it felt like a smack in the head.

Shoving Donny aside, I stood up straight and raised a shaky hand. "I said it."

Silence swept across the courtyard, and the deans on either side of the old woman frowned. All except the speaker, who said, "You are not entirely wrong. I really am quite old!" She laughed the way I had, and even harder.

"Please, do enlighten me, what is your name, young one?"

I forced myself to stand up straight, as everyone was looking at me. "My name is Shad Hadid."

"Hadid? I've had Haddads, Houssans, and Hariris," she said, "but never a Hadid. As for me, I'm Dean Abdullah, the head dean. And next time, Shad, be more careful about speaking during an Academy event, okay?"

I was ready to be so careful that I'd never speak again. How could anyone know there were noise amplifiers nearby if they were invisible? What even *was* a noise amplifier?

"As I was saying," continued the head dean, "although the Academy is the world's foremost math and science school, we must still respect tradition. The uniforms you will wear are hand-knit sheep's wool, like those of the original scholars. Now, standing behind me are the deans for each of our school's six grades, but allow me to introduce *your* class dean, Mr. Farouk Saba."

Everyone applauded Dean Abdullah as she stepped down from the podium, joining the dozen or so teachers gathered off to the side. I turned to Donny, who was still gaping at me. His lips formed the question *Why?*

I didn't have an answer. It just felt like the right thing to do. I felt the pressure of being watched from all around the courtyard. Any chance of going under the radar was squashed. The attention could help me find friends who thought the joke was funny. Yet being noticed by my classmates meant the bullies now knew who I was too.

Speaking of attention, it was impossible to miss Dean Saba, who stood out among the other five deans with his shiny bald head and especially dark skin. "Hello, y'all!" he began with a perfect American accent, much to my surprise. "First off, shout out to Dean Abdullah. She's the Queen of Calm, the Idol of Intelligence, and we salute her."

I didn't think the dean could get any worse, but he followed up his words with a dab. Several of the students shook their heads. Others visibly cringed. It really was *that* awkward.

"Two quick ground rules," he said. "As you all now know, no cell phones on Academy grounds. Get caught with one and you will be on bathroom-cleaning duty until you graduate! Second, no wandering after eight o'clock. If you need to wee-wee, then do it at 7:59, got it?"

We all turned to one another, and even if no one said it, we were all thinking the same thing. *Did he just say wee-wee?*

Dean Saba paused, and he looked like he was waiting for something. Then he said, "I can't hear you!"

Everyone sighed as we all said, "Got it."

The noise amplifiers turned our answer into a loud *BOOM* and I clutched my ears.

"Now that's what I'm talking about!" Dean Saba's

dangling earrings danced as he clapped his hands together. "Go forth, finish unpacking, and make friends. I'll see you all at dinner!"

The deans disappeared into one of the many hallways leading out of the courtyard. Students grabbed their luggage and got to following Dean Saba, me included. Donny dragged his suitcase by my side, and we passed a teacher with a wild brown beard arguing with a group of students.

"I don't know why the prototype keeps failing, Mr. Fares," said one of the students, clearly a few years older. "Maybe we need to give it more power?"

"Well, I can assure you it is *not* that," began Mr. Fares. "During our next robotics class, you can bring your invention and . . ."

I didn't hear the rest of Mr. Fares's order, as I spotted Sarah across the courtyard. A full head taller than nearly everyone else, she marched through the students in her way. Whoever got chosen to be her roommate was in for a real treat.

I trudged along grass and stone, following some of my classmates. A fountain sat in the courtyard's center. In the middle of it, a statue of a boy held what looked like a weird teapot . . . no, a lamp. It was Aladdin, from Teta's nighttime stories. Jinnis didn't exist, of course, but maybe Aladdin was using alchemy to make it seem like he had one. That was what Kahem had thought.

Remembering my teacher's mission, I grabbed *The Alchemist's Hand* from my back pocket as I rounded the fountain. But why had Kahem told me to guard it so carefully in the warehouse? What use did the necromancers have for a dusty old thing like this? Especially if they couldn't even read it.

I gripped the book tight. It calmed me, a reminder that my family remained close to my heart, even at a place like this. But while shoving it into my pocket, a shadow swept over me and I nearly bumped into Dean Ibrahim. He glanced down his strange purple sunglasses at me. The hairs on my neck stood up, and then he tipped his chin down to the book in my hands, which I quickly hid behind my back, shoving it into the pocket by my right butt cheek.

"Hello again," he said. "What was that you were just holding?"

"I–I wasn't holding anything," I lied, raising my empty hands.

The dean leaned in closer. I saw wide eyes in the reflection of his glasses as he said, "Yes, you were."

My heart thumped as I stepped back, but he kept coming closer and closer. This guy was *definitely* not my friend, and something about him made my stomach turn.

My necklace began to tingle, the charm that had been Baba's. That had only happened when that creepy necromancer showed up at my home. Could they be here too?

No, it must have been something else since the Academy was protected from those evil alchemists.

"Uh, I'm a student here," I said, fumbling my words. "I came to study alchemy, umm . . . I mean, to study math, just like everyone else."

Dean Ibrahim quirked up a bushy eyebrow. "Young man," he said, frowning. "There was a nasty rumor that we taught alchemy years ago, but that was all it was . . . a *rumor.* This is a school for math and science. Remember, an imagination like yours can get you into trouble."

My legs began to shake, the knot in my chest tightening as I raised my eyes to meet his. Only, the dean had vanished. I swung my head in all directions, but he was really gone, as quick as Kahem had disappeared the last time we were together.

Many of my classmates were chatting and laughing and making friends with other students. Standing among them, I wondered where all the alchemy was and why no one had any idea what I was talking about when I brought it up.

As I headed through the halls back to my room, the older students passing me only carried thick textbooks. That and the occasional backpack or gizmo, like the dragonfly drone. No alchemy coats or belts. No pockets full of ingredients like Kahem described. Could there have been a different Alexandria Academy on the other side of the desert? I already had a few questions for Kahem, and

I'd need to find a way to reach him without a phone.

Of course, he'd promised to show up, which eased my worries as I slouched my shoulders and—

Ding!

The bell above us chimed and I jolted. All around the courtyard, students slowed to listen to the chimes while a strange itch crept up my neck and Dean Ibrahim's words echoed in my head.

An imagination like yours can get you into trouble.

Chapter 14

I followed the other first-years across the hallways and hallways of books. Along the way, the shelves were labeled. One section was titled *Animals of Asia* while, turning the corner, we passed *Plants of the Amazon*. Eventually, the bookshelves transitioned to ordinary walls. We entered a new wing of the palace, a hallway with all our rooms. I peered into each one and stopped in a room where, facing the door, a placard hung over the bed with *Hadid* etched on it.

Cramped, the room held two beds, but barely enough space to stand. "Lucky me," I said quietly.

White bedding, along with a T-shirt and wool pants of the same color, were folded atop my mattress. I dusted off my jeans and shirt before reaching into my pockets to remove the invitation and *The Alchemist's Hand*.

Sand from my pocket flitted onto the floor as if I were trying to bring the desert into my room with me.

That was how I knew I wasn't in Lebanon. Nowhere in my home country were there deserts like the one I'd just walked through, but I still knew from the beaches that sand found a way into the oddest places. Places where rough sand should never be.

I shook the last few grains out of Baba's book while being careful not to rip any of the pages. I flipped open the cover and read a few of the basic recipes. Paper-Cut-Sealing Elixir, Mosquito-Repellant Mist, a Relaxation Charm. Nothing jump-started my confidence like this guidebook.

I hid it under my bed and changed. The other bed had already been made, and an Egyptian flag hung above my roommate's placard, which read *Shahar.*

A knock came at the door and Sarah stepped in, blocking the daylight coming through the hallway sunroofs. She was like the moon during a solar eclipse.

"Could you move?" I asked. "I'm trying to unpack here."

It made me nervous that, had she come just one minute earlier, she would've seen me in my underwear. Next time, I needed to lock the door.

Sarah laughed. "Come on, we both know that you've got nothing to unpack."

I swallowed, my throat going dry. Was this Sarah's way of saying she could blackmail me? That she could tell everyone that I had no money and nowhere else to go?

All I could remember was how the boy had bullied her in the courtyard, and that she might be looking for ways to regain control.

"Go ahead and tell everyone," I finally said with only a bit of hesitation. "I'm not scared of you or any other bullies. Oh, and I hope you called your parents. You won't get the chance for a while since the school took everyone's phones. Not that it matters since they probably didn't answer."

Sarah stiffened. No snarky response. No quick comeback. My heartbeat slowed and I felt like I'd just broken something between us. Like I'd crossed some imaginary line, even between sworn enemies.

"I was wrong about you," she said. "Or rather, I was *right* the first time."

I grinned, ready for an apology. Maybe I'd earned her respect by standing up to her. Or maybe she was trying to start fresh here. I didn't trust Sarah, but I imagined her being kinder. A Sarah who would rather give me compliments than cruel insults, winks and not wedgies. Hope filled my belly as I awaited her response.

At least until she rolled her eyes. "Back in the Instant Oasis, I thought you were trying to impress everyone, like Herman. Now I see that you're just a nut, Shad. You mentioned alchemy in an invitation? I never even got an invitation!"

"You're the nut!" I snapped back. "Don't compare me to Herman, that fig-faced little . . ."

I stopped just short of saying some words that would have made Teta wash my mouth out with soap. Sarah was the third person, after Deans Ibrahim and Hayek, to suggest I didn't belong.

Sarah opened her mouth to say something else when a boy my height walked into the room. "Did someone say nuts? I'm pretty hungry."

Both Sarah and I asked, "Who are you?"

He grinned a wide smile with his dark brown lips. "Why, I'm your roommate," he said, pointing at the name tag beneath the Egyptian flag.

"Oh my molecules," said Sarah. "I knew it. We *are* in Egypt."

But my roommate shook his head. "My Instant Oasis took too long to get here for us to still be in my country. Based on the direction we went, I'd say we're somewhere in Jordan."

"What's your name?" I asked. "I'm Shad."

He chuckled. "Trust me, after what happened between you and Dean Abdullah this morning, everyone in the school knows who *you* are. And my name's Ramon, but you can call me Rey."

I tried not to be terrified that other students were talking about me. Rey didn't seem to care, though. He had dark skin with cheeks covered in freckles. When he took off the beanie he was wearing, long, curly hair fell down his shoulders.

"Well, that's different," Sarah said, "I wish my hair curled naturally like that."

Rey grinned and continued to unpack his clothes. Meanwhile, I tilted my head, making sure it was Sarah who was standing at the door. The Sarah I knew never gave out compliments. It made a lot more sense when, right before turning to head out the door, she stuck her tongue out at me. I stuck mine out right back.

Sarah may not have been bullying me lately, but that didn't mean I trusted her not to ruin this chance for a fresh start.

I walked over to Rey's side of the room. My roommate was rummaging through a drawer full of beanies, each with a unique design: rainbows, smiley faces, sushi rolls, and things that just plain didn't make sense on clothes. And then my eyes locked onto one of Rey's hats. It had pictures of someone I never expected to find at the Alexandria Academy, and I pointed into the drawer.

"Like my limited-edition Sultan of Slam beanie?" he asked. "Yeah, I know pro wrestling is kinda silly, but I grew up with it. My parents think it's weird to like that sort of stuff too."

"Are you kidding me? You are officially the coolest person at this school! Did you see his last fight, where he—"

"Beat Serbian Stingray by whacking him with a banana? Of course I saw it!"

"And then Rocky Roulette tried to come after him, but the Persian Punisher rescued the Sultan and—"

"They tag-teamed Rocky and Stingray, throwing them both out of the ring! Dude, my friends in Egypt and I are, like, the biggest fans of all time."

Rey chose a bright yellow beanie and wore it over his hair, again hiding the long black curls. He checked the time, which was projected right above the door, and said, "Dinner's in an hour. I'm going to use the bathroom and chat with some classmates."

"I'll catch you later." Sighing from exhaustion, I fell back onto the bed. "I'm just going to lie here for a minute..."

On top of my dresser, I could see the Academy had provided extra pairs of underwear, a toothbrush, shampoo, and basically everything I'd need to get by. It wasn't clear how they knew I needed all that. Could it have been Dean Hayek, who'd seen me come without luggage?

Soon, my eyelids grew heavy. The baggy uniform felt like wearing a cloud. And although sleeping probably wasn't the best idea, I closed my eyes, slowly sinking into my pillow and turning my back to the daylight.

Yup, a quick nap would do the trick.

Chapter 15

*N*o part of me wanted to get up, but the nagging grown-up voice in my head told me I needed to. My stomach began to growl, which meant it was probably dinnertime. I turned to look at the clock and my eyes needed a few seconds to adjust to the darker room.

7:00 p.m.

"Holy cannoli!" I yelled. Dinner began fifteen minutes ago.

Rolling out of bed and scrambling onto my tired feet, I dusted off my plain-white uniform and laced on the school-provided sandals, which were somehow my exact size. Without skipping a beat, I sprinted down the hallway. Being late to dinner meant I might get a detention. Or sent to see the head dean.

The student dorms were on the second floor and had so many hallways, all tight and narrow like a maze. No walls stuffed with books, but digital clocks projected at each corner, reminding me how late I was. I began to see holograms of other things, like a table of elements and, in a separate hallway, a sign that read *Welcome Back, Second-Years.*

Another sign read *Kharaj*, which meant exit in Arabic. I rushed toward it without a clue if I was exiting the Alexandria Academy, or just the student dorms.

Thud!

Something shoved me, and that was the noise my back made when I crashed into the concrete wall. Butt hitting the tiled floor hard enough to hurt, my thoughts were scrambled for a few seconds before I realized what had happened.

"Who let this *bahle* into school?"

I shivered at that voice, closing my eyes as memories I didn't want to remember flooded in. Memories that had become nightmares and had haunted my sleep for months. No, years. It couldn't be real, of course. *He* couldn't be here. Could he?

The hands gripping my collar lifted me up. "What's the rush? You don't look so happy to see me."

I opened my eyes and faced my oldest bully. My stepbrother, Yakoub.

Trying to find my footing, I scrambled to say, "W-what brings you here?"

"My baba was a student here," he said. "The Monsour family is one of the oldest and richest in Lebanon. Not like the Hadids, who were a bunch of poor farmers. Tell me, how does it feel to find out that you aren't the most special boy in the world?"

I'd never said I was special, but I'd also never considered that my stepfamily was special either. How could I have known that Yakoub's baba, my stepfather, was also a descendant of one of the Alexandria scholars?

Yakoub punched my shoulder and I yelped. "Since you left five years ago, your mama's never mentioned you once. She didn't even care when I told her you were coming to my school."

I squirmed in Yakoub's grip. "You're lying, and this isn't your sch—"

Yakoub delivered another hit to the gut as I groaned. "Don't worry," he said. "Unlike Mama, I plan to take *really* good care of you."

Hearing Mama mentioned sent a wave of sorrow through me. Never would I joke about Yakoub's mother, who passed away when he and my stepsister were too young to remember. Unlike him, I wasn't evil.

Being face-to-face with my stepbrother reminded me of all the nasty things he'd done, like putting worms in my school lunch. Or how he and my stepsiblings would joke that I'd never make any friends.

Choosing not to let him see my fear, I widened my eyes and whispered, "You must still be jealous that my baba loved me more than your baba ever did."

It became clear right away that bringing up *that* part of our past was a mistake. Yakoub's expression changed. His smirk twisted into a frown.

If I wasn't dead lahme before, I sure as figs was about to be. After all, my stepfather had always been Yakoub's sore spot. Seeing how my baba always brought me Arabic sweets while his never brought him a thing, or how mine took me to the beach while my stepsiblings were stuck at home . . . it had made Yakoub jealous and everyone knew it, especially him. It was probably why he loved to bully me in the first place.

"How about we play a game?" he asked. "I'll hit you in the face until I collect enough teeth for a big chunk of money from the tooth fairy. That will make up for all my birthdays that you missed, eh, brother?"

"I–I'll tell one of the deans," I said as he laughed. "Seriously!"

I tried to think, *What would an alchemist do?* But I had no ingredients to use, no elixirs or charms either. Alchemy didn't have my back this time, so I closed my eyes and braced for the worst.

But before I got a knuckle sandwich, something smacked into Yakoub's neck and he crumpled. I landed on my feet. Yakoub lay flat on the floor, frozen with eyes open wide. In the meantime, someone else walked down the hall. As they stepped forward, I noticed white hair and a *very* red outfit before a familiar scowl greeted me.

"Are you going to be trouble for me this year?" asked Dean Hayek. "No need to answer; I watched you make a mess of yourself during the assembly."

Not even the desert sun could have prepared me for that burn. Despite the insult, the dean was my new hero for saving me from Yakoub. I smiled and she returned it, briefly, then she reached out and plucked a small black chip from Yakoub's neck.

"Since this allowed me to test a project some of the last-years are working on," she continued, "I will let you off the hook just this once. The boy will be fine when he wakes up shortly, but you better get to dinner before I change my mind and issue a detention."

I didn't need her to say that again. Seeing the type of tech that students six years older than us worked on brought a nervous sweat to my forehead. I hurried toward the exit, leaving Yakoub on the floor. It took maneuvering through several hallways before my nerves settled.

I stumbled toward doors large enough to fit an elephant at the end of a long hallway. With different last names, nobody would suspect my stepbrother's relation to me. Yet that didn't change who Yakoub was, and that I was trapped at this school with him.

My nightmare had just become a reality.

Chapter 16

As the massive wooden doors to the dining hall opened on their own, the noise from inside rumbled and I gasped.

In a way, this cafeteria was like the one in Portland Middle, except it was the size of a movie theater. More bookshelves sat along the walls on the other side. A wooden sign labeled one end as Alkhubz and the other Tabakh, along with their English translations, Baking and Cooking. I first passed the tables full of older students, teachers, and administrators, who sat off to the side. My classmates packed the other tables in the hall's center. They all wore the same soft white T-shirt and pants, kneeling on fluffy patterned rugs. Up to six students sat around the low tables, which were each covered in empty plates.

Students began looking at me when I passed, my name being whispered across tables. Like Dean Hayek, my classmates hadn't forgotten the whole welcome-speech incident.

Finding an open seat wasn't easy. The large bully I'd confronted earlier, who I'd heard called Jad by one of his friends, sat around a group of equally mean-looking students. They flung food at other tables. A chunk of kibbe almost hit Selma Aboud from New Mexico. She now sat at the table next to Herman Reyes from actual Mexico, both having been on my Instant Oasis. I remembered them mentioning their families had immigrated from Jordan, the country where Rey thought we were now.

I spotted Sarah at the other side of the hall, which was brightened by lamps hanging along the walls. Directly behind her, large vases held even larger plants, almost as tall as trees. They'd make good cover if I ever needed to hide from her. Only, it seemed the opposite would happen because one of the only empty seats was at her table.

My legs grew wobbly as I neared my former bully. We hadn't exactly started off on the best terms earlier today. Thankfully, she didn't kick away the floor cushion opposite her as I approached. Bending, I sat with crossed legs and the table came up to just above my belly button.

A student was asking her, "So, if your parents are not Arab, North African, or descendants of a founding scholar some other way, then how did you get into this school?"

Sarah shrugged, reaching for another spoonful of hummus instead of answering. Meanwhile, I glanced at the student who'd asked the question, with her ball of poofy hair and a face that looked much younger than the rest of the first-years'. My mind flashed back to the courtyard assembly, where I'd tried to defend her from that bully, Jad, and almost gotten thrown across the field for it.

Eyes widening, she said, "Oh, it's you!"

"Yup, I'm Shad," I said. "Glad you still remember me."

"I'm Hayati," she said, "and I never forget a face. Besides, it's only been a day and you are already more well-known than anyone else in our class."

Her voice squeaked like the pet mouse back in Portland Middle's science lab. "Did you know your tardiness reduces your odds of graduating? Studies show that teachers notice these things, so you should see that such recklessness does not become common practice."

I scratched my head. "Um . . . thanks?"

In the seat opposite us, beside Sarah, the sleepy boy from earlier, Donny, munched on kousa. It was the very same stuffed eggplant dish Teta and I prepared together a couple months ago. Thinking of that night had my eyes beginning to burn. I distracted myself by watching Hayati carefully feed herself over a napkin, taking baby bites.

"So, as I was saying earlier," she began. "That's the teachers' table. It's a little bigger than all the others."

"I met Mr. Boutros in the courtyard earlier," said

Sarah, pointing at a man with gray hair who was only an inch or two taller than me. "He'll be the Arabic teacher for most of the first-years. I told him I don't speak it, but he said that's normal since students come from all over the world."

"My sister had him as a teacher when she was a student," added Hayati, gesturing toward a woman with hair down to her butt. "That one is Ms. Marakesh, one of the math teachers for the higher grade levels. My sister had her too."

"I wonder how many librarians there are," I said. "There are books *everywhere* in this place, more than in my former school library."

Hayati nodded. "That's because the Alexandria Academy *is* a library. At least, it used to be thousands of years ago. One of the older students told me that this dining hall is the cookbooks section."

Donny nodded and said, "Back in Chicago, my aunt told me this place is old as bones. That there are secrets hidden with the school and stuff too, like a . . ."

Yawning, the boy bent over and placed his head on his hands, which rested on the table. We all gave each other confused looks when he began to nap, but then I tilted my head toward the shelves along the wall.

The dining hall was part of a library? Although hard to believe, I couldn't deny all the books. There were more than I could count in this room alone.

Around us, dinner was clearly winding down. Students across the tables were setting down their forks, knives, and fingers, since lots of Arabic food was eaten by hand. Luckily, there were still a couple of pieces of grilled eggplant and some fattoush salad. I used the last small loaf of pita bread to scoop some creamy garlic sauce and got to work stuffing my face.

Someone cleared their throat near the front of the dining hall, loud enough to make an echo. I looked up from my plate while still chewing to see that Dean Saba had arrived, and a group of teachers stood around him in a semicircle. The sunlight pouring in from the glass dome above had softened. Still, it didn't stop Dean Saba's bald head from shining like a lighthouse.

"Students, I hope you are enjoying your first meal with new friends," said the dean. "Like the food before you, the Academy's founding members came from all over the Mediterranean to share their knowledge and make new discoveries. Now, we like to honor one of their traditions with a first-year science fair, which you'll be working on this semester! For that, I'm bringing two of our lovely teachers, Ms. Wassouf from the science department and Mr. Fares from the math department, to share the details."

As the dean spoke, two adults approached. The first of the two, Ms. Wassouf, wore large glasses and had crooked teeth, her dark skin folded into wrinkles. Meanwhile, Mr.

Fares beamed at us from under his single bushy eyebrow.

"Hello, everyone!" said Mr. Fares. "To begin, you will be split into groups that will present a project in the courtyard where you had orientation. Each project must be unique and based on a topic you can research in the library."

"There won't be a winner," continued Ms. Wassouf. "But teams that do well *can* receive extra credit in both science and math."

"Finally," said Mr. Fares, "since the point of the science fair is to test your ability to solve challenges, you can only use supplies that are found in our science labs, and no older students may help!"

The two teachers smiled at each other with more enthusiasm for science than I'd ever felt. Dean Saba stepped forward again, gesturing them back to the teachers' table.

"Now," he said. "You'll have until the end of the month to find a four-person team for the fair. Working with these classmates through October and November, you must prepare to present your projects to the deans just before winter break in December. Is that clear?"

We all collectivity murmured, nodding in understanding.

"Good," he said, clapping his hands together. "Now, choose wisely . . ."

We all looked at each other and then chaos erupted in

the dining hall. Like a pop quiz, it spurred everyone into a frenzy. Some of these figs shouted random math problems at potential teammates, while others tested classmates in biology and chemistry with trivia facts. They wanted the best students on their team.

"Well, well, well," said Dean Saba, arriving at our table. "Today is a historic one at the Alexandria Academy, with our youngest ever first-year. Welcome, Hayati!"

Dean Saba reached down to pat her on the shoulder like Kahem used to with Yolla. Hayati shrank away from his hand. There was no denying she looked younger than us. Still, the youngest first-year in the school's history? Dean Saba left us, and before I could ask her about her age, Sarah wrapped an arm around Hayati's neck.

"You and Donny are going to be on my team," she said. "Shad, you can go run off. Find whatever group you want."

Hayati fought against Sarah's much larger grip. "I don't want to be on your team, let me go!"

It surprised me how much it stung not to be chosen by Sarah. Even back in Portland, no one ever wanted to partner with me. My classmates always complained when the teacher assigned me to their team. I'd never let them know how awful it felt. Never let them see my tears.

But as Hayati and Sarah eyed me, waiting on my next move, I wondered why I should brave all those awkward smiles and fumbled introductions. A student approached

Sarah from behind and I flung a carrot at their head so they'd turn around.

"I've already chosen my partners," I said. "You all need a fourth person, and I need a team. Catch my gift?"

"The expression is *catch my drift*," Donny clarified, coming to sit down. "Oh, and I just joined another team as I was coming out from the bathroom."

"Well, I will join your team," said Hayati.

Sarah and I both asked, "You will?"

Hayati nodded, adjusting her glasses. "No one has ever stood up for me like you did at the assembly, not even back in Morocco where I grew up. Besides, you clearly do not have the science expertise. Leaving you to figure out a project would just be cruel, and probably a bit dangerous."

That answer sounded more like an insult than anything else, but I just shrugged and said, "Sweet, my first team member!"

While Sarah growled at Hayati and Donny, the excitement of joining up with Hayati spurred me to begin glancing around the table. Kahem loved to say that the ancient art *was* technically science, and we were already talking about the fair, so this seemed like the perfect time for a demonstration.

Only, this alchemy had to be something the deans couldn't catch me doing. Dean Hayek yelled at me just for mentioning it, so I needed to be careful.

"Who wants to see something cool?" I asked.

Sarah scoffed. "You're about as cool as the desert, Shad."

"Well, then prepare to watch a desert become an ocean," I said, bringing several of the plates closer to me. "You won't want to miss this."

I swallowed back the pressure of doing alchemy in front of anyone other than Kahem for the first time.

"Hey, everyone!" Rey came to crouch beside us. "Just wondering if . . ."

My roommate's voice trailed off as he noticed me dipping a finger into the olive oil that lingered in the hummus bowl. With my other hand, I grabbed the salt-shaker. Swirling an oil-covered finger into a cup of soda, I began to add in the salt, stirring it all together. Then I waited. . . .

"Is something supposed to be happening?" asked Rey.

Hayati adjusted her glasses. "It appears to be some sort of experiment."

A few seconds had drifted by and the fizzing hadn't even begun. Of course, the elixir I was mixing wasn't a dry one, so there needed to be fizzing. This had always happened with Kahem in the warehouse. I'd goofed some-where, forgotten something. But what?

Sarah shook her head. "Guys, Shad is full of–"

"Aha!"

I spotted the dandelion earrings that Sarah wore and remembered what was missing. The right ingredient was crushed rose petals, of course, but we didn't have that. It was as if Teta were whispering in my ear–I knew to scan the table, my imagination guiding me to a replacement.

I grabbed the small bottle of rose water that, like in any reasonable Arab kitchen, sat next to the condiments. In the back of my head, Kahem's voice told me what I was about to do was wrong. That the mixture wouldn't work. Sure, I wasn't using the exact same ingredient as what the recipe called for, but what was the harm in trying? I splattered several drops into my cup and, concentrating, I waited until something started to happen.

Fizzing, foaming, the drink began to evaporate like fog from a lake. Lifting both hands, I shoved the foggy mist into Rey's, Donny's, and Hayati's faces.

"Hey!" Hayati groaned, leaning back.

It was too late. She'd breathed it in, and her nose scrunched up in disgust, at least until the mist's effects kicked in and displayed the hall–and everyone in it–in a shade of green.

"That is *so* rad," Donny said, eyes wandering around as he laughed his way into a nap.

Hayati leaned in and said, "Give me more!"

Sarah followed Hayati's lead and took a big whiff too. Soon we'd all breathed in the mist and were seeing the entire hall, the students, everything in a bright green shade. In the guidebook, this was the Green Eyes Mist. And, if I remembered correctly, it would last for only a minute or two and helped to see things in the dark. After that, our eyesight would return to normal.

Hayati and Rey kept on giggling while Donny snored comfortably.

"Call me a comet," said Sarah. "Shad, what did you just do?"

I gazed around, taking in the students, teachers, and everyone in between. When the mist began to wear off, I gave Sarah my most honest answer.

"Exactly what I came here to do," I said. "Alchemy."

Chapter 17

"*What the figs!*" I shouted, awakened by an earspliting croak.

After wowing my classmates with an alchemy demonstration last night, I'd come back to my room and gone straight to sleep. No shower. No brushing my teeth. Not even a pre-bed pee. And now I couldn't do anything other than hold a pillow over my head to block that terrible croaking noise.

"Don't mind the roosters," said Rey. "You get used to them eventually. But hey, check out the clock!"

The digital clock in our room had become a projection of the words *Alexandria Library Hallway 21, Room 18*.

"Where's that?" I asked, stretching out of a yawn.

"Get your clothes on," he said. "I got here several days early and taught myself how to get around."

I threw on our sheep's-wool shirt and pants uniform while he slipped into another beanie. He'd agreed to work with me after I told him about Hayati, bringing my science group number to three. Although it was just the second day of the Alexandria Academy school year, most students were apparently scrambling to find partners for the fair, nervous about locking down the right team. Rey wasn't a big fan of the first team to offer him an invite, and I didn't blame him since Herman was on it.

It only took a few minutes for us to get to room 18, but it felt like an hour. I made us stop at every hallway intersection since I couldn't risk running into Yakoub. My stepbrother knew how to hide, and he loved springing traps.

"So, who should we ask to be the fourth member of our science fair group?" asked Rey.

"Not sure yet," I said. "We have until the end of the month, and I have a feeling that whoever it is, they'll find us when the time is right. Besides, they won't be able to say no once I show them some more neat alchemy."

"Show them *what*?" asked Rey.

"You know, what I told you about yesterday," I explained. "The Green Eyes Mist."

Rey shrugged. "Got no clue what you're talking about, dude."

I snorted, thinking Rey was only messing with me, but his confused expression never changed. Could it be that he'd already forgotten?

A sense of unease filled my belly. I still hadn't heard anyone else mention alchemy, and I wasn't going to stop bringing it up. After all, if the school had somehow lost its way, it would be my responsibility as an alchemist to remind everyone just what the ancient art was. Hopefully Kahem would get here soon so I wouldn't have to do it alone. . . .

But I didn't mention it again as we trekked to class, arriving to find that it wasn't going to be in just any ordinary room. No, this was an enormous hall full of books, like a library within a library, and the second floor had been knocked down to give more space to the towering shelves. There were hundreds of those stacks, too many of them to count. Even a professional basketball player would need a ladder just to reach the top.

"There must be a million books in here," I said, my voice leaving a small echo.

He adjusted his beanie, which had a map of Egypt embroidered on it, and shrugged. "Actually, there are 2,768,532 books here. Says it right there."

The center of the room was as wide as one of the Academy's four courtyards. A two-sided television monitor hung down like a chandelier, and it displayed a count of the books on the shelves, the ones taken out, and who had them. The list seemed endless.

"Welcome, my first-year students!" A man as old as

dust stepped out from behind a large counter. His beard nearly touched the tiled floor, and he didn't have any teeth when he smiled. He spoke with a wrinkly grin that reminded me of Teta's, and asked, "Surely you realize where you are standing?"

Rey scratched his beanie. "Um . . . in a library?"

The answer made the old man's shoulders droop. "Oh Allah," he said, his gummy smile disappearing. "Well, you are not entirely wrong. The Alexandria Academy is indeed a library. The key is in the name. This palace was once known as the Library of Alexandria–ring any bells?"

I turned to Rey, who was shaking his head. Kahem had never mentioned it during his lessons on alchemist history either.

"Surely you have heard of the Library of Alexandria. It was the oldest in the world!"

And you are the world's oldest librarian, I thought.

The old man gestured to the stacks. "This is one of history's wonders, now believed to be lost. Some will claim our palace was burned to the ground during the second century, but the descendants of the founding scholars were able to preserve it, keeping it secret and safe. Since then, thousands of their smartest descendants have come to learn here, studying science, language, mathematics, and much more."

"We had a library in Cairo," said Rey. "Never went there, though. It was filled with rats."

The old man stroked his long beard with both hands. "That's troubling, young one. Although some of these books have been preserved for thousands of years, I can assure you that we do not have rats."

"It doesn't look so old," said a girl who was just walking in.

"And you do not look so bright!" said the man, belly-laughing as if he'd told the world's funniest joke.

The girl furrowed her perfectly plucked eyebrows. She stood by Jad, the same student who'd made fun of Sarah in the courtyard. They all looked the same—manicured, mischievous, and mean. I couldn't vibe with that. What I *could* vibe with was seeing one of the bullies squirm at being the butt of a joke, and I belly-laughed too. Rey also seemed to find him funny, and he giggled beside me.

The old man wiped away a tear and said, "Only joking, dear. What do we have if not our sense of humor, right?"

The bullies made a face at me and the old man, but now a dozen other students had gathered around us, and the hall in the library was quickly filling up.

Ding!

The Academy's bell chimed and everyone stiffened. Even Rey looked like he'd just become a statue, and I reached out to touch him. Before I could, the sound of the bell went away. He returned to normal and gave me a look.

"That bell marks the beginning of your very first

class," said the man. "It rings eight times per day. Once after every class is finished, and after each of the three mealtimes. Now, welcome to the school's history department, the hall with the single largest collection of books in this palace. I am the head librarian here, but I shall also be your history teacher when you have this class. The Academy uses a rotating schedule, which means there are days when, sadly, we will not meet. Now, you may all call me Mr. Saud, but I prefer Moussa."

"Moussa?" asked Rey, raising his hand. "What in the world is *that* thing?"

Perched above one of the stacks, looking down at us, was a monkey in a vest. One of the students stumbled back in surprise. They nearly fell into Jad's arms, but the boy stepped aside and let them crash into another student behind him. He chuckled and dusted off his clothes.

"Oh, you all are such children," said Moussa, walking bowlegged to the stack with the monkey. "Get out of here, you miserable ape. Stop interrupting my lesson!"

The monkey bared its sharp teeth, then it turned and leapt onto another stack. At this point, I wasn't sure what the figs to expect. Pretty much nothing made sense here. Instinctively, I ran a hand over *The Alchemist's Hand*'s cover, tucked under the waistband of my pants. Just touching Baba's book sent a rush of memories through my bones. Like I was back in Kahem's warehouse, my teacher standing over me and yelling that I used the wrong measurements or confused the salt with the sugar. Still, it felt . . . comforting. Like I wasn't alone.

"Pop quiz!" announced Moussa, the side of his lips twitching into a toothless smile. "What is the standard system used to keep books in order at most libraries?"

We all turned and looked at each other. I had no clue. I'd never set foot in a library by choice, and usually never got farther than the computer room, where I schooled some figs in online backgammon.

"The Dewey decimal system," said a quieter voice from the back of the group.

Hayati. She was so small that I hadn't even noticed she was in the room. Her shirt and pants sank down her body, way too big for her. Her legs shook at the attention she was getting, and she hiked up her glasses with her fingertips, clearly trying to look like she wasn't nervous.

"Whoever said that, please get over here!" said Moussa. He waved his arms and made a welcoming gesture.

"What a dork," said someone near the back.

I turned and heard a boy, another one of my bully classmates, whisper, "Heard she's some kid genius who got a special invitation. Yakoub would want us to put her in her place."

The mention of my stepbrother set my nerves on fire. It concerned me to know he was influencing my classmates, turning them into his little minions.

As Hayati passed, I gave her shoulder an encouraging

pat. She spun and glared, though her face softened when she saw me. Unlike my evil twin stepsister, Layla, who always lied about me calling her names just for the joy of seeing me in trouble, I wouldn't have minded having a younger sibling like Hayati.

"What is your last name?" Moussa asked, lifting his bearded chin and not quite smiling.

"El . . . El-Sayed," whispered Hayati with her mouse-like voice.

"Ah, you have a sister here. Very well." He fished out what looked like a flash drive. "Usually, teachers here will keep scores using their Academy-provided tablets. As for me, I prefer to have some fun with our grading. I use this cool gizmo that I call a point tracker."

Moussa clicked the button on the rectangular device and a hologram sprang out. All the student names in the class were displayed, twenty in total. Moussa poked one of two holographic buttons and a one hundred appeared right above Hayati's name. All our eyes were glued to the sweet projection, so when Moussa started clapping, I jolted in surprise.

"Hayati has been awarded the maximum participation points," he said. "Full credit for class participation!"

I joined in on the clapping, worried I might lose points if I didn't. Then I realized something that made me gasp. Holy cannoli, was I beginning to care about school?

Slowly, I snuck through the crowd of standing class-mates, making my way over to Hayati. She grinned as I approached. Waving, I found a place by her side, pretend-ing to listen to Moussa's continuing lecture.

After Rey was acting weird around alchemy earlier, I couldn't help but double-check that my trick got the attention it deserved, asking, "You remember that alchemy I did during dinner, right?"

Hayati shook her head. "Alchemy? No, we discussed the science fair."

I scratched my head, a hint of worry nipping at my thoughts as I whispered, "Yeah, I also crafted that mist. You were seeing things in green, we were laughing, and it was great!"

"I don't know what you're talking about," she said. "I have an impeccable memory, so I would've remembered that."

"*Shhhh*," said another student, to which I stuck out my tongue.

How could anyone forget something as special as alchemy? I remembered each mixture I'd ever crafted, every lesson Kahem gave. Something about Hayati's and Rey's responses didn't add up. . . .

A tingle from Baba's charm stole my focus away from the issue at hand. The sudden sensation came from the back of my neck, and an instinct urged me to spin around.

Nothing was there, only the endless stacks of neatly organized books.

We have been observing you, a voice whispered, like someone was saying the words into my ears. *Join us, alchemist. We can help you. Strengthen you.*

I spun in both directions. "Did you hear something?" I asked Rey.

He shrugged. "Hear what? The clapping, or Moussa speaking?"

"Never mind Moussa," I whispered under my breath.

Shaking my head, I patted *The Alchemist's Hand* and turned back to where I'd thought I spotted movement.

Right at the end of the stacks, where the lights were dimmest, a shadow swept from one column to the next. At least, I could've sworn I saw one. In an instant, the voice had gone silent, the movements vanishing.

While my classmates listened to the lecture, I couldn't help but wonder if we weren't alone in this ancient school, and the thought chilled me to the bone.

Chapter 18

Kikeek-kikeekee!

Roosters woke us again, as they'd done nearly every morning since I'd arrived two weeks ago. One of the Alexandria Town residents basically kept a farm's worth of animals in a stable just outside the school and, while annoying, it reminded me of Lebanon. The difference was that back then, even the annoying parts of life didn't feel so bad since I got to spend them with Baba.

"Rise and shine," said Rey, already having changed from pajamas to the nearly identical school uniform. His bed head was brutal, and he was working his curls with a comb.

"Good morning to you too." I yawned as I stretched, my arm hitting *The Alchemist's Hand.*

Quickly, I swept it under the pillow and hoped my roommate hadn't noticed. The guidebook had been open to a section on Communication Alchemy, recipes that might allow me to reach out to Kahem and ask where in the figs he was because something strange was definitely going on.

Ever since that first class in the library, I'd been wondering if my mind had just been playing tricks on me. The voice I'd heard sounded *so* real, its eerie whisper unforgettable. Yet when I'd looked every class since, there wasn't a single sign of the shadows. No indication the necromancers were here, or that there was any other alchemist around, for that matter. Still, I wanted to tell Kahem about the voice I thought I'd heard, as well as how no one seemed to know anything about alchemy.

My classmates refused to believe me when I explained why the grass in the courtyards never grew past several inches. That someone had mixed Evergreen Dust, an advanced alchemy, into the soil so the grass never needed tending. Or that the strange steam in the bathrooms had to be some Odor Mist, which explained why the centuries-old toilets didn't stink.

Maybe I should drop the necromancer hunt, but if I gave up on bringing alchemy back to the Alexandria Academy, I'd be giving up on more than just my dream. I'd be giving up on carrying on the Hadid family legacy. *Baba's* legacy.

Fluffing my pillow, I said, "I've been working on mixing a pretty advanced elixir. Want to try it in the dining hall sometime?"

Sighing, Rey shook his head. "Not sure how many times I need to say it, but elixirs aren't real."

"They are too," I argued. "You just haven't learned to make one."

"If they *are* real, then you must have drunk an elixir that makes you irresponsible. That'd explain why you haven't done any homework assignments."

Rey was right. I hadn't been doing my homework because most of it made about as much sense to me as a cake without frosting. And that would soon become a problem since, according to the student handbook that Moussa made us read, any grade below a C meant expulsion.

I wondered what might happen if I got expelled. Would they send me back to Lebanon, to Mama, who never bothered to listen when I told her my stepsiblings were bullying me? To my stepfather, who laughed whenever my stepsiblings snuck extra spice into my food at dinner, watching me gulp down glasses of water in pain?

Maybe I could live somewhere else and work at a bakery or help in a restaurant kitchen. Anything would be better than sitting in math class, pretending to listen while guessing when my alchemy teacher might show up.

But it was for the sake of Kahem's mission that I had to stay. I had to find out what was going on. And one of these days, he'd show up and prove to everyone that alchemy existed.

"Stop moping around," said Rey. "You're slower than the Serbian Stingray after the Persian Punisher hit them on the head with a sack of potatoes."

He stood in the hallway and pointed up at the clock, which read 7:20. We only had ten minutes to get to class, which meant I only had five minutes to poop and grab my textbooks. Gym class was first on the schedule today, and the gym was across the Academy. Just thinking about all that walking made my legs sore.

"Wish I was the Serbian Stingray," I mumbled under my breath. "At least he doesn't have to play sports with annoying virtual equipment, like simulation volleyball."

Rey kept bugging me while I hurried through my morning routine. He led the way out, telling me about his language arts class, which was in the ancient literature section of the school. The gym was only a few hallways down from that.

Like every other student, my roommate was an over-achiever. All my classmates were suck-ups, most of them taking enough notes to write their own textbooks. They also raised their hands to answer almost every question and, because of how much each student cared about their grades, most tended to arrive in class at least ten minutes before the bell. That was a good thing for me, though, because it meant the hallways were clear right before class.

I nudged Rey with my elbow. "How do you manage to get up so early anyways?"

He shrugged. "My parents always used to wake me up for school. Didn't yours?"

Shaking my head, I admitted, "Not really, no. Guess yours were really strict."

"You can say that again," he said. "And in more ways than you can imagine. . . ."

My friend's voice dipped, and I could sense sadness in his tone, though I didn't press him on it. Nor did I tell Rey that I hadn't been living with my parents. That I hadn't seen Mama in forever. The thought only made me miss Teta more. Her love had protected me like the shade of a fig tree, and I didn't realize it until she was gone. It was torture knowing that every student had a home to return to.

Everyone but me.

After we'd been walking for a minute in awkward silence, Rey whispered, "So, are we not going to talk about the smell?"

He didn't need to whisper. We were the only ones in the hallway, except for some of the older students who had a free period.

Shrugging, I said, "I never noticed a smell."

"Shad," he sighed, sounding annoyed.

Of course, I knew exactly what he was talking about. I

wished I didn't have to lie to him; it was hard to not have anyone to talk to about baking, let alone alchemy. Still, I'd never admit to sneaking garlic, salt, olive oil, and a few other ingredients out of the dining hall. You never know when you'll need some quick alchemy.

"Come on," he pressed. "What's causing that gross smell coming from your side?"

"Seriously, what smell?" I asked, snorting. "I mean, I fart in my sleep, but that's completely natural and . . . oh, look, isn't this where your class is?"

"Wait, we're not—"

A group of older students led by Yakoub approached and both of us went stone silent.

"What a fun surprise," said Yakoub, patting his friends on the back. "This is Shad, my baby brother."

"I may be younger, but I'm not the baby," I snapped without thinking.

Rey turned with wide eyes, and I knew I'd messed up. Yakoub's grin contorted into a frown and I wondered what the odds of me getting away were. Enough distance sat between us and the bullies for a good head start, but it was one that wouldn't last since they were bigger *and* faster.

"Get them both!" snapped Yakoub, his friends lunging.

But before the bullies could do a thing, I turned and belly-bumped Rey into his classroom right beside us. As

I sprinted away, the bullies giving chase, I yelled, "Sorry, you'll thank me later!"

Sunlight streamed in through the courtyard where we'd had our assembly as Yakoub chased me through it. I rushed into a nearby hallway, pivoting behind a bookshelf, waiting until he and his friends zipped right by.

Ding!

The bell chimed and, catching my breath, I'd started back toward my class when a sudden chill crept up the back of my neck. A lesser tingle from Baba's charm.

Oddly, it vanished as soon as I turned. The hallway stood empty and, since I was only a few steps away from the hallway where the gym was, I slowed down my stride. Ms. Najoom, our gym teacher, had flat-out rejected all my requests to keep score rather than participate in the class activities. Maybe today, she'd change her—

My necklace sent a much stronger shiver down my spine. Like at the library a couple of weeks earlier, I twisted around. The hall was empty, except for a single person among the bookshelves. A woman in a long black coat whose cold gaze froze me still.

"You there," she said. "My order wishes to speak with you."

"Order?" I asked, taking a step back. I'd only ever seen necromancers dressed in all black like that. "Like a school club? Sorry, but I'm already late to class."

Frowning, the woman shook her head and reached into what turned out to be an alchemy coat. The many pouches visible, she took a step forward and tossed down some dust, transforming into a giant black ball as large as the hallway itself, shadowy tendrils reaching toward me just like the necromancer in the alley.

"You?" I shouted. "You figs are *here*? Someone help!"

Bullies and homework and all my other worries vanished as my suspicions turned out to be true. Two hands stretched out from the darkness and chased me down the hall.

The necromancer drew nearer and nearer, reaching for the back of my shirt. I knocked down books from the shelves, weaved around pillars, and even farted. Nothing I did seemed to slow her, my lungs burning as I hurried away.

"There is no need to run, child," said a raspy voice, echoing from the darkness. "We can shield you from the bullies, make you powerful beyond your dreams. . . ."

"No thanks," I said, pointing back down the hall. "The bullies went that way, why don't you go talk to them!"

"Do not resist us," she said, a tendril brushing my neck. "We know what you are!"

I hurried around a corner, rushing into the school gym just before the necromancer could grab me.

"We are honored that you decided to attend class today, Mr. Hadid."

Ms. Najoom waved from across the court while I hunched over, catching my breath.

With Baba's charm continuing to send tingles down my spine, I tried to explain, "Shadow monster. Really big. Outside. Right now!"

"I'm sorry," she said in her kind, soft-spoken voice. "Monsters, though? That is one of the oddest excuses for being late I've heard in years."

"Ms. Najoom, I *swear* that this time it happened!"

She shook her head and said, "I know gym can be tough, but it's not fair to the other students if you don't participate. Now, go get changed and be sure to take off that necklace like I told you last time. It's against the gym class dress code."

Shaking out all my tight nerves, I turned away from my skeptical gym teacher, gazing out at the dodgeball game ahead. Although not as strict as some of the other teachers, who would have given me a detention for being late, Ms. Najoom sure enjoyed making us play this aggressive game.

Three years ago, a group of last-years had presented a prototype of the virtual balls for a class project. When they attached a few lightweight projectors to a foam ball, it could appear much larger, and sense when the projection touched someone. The deans liked it so much that, in addition to giving the students straight As, they ordered dozens of the balls created.

Now students traded swings on either side of the court. Many of my larger classmates had the advantage of size and power on one side. Yet Sarah resisted on the other, dodging balls and easily tagging out her opponents as if on a one-person team.

Along the middle, all alone, Drowsy Donny sleep-walked with balls soaring overhead, finally bumping into the wall, a bookshelf full of exercise guides that probably reeked of sweat.

But the balls and the books didn't matter now that I had concrete proof the necromancers were here. The voice from the library hadn't been in my head. All of it was real. Baba's charm had been trying to warn me about them both here and in Moussa's class two weeks ago.

I heaved out a breath, stretched out my legs, and headed into the locker room. Being Kahem's *eyes and ears* was turning out to be a lot more than I signed up for when I accepted this mission. My alchemy teacher had lied. Or, at least, he was wrong.

The Academy wasn't safe. There were necromancers lurking, and they knew about me.

Chapter 19

"Just try and come for me, necromancers," I said, biting my lip while placing a Vomit Charm on the dresser beside the door.

My attempts to communicate with Kahem using the recipes in my guidebook continued to fall flat. Whether thanks to bad mixing on my part or my teacher hanging out somewhere that warded off such alchemy, I decided that the best next step would be to protect my room.

Ripping off tape I'd snuck out of a supply closet down the hallway, I added another decanter, the type of mixture meant to repel other alchemy. It fit nicely with the line of ornaments now hanging over the door from the inside. Not the prettiest decoration—I wouldn't blame Rey for complaining—but that didn't mean they could come down.

Would these charms make the room impenetrable? No, but they would ensure that, if anyone with a hint of Shadow Alchemy tries to come in uninvited, they'd at least be *very* uncomfortable.

Besides, I didn't want to completely cut off alchemy in here. For one, I practiced whenever Rey wasn't around. And I'd still want a Communication Mist to be able to come through. After all, Kahem might end up trying to reach out to me . . . at least, I hoped he would.

I walked over to the ingredients strewn about my bed and sighed, starting to shut the pouches of metals, salts, and dried foods. To cap the jars of oil, chemicals, and water. All of it fit neatly under the bed with the other things I kept carefully hidden, like *The Alchemist's Hand*. Over time, I hoped to add to the collection and, maybe, come as close as I could to an alchemy workstation.

"Kahem, where are you?" I said, lying back against the pillow.

Outside, the halls sounded empty, which made sense. All my classmates should be in the dining hall since it was the first-year lunch period. Rey and Hayati would probably be discussing the science fair, or some cool tech they saw the older students building. Meanwhile, Sarah probably sat with her new bully friends.

I'd head over in a sec too. My belly *was* rumbling, but the last few hours since the necromancer attack had been too stressful to focus on anything else. Even eating took a back seat to the danger at hand.

If only I could explain to the deans, teachers, and

my classmates just how serious things were. But no one would believe me. No, even my alchemy demonstration hadn't worked. I closed my eyes and wondered what Teta might tell me to do. She would know what the right move was, unlike me.

But she wasn't here.

Loneliness crept up into my chest just remembering our practice cooking sessions and being back in Portland, the two of us together again, until my belly began to roar. Climbing out of bed, I studied my newly charmed room once more before opening the door and leaving.

"Let me get this straight," said Rey. "A ghost attacked you in broad daylight on your way to gym class?"

"Yup, only it wasn't a ghost," I said. "They are called *necromancers*, and they are evil alchemists who can disguise themselves in shadows. And I believe there was one during history class a couple weeks back!"

Hayati shrugged. "Maybe try telling Dean Saba, or Dean Abdullah?"

"I tried telling Ms. Najoom," I admitted. "But it didn't work. The deans will probably just think I'm trying to get out of doing classwork like she did."

The cafeteria clamored with gossip and rumors as I explained what had happened this morning. I had quickly realized the only similarity the Alexandria Academy had to Portland Middle was my gossiping classmates. Everything else, from the uniforms to the accents, was different. Even the food tasted better thanks to all the Arabic dishes.

We didn't have required seats, but Hayati and I had been eating together every meal. Saving her from Jad that first day earned me the brainiac's friendship, and sometimes she'd shed her serious demeanor, but only when the two of us were alone.

Aside from Hayati, Donny sometimes joined, but Rey took Sarah's place after she moved tables altogether.

Two days ago, she'd almost attacked another student who'd tagged both of us out during simulation dodgeball. The brutal game would've put me in a coma had the virtual balls been real. Oddly, threatening another student had led Sarah to be welcomed into our class's little band of bullies. She'd clearly forgotten that, in the first week, some of them had singled her out for not being Arab.

Rey said, "Shad, yesterday you were trying to convince us that the fire burning across every Academy tower is from some kind of Eternal Heat Gas, or whatever you called it."

"It's an Eternal Heat *Mist*," I corrected him, "and yes, that's the reason those flames never go out!"

"Good one." Hayati giggled, continuing, "There should be a perfectly scientific explanation for it. My hypothesis is that birds bring tons of wood up there because they make the perfect nests. Since the desert temperatures get so high in daytime, that wood constantly catches on fire."

"Well, I don't know what a *hippo-thesis* is," I said, "but that doesn't explain why the flames are still burning when it gets dark outside!"

"Yes, science can!" she insisted.

I couldn't hold in my groan. Science this and science that. What didn't they understand about alchemy being real? It seemed simple when Kahem explained it to me. If he were here, he'd know exactly how to convince everyone, even my skeptical science fair partners.

"Let's say these *necro-manders* or whatever you call them weren't made up," said Rey. "How does that explain why you always manage to show up to lunch so late?"

I dipped a carrot into the bowl of baba ghanoush. "I like going to the bathroom after class is all."

Rey had already returned to eating, but Hayati's gaze lingered. I wondered if she'd inherited the ability to tell if someone was lying from her grandma. After all, Teta could always tell.

She set aside her plate. Her ten-year-old belly couldn't fit more than a kabob, so she always finished first. "For the science fair, how about a solar-powered Jet Ski for driving across the desert sand?"

"Then we can have Jet Ski races," I said. "Let's do it!"

But Rey shook his head. "No way the teachers would allow that. Too dangerous. Maybe a robotic hand that can reach up to the tallest library shelves. That way we don't need ladders!"

Hayati shook her head. "What about using the technology in Eddie Azzar's floating wheelchair to build a real-life flying carpet!"

"I don't think you can call it a wheelchair if it floats," said Rey, "but I like where your head is at."

Interrupting both members of my incomplete science fair team, I whispered, "Speaking of school stuff, do you think you can help me with the homework for our history and algebra classes?"

Hayati nodded. "As long as we are not giving you answers, the school handbook would not *technically* call it cheating."

While my friends both agreed to help because . . . well, they were my *friends*, I caught Sarah squinting at me across tables. I couldn't tell why, but unlike some of the other bullies, she hadn't started picking on me again. Still, others took her place, like Herman, who judged me for not coming from a rich family, or Pascal, who I'd caught shoving Hayati around the Academy's math wing.

Pushing the bullies out of my thoughts, I studied all the ingredients and said, "Enough about boring school stuff. Food alchemy 101 is back in session and today, we're going to cool down."

"What does that mean?" asked Rey, stiffly observing me. "When have you showed us food alchemy before?"

I didn't bother trying to remind them *again*. Words wouldn't restore alchemy. Heck, maybe nothing would. Maybe the necromancers, whatever they were planning, were responsible for the alchemy not being a part of the school curriculum.

Although I didn't have Kahem around, my teacher would want me to put up a fight, and for now that meant doing demonstration after demonstration until people understood.

All I needed was three pinches of pepper, one pinch of iron, two spoonfuls of dirt, and half a cup of cold water. Cooling Dust was a surprisingly quick mixture, even if dust alchemy tended to take longer. Pepper and water were already on the table, dirt came from a quick trip to one of the plants by the bathroom, and the iron was in my pocket. That last ingredient was not easy to find, but I traded a student who took iron vitamins for their deficiency. In exchange, I'd given them my share of last week's Sunday pudding.

I emptied a porcelain jar and, with my tongue jutting out of my mouth, I got to mixing. To me, making this alchemy felt as natural as a tuna swimming in the water, or a dog pooping on someone's front yard. The mix was ready in less than two minutes. A hundred and twelve seconds, to be exact.

"You are not following proper safety rules," said Rey, adjusting his beanie. "We should be wearing safety goggles."

"Don't you trust me?" I asked.

Hayati and Rey gave each other uninspired looks. I had to admit, although two weeks had passed, it still crushed me a bit that no one remembered my last trick. Still, Jiduh always said that the toughest customers to earn became the most loyal.

I raised the porcelain jar over my head, closed my eyes and pictured the snowiest winter day back in Portland, then said, "If you don't trust me, then trust—"

"What's that smell?" asked Rey as everyone suddenly pinched their nose.

I lifted the lid of the jar and gagged, realizing I'd messed up, accidentally creating a stink bomb. Kahem had warned me this could happen, but he'd also taught me the solution. I hurried to add some more pepper into the mixture, pinching my nose as the smell neutralized.

Before anyone could duck, I whipped around the porcelain jar, covering my two lunch-mates in a black-and-white powder, Cooling Dust. It instantly dissolved across their faces, arms, anywhere that it touched. I counted *five, four, three* . . .

Rey hugged his body, teeth chattering. "Co-co-cold!"

"What in Newton's apples?" asked Hayati, shivering.

Sarah was turned around again, peering over at our table with wide eyes. I turned back to my friends, the classmates who *hadn't* left me, and said, "So, how about we discuss some of that homework I've missed!"

Chapter 20

"No, Shad, the scientific method does not include using your imagination."

The bell rang just as Ms. Wassouf shut my answer down.

I hurried out of the class and into the courtyard. After three weeks at the Academy, the days had begun to shorten, and the afternoon sunset cast the hazy sky a hot pink. Rey would've loved it. As for me, I focused less on the view and more on checking for necromancers in the darker corners of the hall.

Luckily, students filled the walkway and, so far, necromancers hadn't seemed to appear in crowded spaces. I walked toward the library where Hayati and Rey waited to discuss who we'd ask to be our science fair group's fourth member.

"Hey, look at what we have here!"

I stopped, Yakoub's voice causing my body to go stiff.

I didn't see anybody remotely as big or menacing as my stepbrother, not until I noticed one of the pillars separating the hallway from the courtyard.

"He's sound asleep," said someone. "What should we do with him?"

Yakoub stood with two other students, one a first-year bully. As more heard the noise, a small crowd began to form around Donny.

"Seems like this first-year should take a bath with Aladdin," Yakoub offered, to which his friends cackled.

My friends were waiting on me, but I couldn't let these bullies mess with Donny. I pulled *The Alchemist's Hand* from my back pocket and flipped to a recipe that made sense. One that I could mix with what I had on me.

"Hey, what's going on?" asked Donny.

"Quiet," said Yakoub. "It's bath time!"

The growing crowd watched Yakoub bend over to pick up Donny. I rushed back into Ms. Wassouf's classroom, the students still pouring out after an evening lab session. Inside, a few squirts of hand lotion gave me enough of the aloe plant extract that the mixture called for. I rushed back outside, where I crushed some lavender from the courtyard in my hand. Without water, I spat into my palms, imagining what I hoped the mixture would become. Soon, tendrils of yellow blossomed from my fingertips.

Thirst-Inducing Mist.

I walked into the crowd just as my stepbrother hoisted Donny up and everyone fell silent. As my mixture began to permeate across the hall, faces contorted, people placing hands on their throats. Those who didn't have water bottles to chug quickly hurried to the fountain, bullies included.

Yakoub held out for a few moments longer. Eventually, he also set Donny down and followed, but not before glancing up at me. His eyes widened and I backed away from the moving crowd. Reaching out his hand, he nearly caught my shirt, but that only made him breathe in more of the mist.

"Next time," he said, and rushed to gulp water from the fountain just like the others.

My heart thudding a million beats a minute, I let out the breath I'd been holding as the mist at my fingertips vanished. I hurried to pick up my textbooks before my stepbrother could drink his fill.

"Oh, hey, Shad!"

Donny called to me from behind a pillar, one of his hands gripping a water bottle that he sipped, the other beckoning me closer.

"Why were you sleeping here?" I asked, pointing at the grass beneath his butt. "You almost got thrown into the fountain."

Scratching his head, Donny said, "That *was* a close call. Guess I just really like napping. It's funny, I feel like I wanted to tell you something, but . . . uh . . . well, I forgot."

I sighed, but at least he admitted he forgot what he wanted to tell me this time. A step in the right direction from the last time, when he just passed out mid-sentence.

"Stay here and see what Yakoub does," I said. "I'm headed to the library for a study session."

I made it a few strides down the hall before the sound of footsteps caused me to turn and find Donny half-sleepwalking behind me. "Library, that's where I meant to go! At least, I think that's where. . . ."

"Whatever, just keep up."

The library halls were always packed around dinner-time. Students loved coming here to study. Not only did it have the most research books for class, but it was almost always quiet. Perhaps that was why Hayati insisted on meeting here for our project.

Donny followed like my shadow as I searched the tables in the library's hall for Hayati and Rey. Students packed the space, their chatter filling our ears. Chains as long as the gym court hung down from the ceiling, holding burning lamps above everyone to brighten up the tables and nearby stacks.

Like back in the hallways, I glanced across at the ends of the library where the lights didn't burn. Even Moussa must not have gone there, at least not without a flashlight.

All that came to sight was darkness. No necromancers.

"I don't follow anyone else, even if they are a second-year." Sarah's voice floated from behind a stack we were passing. My curiosity getting the best of me, I stuck my ear to the row of books.

"You don't get it," said another girl. "This second-year, Yakoub, he bullies some of the scariest students in the Academy. Apparently, he gave a fourth-year a wedgie on his first day!"

I shivered at the mention of my stepbrother, but that fear was eclipsed when someone yanked one of the books out of the other end of the stack. Sure enough, the group of classmates who I was eavesdropping on saw me through the newly made opening.

Sarah furrowed her brows. "Shad?"

I yanked Donny's shirt and darted through the study area. Footsteps came from the other end of the stacks as Sarah and her friends rushed to catch us. To catch *me*. Luckily, we had enough time to cross through the study hall, heading toward a bright pink beanie that stood right out.

"No, I *promise* that the robotic book-grabbing arm is a cool science fair project," said Rey as we approached.

"And I'm telling you that my solar Jet Skis will earn us a higher grade," said Hayati. "Let's ask Shad when he—"

"Come on," I said, interrupting them with a whisper. "Both of you!"

They jolted when I arrived, glancing at me funny until they noticed the bullies approaching from across the study area. I squatted down and came to rest on hands and knees, Donny and my science fair partners doing the same, only with books in their hands as we maneuvered by the feet of students too focused on their work to care.

"Where's Moussa?" I asked.

"He and his monkey went to grab a bite from the dining hall," answered Rey. "Says so on the sign at his checkout counter."

Reaching the end of the study area, I crawled around a stack on the other side, standing to dust off my knees. The others hurried after me. Hayati squatted, one hand around a couple of books and the other keeping her giant glasses from falling. Rey's beanie swung left and right with each move as he breathed heavily under an over-stuffed backpack. Donny came last, basically doing the worm in a half-sleep crawl.

"Shad, you have some explaining to do," said Rey, re-adjusting his beanie.

Hayati shot me a look. "All the germs on the floor, added to my rising heartbeat . . . are you trying to give me cardiac arrest?"

"Sorry," I said, still trying to catch my breath. "A few figs were after me. Ones who would've hung us from the top of the stacks by our underwear."

"Say, that's a pretty good idea."

I twisted, gasping as I saw Sarah standing behind us. She approached alone as we all squirmed together. "Relax, I won't hang anyone by their underwear," she said. "What are you doing here?"

"Napping," said Donny, still on the floor, eyes closed.

"Studying," I corrected him, ready to turn and run at a moment's notice. "Looking into science-y stuff for the fair."

I didn't say too much. Sarah may not have been going after me and my friends, but she still hung out with the students who did. That meant I couldn't trust her.

Hayati, on the other hand, didn't seem to think that way. Stepping forward, the girl said, "Technically speaking, we are supposed to be planning our project *and* exploring which student would make a good fourth partner."

As Hayati explained our progress to Sarah, a warm sensation came from Baba's charm. Not a tingle like when that necromancer tried to grab me in the halls. This warmth felt soothing, and I searched for its source.

A glow illuminated a shining book several stacks away. No part of me wanted to venture deeper into the stacks, farther away from the students and lights. But I had to know what was causing the glow and how it was connected to my baba's charm.

". . . and that was why, after one smell of Shad's fart, she decided to leave our group," Hayati was saying. When she saw me, she asked, "Shad, where are you going? We still need to talk about the science fair project!"

I ignored them, cautiously moving to the end of the stacks, underneath ladders. The warmth at my neck spread across my body as I approached the glow. It wasn't the book, I realized, but a single page inside.

"What is that?" asked Sarah.

I jolted to see her and the others following behind. Judging by their faces, they could all see the glow and were equally concerned. Even Drowsy Donny watched on, mouth hanging open at the sight. They kept their distance as I moved in toward it. Swallowing, I stretched out my hand, fingers pinching the shining page.

My whole body surged with energy as I held it in my hands, returning the book and keeping the page. Only, the words were written in an Arabic script I couldn't understand.

"Can any of you read this?" I asked, raising the yellowing paper for all to see.

Everyone but Hayati shook their heads. As for my youngest classmate, she stepped forward timidly, holding out her hands where I placed the paper. Adjusting her glasses, she cleared her throat and began to read.

"It's written in an old style of calligraphy," she

explained. "It says that 'she discovered the ways of necromancy during the thirteenth year of the Great Library's opening. Rejected by the rest of the founders, who called her style of alchemy a great evil, they ordered her not to spread her teachings. She defied her fellow alchemists. In secret, she would make followers out of her students, promising an elixir that would grant immortality. But she died before she could see her goals realized, defeated by the other alchemists determined not to allow the ingredients for the Elixir of Immortality to be passed on. It is said the burial site appears every tenth winter solstice once the moon is shining. . . .'"

"Wait, every *tenth* winter solstice?" Sarah cut in, scratching her head. "A winter solstice only happens once a year, so that means her burial site is revealed once every ten years?"

Rey nodded. "Not only that, but the solstice falls on December twenty-first, which is the day of the science fair."

Donny raised a finger. "It's also the darkest day of the year, the best one for sleeping!"

"Indeed it is!"

Sarah yelped, and we twisted to find Moussa standing right behind us. He grinned and scratched his wild gray hair. I almost asked where he'd come from, but he cut me off, whistling. Noises came from up high on the stacks as a shadow fell upon us. The monkey. It leapt onto Hayati's head, snatching up the paper, and leaping overhead.

Once the monkey landed back on Moussa's shoulder, the librarian accepted the still-glowing page from his pet and smiled. "Don't you students have studying to do?"

"No, we were just—"

"I asked if you had some studying to do!" he snapped.

We all got the message, scurrying back into the study area. Students lifted their gazes from their textbooks to see us first-years hurrying to our table. The warm feeling at my neck vanished and I didn't dare glance back.

My heart raced with excitement about our discovery, but also disappointment over losing the glowing page.

Still, I couldn't stop thinking about the excerpt Hayati had read. What were the odds that something to do with necromancers, a winter solstice, and the science fair were all happening on the same day?

That couldn't be a coincidence.

Chapter 21

*W*e *watch you every day and every night. Join us, Shad.*
"Cannolis on fire!" I shouted, jerking upright. "Cannolis on hot charcoals, sugary stickiness all over. . . ."

Mumbling gibberish was all I could do not to have a total freak-out over my dream. It started out great. A kitchen, my trusty old wooden spatula, and even Teta there to help me. I was preparing the dough for manoush, rolling it flat and thin so it would come out from the oven nice and crisp.

Then the kitchen went black. Teta was gone, and in her place . . . a massive shadow.

"It was just a dream," I whispered. "It was just a—wait, this isn't my room!"

Looking left and right, I saw it was dark outside. A nearby projector displayed the date and time: *October 12, 9:05 p.m.*

Bookshelves surrounded me, strange beeping machines too. The rapping sounds of wind on glass gave me tingles.

I recognized this place, having come here once after running into another student during simulation dodgeball. This was the nurse's office, located in the section of the Academy with all the biology and medicine books.

Twisting until I freed a hand from under the sheets, I snatched a clipboard from off the table by my bed. The nurse had scribbled a bunch of medical mumbo jumbo. None of the numbers and words made any sense until I got to the bottom, where the nurse had written:

> Student found unconscious between class periods. All tests show good health, no injuries. Cause of issue undetermined at this time. Student allowed to return to his room pending follow-up tomorrow.

"I was unconscious?" I wondered aloud. "How the fig did that happen?"

A feeling told me it was the necromancers, but I couldn't remember. I could barely think without my head feeling like it was going to burst, which meant I needed to make like a banana and split. Being all alone was the last thing I wanted with shadowy alchemists lurking about. This nurse's office had evil eye aura all over it, from the creepy beeping to the red lights coming from machines in the corner, like the eyes of a monster watching me sleep.

Since I was still basically a mummy, it took all my

effort to squeeze the rest of my body out from the sheets. Soon, sweat dabbed my cheeks, and my fingers were sore from pushing against the mattress, but I wormed my way out. Only then did I feel the needle in my arm.

"You're twelve," I told myself over and over as I reached for the tubes attached to it, connecting to a plastic bag of some clear liquid. "You're twelve," I said one last time, then I pictured a giant peanut-butter cupcake and ripped out the needle.

It really didn't hurt *that* much. I mean, I only squirmed for like ten seconds. Totally nailed it.

I rolled off the bed and fell splat onto my belly. "Smooth as a sikini," I said, trying to gracefully get up.

There was a picture of a dog with a stethoscope and the words *Feeling tired? Take an afternoon nap.* Instead of *noon*, there was the Arabic letter, which was pronounced "noon." The pun had me chuckling all the way to the door, when a voice coming from down the hallway stopped me cold.

In the dark, it was hard to tell exactly where it was coming from. I carefully crept out the door and into the hallway, heading toward the literature department. As I snuck by the room where our language arts class was held, I remembered that I had five book quizzes due before winter break, so I should probably think about reading at least one of those books. That was, if I could stop what-ever the necromancers were planning in time. Otherwise, a book quiz would be the least of my worries.

"Why are you so caught up with this first-year?" asked the voice. "I heard about him getting in trouble, sounds like a real butt-for-brains."

"Don't be fooled," came the response. It was Yakoub. "This kid isn't like the others. He and I, we have unfinished business."

Yakoub's voice made my legs noodly the way Sarah used to back in Portland. I still couldn't believe he was a student here, and that my no-good stepfamily carried the blood of the founding scholars. No doubt I was the first-year they were talking about. Who else could it be?

I sucked in a deep breath and tiptoed through the eerily quiet, dimly lit hallway, even if I was creeping closer and closer to my stepbrother. No one suspected that I, Shad Hadid, was as subtle as a fish in the sea. A Lebanese ninja. I had sharpened my skills from years of sneaking into our apartment without waking Teta.

"Business?" said the voice, just as I approached the edge of the hallway. "You mean, like, you two are opening a business?"

"No, you dope," said Yakoub. "Just be quiet and follow me. We can't be caught wandering the hallways at night."

My stepbrother and his friend were rounding the corner. Once, back in Lebanon, Yakoub sprang up on me on the way back from Baba's shop. He'd sent me home wearing my shirt as pants and my shorts as a headscarf.

My legs shook at the memory, but Kahem had a saying for times like these. *An alchemist works with all five of their senses.*

I obviously couldn't taste Yakoub. Couldn't see him either. So, closing my eyes, I listened instead. While the footsteps came closer, I snuck into one of the dark corners of the hallway, behind a large plant next to bookshelves that smelled like dusty old paper. Sure enough, Yakoub and another older boy turned into my hallway and walked right by me.

"What are you going to do if you ever corner this kid?" asked my stepbrother's friend, now in my line of sight. "You already have all those first-years doing whatever you want; can't they take care of him?"

Yakoub stopped and thought for a second. "No, that would be too easy. Been a while since I lived close to my stepbrother, so I want to personally remind him who's in charge in this school, and in our family. As for anyone else who considers themselves as tough as me, my baba always says if you are not the predator, you become the prey."

I rolled my eyes. He hadn't changed a bit. Yakoub always wanted to be the king of everything, just like my stepfather, his dad. Only, taking charge of the first-year bullies must have meant he was getting close.

"Yikes, I wouldn't want to be him," said Yakoub's

friend. "All right, let's finish before we're caught. There's a geometry test tomorrow, so I want to be in bed before ten."

I waited until both boys disappeared into the dark, then I sprang out from behind the plant. My victory dance was a quick one-two dabke step that Baba used to do at parties.

As I continued back toward my room, the stars cast a glow over one of the courtyards. Those blue flames still burned within each of the palace's swirling towers, which kind of looked like upside-down squid tentacles. There was no way Rey was right about them. The magical glow had to be alchemy. I puffed my chest and marched down the hallway, picturing myself here one thousand years ago. In my imagination, torches burned in place of the lamps, and all the benches were cushions lying against the walls.

Daydreaming, or rather night-dreaming since it was dark out, caused my head to ache. I placed a hand on my forehead and felt a bandage right beneath my hair. It was the first time I was noticing it. Was it from face-planting on the Academy's cement floor, or from the necromancer's touch?

Picturing those shadowy figs shocked Kahem's mission back into the front of my mind. I mean, it wasn't off to the *best* start, if I was being honest. Weeks into the school year and Kahem still hadn't shown up. I wanted to stop whatever the necromancers were doing, but how could I fight them without so much as my alchemy belt?

Still, although he hadn't even sent a box of baklava to help curb my sweet tooth, I wouldn't let my teacher down.

Stopping in the hallway, I almost turned toward the staircase that led to my room. There, I had a slowly growing number of ingredients hidden in my dresser thanks to our chemistry lab sessions. Not much, but enough to craft a charm that might make Yakoub think twice before messing with me.

But maybe this was the best chance I'd get to explore the Academy. To find another clue to what the necromancers were doing here. I swept through the halls with a renewed excitement and gazed across the countless books and thousands of shelves housing them.

Maybe I'd find a hidden passageway, or nothing at all. While I was sneaking by the Eastern Courtyard, I noticed the Academy looked to be lacking security, no guards or hall monitors like in Portland. Only a red light beamed out from inside a bush. Then another.

My heart stopped as a rooster teetered out of a collection of flowers. I looked left and right, wishing there was someone to see what I was seeing. Were roosters supposed to have red eyes?

"Oh crud," I said, noticing the metal legs.

That was no ordinary rooster, but a robot. One that I'd heard had very sharp teeth to make sure any student who snuck out at night *never* did it again.

Without hesitating, I sped down the hall. Robotic sounds came from the courtyard and I turned. The fake rooster was hot on my tail, and it had a small army of robo-roosters following close behind. Their red eyes were trained on me and I could just picture the bullies laughing during my funeral, telling everyone that I should have listened.

"Darn it, Shad, you really messed up," I said. "Think, think, think . . ."

I rounded a corner into another hallway. My legs felt like they were going to give up on me any second. From behind, red eyes swarmed like a nest of bees whose hive I'd just kicked. I was still glancing back when I slammed into the dining hall door and stumbled inside.

I shut the large door and, using all my strength, I slid the super-old latch to seal it closed. Then I stumbled back and listened as, one by one, the roosters crashed into the wooden slab with a *bang*, like exploding popcorn.

"Note to self," I said, gasping for breath, "don't underestimate the security in a school where students build robot dragonflies."

Up above, stars glittered through the dining hall's glass

dome. My head was aching, my legs were sore, and worst of all, my stomach growled in hunger. Still, I couldn't help but smile since Baba, Jiduh, and now Teta were probably watching me, and I didn't want them to see me scared.

"What do I do?" I asked the stars. "Give me a sign, or maybe a bowl of vanilla custard."

The stars didn't give me custard. They didn't do much other than shine. I tried to remember one of the constellations Jiduh had shown me back in Lebanon, but my brain was too fried for even that.

Suddenly, a sharp tingling sensation rushing through my hands and feet.

"Oh no," I whispered, getting on my belly and crawling to the table reserved for the deans.

I rolled underneath. Beginning with Baba's charm at my neck, a shudder swept through me, running up and down my spine.

That feeling could only mean one thing—and it wasn't good.

Chapter 22

Necromancers.

The kitchen door swung open as lanterns sprang to life all throughout the dining hall. "The robot roosters were awakened, you say? Deactivate them and locate the culprit. We can't have anyone finding out about our plans."

I couldn't make out the voice, so, keeping quiet, I peeked out from under the table and a chill seized me. One by one, nine necromancers came out from inside the kitchen. They formed a semicircle in the middle of the hall, mirroring the shape of the moon above. All of them adults, they wore full-on alchemy coats, hoodies and all.

"Time is quickly running out," said the necromancer at the center. "What is our progress on securing the final ingredient?"

He held something in his hand, and I didn't know what it was until he placed it around his waist and fastened the buckle–an alchemy belt.

"We have yet to locate it," admitted a necromancer. "We have spent years scouring the stacks of books across this school. Years gathering clues hidden by the original alchemists that might help brew our mixture. Perhaps the deadline is too ambitious?"

There was silence for a few heart-stopping moments. The necromancer standing at the center reached up, grabbed their hood, and pulled it off. I nearly shrieked from under the table.

"Ambitious?" asked Dean Ibrahim, raising a finger to his face. "Tell me, do you wish to delay my plans? *Our* plans? The others and I have worked tirelessly to ensure no alchemist may interfere with our work here. And now, after all this time, you would all just . . . what? Take a break? And then just wait another ten years?"

The necromancers bowed their heads and answered, "No, teacher."

Baba's charm all but shook around my neck, and I realized I'd gotten this feeling around him the first time. *He* had been a necromancer all along. And when he said ten years, could it be that he was describing whatever the page in the library had mentioned happening every ten years on the winter solstice?

"I may not be the leader of our order," said Dean Ibrahim, "but I am *your* leader."

"Yes, teacher," they chimed.

"Good. We have nearly discovered every ingredient for the mixture. In ten weeks, at this location, all that we worked for will be complete. Not a soul will be able to stop us. Now, on to recruitment. Have we designated any new apprentices from among the first-years?"

One raised their hand. "The girl named Zara may serve our purposes. She displays an above-average intelligence, not to mention tremendous athletic ability."

"I vote for Jad," said a second voice, suggesting yet another bully. "We are ordering our apprentices to keep the students in line with fear, and who among the first-years is more terrifying?"

"I would wager the girl Sarah may be better. She seems naturally suited to scare students. Even if she knows nothing of our traditions, as my apprentices tell me, our order seeks valuable alliances with all types of people."

Names began to be called out, nearly all of them were for bullies. I couldn't take my eyes off the alchemy belts, all those pouches. These necromancers were working on something big, and they were using the bullies to scare us, to keep my classmates from discovering what was really happening here at the school. Worse, these necromancers were under the protection of a dean.

Could that be why Yakoub had been out this late? Working for the necromancers would explain him recruiting all the jerks in my class. . . .

No, my stepbrother couldn't have been an alchemist. Living with him for two years in Lebanon, I would've known. Not only was Yakoub a jealous stepbrother, but one who loved to show off, so word would've spread if he was doing Shadow Alchemy for his friends.

I counted off ten weeks from today with my fingers. *October, November* . . . I cupped my hand over my mouth. My count placed us on December 21, the day of the science fair.

My mind flashed back to the glowing page in the library, the story of the first necromancer. Whatever big event they had planned, it would happen during the winter solstice, on the night the burial site would be revealed.

"Determine your new student apprentices by the next week's gathering," announced Dean Ibrahim. "It is important we have enough followers here to help convert the others in this school."

"And what if we can't convince everyone?" asked one necromancer.

Dean Ibrahim didn't hesitate before snapping, "Then we do what we always do and get rid of them, be they teachers *or* students! Once our goals are achieved, we will eliminate anyone who chooses to stand against us. There can be no witnesses."

A pause set in among the group. None of the necromancers surrounding the dean spoke, and I could barely breathe. Had he just said he would get rid of students? Swallowing, I wondered where Kahem was. He'd be able to stop them all, to protect my classmates and teachers.

Dean Ibrahim reached into his pouch, pulling out a marble-sized ball. "Have our current apprentices resume their training tomorrow. Now go, search every corner of this school for whoever was snooping about. I want them to be found and taken care of."

A necromancer stepped forward. "Teacher . . . the equipment in the kitchen. We were in the middle of another experiment."

"Find the student first," said Dean Ibrahim. "Come back and clean up once that problem is dealt with. It is not as if we have the proper ingredients for that particular mixture yet."

Before anyone could answer, he threw down a vial that caused an explosion of black smoke. I shielded my eyes and when I looked back up, the dean and his necromancer friends had vanished.

Nothing stirred in the dining hall as I remained under the table for quite some time. I couldn't risk a necromancer ambush. My eyes could barely hold themselves open, and my body yearned for sleep. Even the glow of the lanterns seemed to have dimmed.

I rolled out from under the table and got to my feet. What was it that the necromancers had been planning for ten whole years? They mentioned an experiment, a mixture missing the proper ingredient, but what?

Carefully, I tiptoed over to the kitchen door, stepping inside. Nearly every meal period, I'd imagined the cooks coming to my table, begging for me to help prepare one of my signature Arabic dishes.

"Holy cannoli."

Shelves and shelves of spices from adobo to za'atar. Sacks of beans and grains and lentils, all the appliances we could never afford in Portland. I might have cried had necromancers not just been standing here a few heart-beats ago.

One of the shelves atop the stove lay cracked open in a way that invited me forward for a peak. I tiptoed over, checked all around to be sure I was alone, and opened it.

Creeeeak!

I stiffened. A still-sizzling pot sat to one side and a vial holder held several unlabeled ingredients on the other. This was an alchemy lab, but where it differed from the ones Kahem and I worked on was the added equipment. Thermostats, digital timers, funnels that opened and closed with the touch of a button . . . never had I used anything so advanced. But since the Alexandria Academy had become some kind of math-and-science-based school, maybe the necromancers were using that to somehow improve their alchemy.

Following one of Kahem's most important rules, I leaned away as far as possible while pulling all the alchemical contraptions out, careful not to catch a whiff that could have me sick for the next month.

A paper slipped out from under a pouch. I set down the pot and vials, snatching it in midair. It appeared to have been ripped out from a book, and as soon as my fingertips grasped it, the edges began to glow. I shook as my necklace, once tingling from all the necromancers, now sent energy rushing through me.

The page contained a list of ingredients. Notes were scribbled along the margins of the page. Unlike my guidebook, the name of the recipe was faded, nowhere to be found. I dropped the note when I read some of the ingredients.

A pinch of salt.
Three drops of mercury.
One drop of sulfur.
Five flakes of pure gold.

"No way," I whispered, reaching down to pick it back up with trembling fingers.

These weren't just any ingredients. These belonged to the Revival Elixir I'd messed up when I tried to save Teta in Portland. The one that had nearly seen me become a necromancer without knowing it. Now, with tears in my eyes, I pictured her wrinkly smile at our dinner table.

Some things in this world are not meant for us to change.

That was what Teta had told me right after I used the elixir on her, and it was true. Kahem had warned me of the same back on my first day of training. And, even now, I still wanted Teta back more than there are grains of sand in the desert, but no one should have the power to bring back the dead. Especially not those who would hurt my friends.

Everything Kahem had told me of the necromancers, and their goal to learn the secrets of immortality, pointed to one reason why they'd need this kind of forbidden alchemy. Why they'd planned to meet on the winter solstice . . .

While the rest of the school was distracted with the science fair, they planned to revive the founder of their order—the very first necromancer.

The page from the library had said the winter solstice was when the original necromancer's grave would be revealed. This had to be the tenth year it had mentioned.

I studied the paper that must have belonged to one of the millions of books scattered across the school. Scanning through the ingredients for the elixir once more turned up a mistake. Well, not a *mistake*, but the recipe left out zaffer, a key part of the mixture. All this time, they must have been scouring the Academy for a clue as to what that missing ingredient was.

My chest swelled with relief. Besides *The Alchemist's Hand*, I didn't know a single place the necromancers would find it. And according to the first rule of alchemy, they couldn't go through with their plan so long as the recipe remained incomplete. A true alchemist could still stop these figs.

Since Kahem wasn't here, *I* had to be that alchemist.

All the equipment sat on the table, nearly everything necessary for them to brew the elixir. Without much time, I did what every self-respecting alchemist would do when trying to quickly ruin a mixture—combine all the ingredients.

The dangerous thing about pouring a bunch of random ingredients into one vial was that it was almost guaranteed to cause a mess, no matter how techy and advanced the setup. So, right after throwing in the brown gunk from the final vial, I tossed in the recipe for the Revival Elixir last of all, watching it melt into the boiling mixture. Then I hurried out of the kitchen and through the dining hall doors with a finger in each ear right before—

"Ah!"

Sarah Decker and I shrieked at the same time. We stood just outside the dining hall for a moment, looking at each other, and that was when the explosion rocked the Alexandria Academy.

The ground shook and the sliver of space beneath the dining hall door brightened as if by a flash of lightning. I doubted anyone would be using that kitchen for at least a few days and, to be honest, that was the coolest thing I'd ever done. But there was still the matter of Sarah. . . .

"Are you one of them?" I asked, backing away.

She looked left and right frantically, holding her chest. "One of who? And what was that noise?"

I hesitated, studying her expression. This was Sarah Decker, the bully and friend of bullies. The meanest wedgie giver in Portland, and maybe the world. Yet she hadn't made a move to catch me, and she didn't shout about my being here. If she'd been a necromancer, she would've already used a Sleeping Dust, or just knocked me onto my butt the old-fashioned way. It wouldn't have taken much.

"Oh, *that* noise," I said, considering whether to tell her that I'd just blown up a secret alchemy lab in the dining hall. "It was nothing."

Sarah gave me her eyebrow-raised look of suspicion, asking, "Shouldn't you be in the nurse's office? I was worried; the word around the Academy is that you fainted."

"Nope, just a rumor," I lied. "I actually tripped on my sh—"

We both jolted at the sound of fast-approaching steps. If Dean Ibrahim hadn't heard the blast, another necromancer would have. Without thinking, I grabbed Sarah's hand and yanked us into the nearest hallway.

Wait, did Sarah say she was worried . . . about me?

She leaned back against a stack of books, shoulders stiffened, eyes locked on our hands held firmly together. Heat rushed to my cheeks and I almost drew my arm back. Only, a single black tendril reached around the hallway, landing right near Sarah's face.

"Come on!" I said, leading her down the hall.

The tingling of Baba's charm told me that the necromancers were hot on our trail. We found one of the staircases and escaped to our dorms. If I hadn't been pee-my-pants scared, I might have laughed; the last time we were both running, she was chasing after me with a carton of eggs.

But now things were different. We were running side by side, almost like a team: the bully and the baker.

Chapter 23

We slipped into Sarah's room since it was right by the stairs. While she closed the door, I collapsed onto her bed, breathing heavily and hoping I wouldn't have a heart attack.

Yakoub, the necromancers, and now Sarah Decker. This evening had been a nightmare cake, where the ingredients were all the people who had wanted to squeeze me like a lemon at one time or another.

"Are you seriously getting sweat all over my sheets?" Sarah said.

A wave of relief came at having the old Sarah back and not the stiff, quiet one from the hallway. But something stirred and we both looked over to the next bed. Lying there, sound asleep, was Selma Aboud.

Keeping my voice hushed, I asked, "What if we wake her up?"

"You don't need to whisper," she said. "Trust me, nothing wakes up that girl."

"Okay, so why were you wandering the halls?"

"Because," said Sarah, crossing her arms.

"Because what?" I asked, leaning in.

"Because none of your stinkin' business, that's what!"

Selma stirred and I almost fell off the bed. Sarah had backed against the wall, and I shot her a *see what you almost did* look.

Sarah held up her hands. "Relax, we're safe. This wasn't even a big deal."

"We almost got caught," I snapped. "Not only that, but robo-roosters chased me across the Academy, my step-brother was looking for me in the nurse's office, and Dean Ibrahim, I saw him—"

"Okay, okay," she said, raising her arms to stop me. "Time out, that is *way* too much information."

"Point is, there are necromancers at the Academy, and they're planning something big on the night of the science fair. You know, the *winter solstice*."

"Are you talking about what we read about in the library?" she snorted. "You realize that was just a story, right?"

"I'm being serious," I said. "I can't explain it, but there are these shadows that keep appearing out of nowhere to grab at me and ask me to join them. And when we bumped into each other in Portland—you know, the day before Dean Hayek showed up—I was being chased by this weird alchemist, Dr. Salazar."

"Alchemy?" she asked. "Like that trick you showed us during dinner? The one that made us all see in green?"

My jaw dropped. "Wait, you remember that stuff?"

Sarah shrugged. "Is there a reason I wouldn't?"

All our other classmates had convinced me that I'd become a majnoon, acting like I'd never shown them alchemy in the first place. It didn't make sense that, of all people, Sarah would be the one to remember. Maybe kids from Portland were immune to what had caused everyone to forget.

Whatever the reason, I said, "The dinner trick is exactly what I'm talking about. There's alchemy like that at work all over the school, but everyone refuses to see it. Good to know someone else believes me."

"Whoa there, I still don't think alchemy's real," she said. "I don't care about what happened back in Portland either. What I want to know is, if you're going to fight these things and make yourself their problem, does that mean I'll be a target too?"

I suddenly remembered that Sarah had ditched our table to sit with the bullies. The necromancers might try and make *her* one of their apprentices. They even mentioned her name back in the dining hall.

"You know what?" I said. "Maybe I should go. . . ."

Sarah leaned in closer and held up a notebook. "I forgot the notes to my Arabic class and was hoping the teacher had left them around. That's why I came downstairs."

I let out a sigh of relief. "Really?"

"This class isn't going so great," she continued. "Arabic makes no sense to me. You write from right to left, and there are strange marks over the letters, and you connect the letters like cursive, but not all the time. I'm definitely not going to pass this quiz tomorrow."

I didn't have much sympathy for my one-time bully, but Teta's words drifted into my head: *We cannot face this world alone, Shaddo.*

Teta was right. Even though I used to think I did everything alone, I wouldn't have become a baker without first spending all those hours outside of Halwa Heaven, or learned a single recipe without Kahem's guidance, or even been able to read that page in the library without Hayati's help.

Sarah deserved my support just the same. Besides, she was both bigger and smarter than me, qualities that meant she could help figure out this necromancer situation, and maybe deal with some of my other problems at the Academy. The *only* advantage I had over her was knowing Arabic.

"Don't worry about the quiz," I said. "What if I helped you to not only pass that class, but ace it?"

"You'd do that?" she asked, her tone softening. Then she coughed, changing back to her deeper voice. "What do you want in return?"

Oh, this was good. She was hooked like the fish Baba

and I used to catch back in Lebanon.

"Nothing at all," I said. "Consider it a friendly favor."

Sarah narrowed her eyes. "You'd help me, even after I bullied you all those years?"

I cringed at the memories. Sarah did bully me a whole lot, but it couldn't have been a coincidence we'd bumped into each other tonight. Teta was probably up there in the stars, working her magic for me.

"Well . . . what if you helped me with some of my homework?" I asked, adding, "And, if you don't have one yet, consider joining my science fair group?"

Sarah stiffened. Butterflies fluttered in my belly, and I began to regret asking until, unexpectedly, she nodded. "Deal."

It hit me that Sarah really might be able to change. That she wanted to earn her place at the Alexandria Academy. She seemed so unlike Yakoub, who had all the bullies under his control. Who believed that he belonged here because of his last name. His fig-faced ancestors probably bullied other alchemists too.

I held out a hand and we shook on our agreement. My Arabic help in exchange for her smarts when it came to other classes and the science fair project. While I never would have expected this, it felt pretty good.

"So, does this mean we're friends?" I asked, maybe a bit too excitedly.

Sarah snorted. "I wouldn't go that far. Let's call it a partnership."

My shoulders involuntarily sagged at the rejection, but I knew better than to press my luck. Heading to the door, I reached for the knob—

"Shad, wait!"

Sarah grabbed my hand. My whole arm stiffened as my fingers intertwined with those of my former bully. Her cheeks had reddened, and she bit her lip, waiting a second before drawing her hand away.

Scratching the back of her head, she said, "I just wanted to say I'm sorry for what my parents said. You know, back when we were younger. It was not okay."

"*You* are apologizing," I asked, my jaw dropping, "to *me*?"

She shrugged. "Yeah, I guess I am. . . ."

It was already a surprise that Sarah had agreed to help me, but I'd *never* expected her to apologize. Ever. My lips trembled, tears threatening my eyes.

I smiled and said, "Apology accepted."

"Okay, let me see if I understand," said Hayati. "So, this time, you were being chased by a robotic rooster?"

"No," said Rey, shaking his head, along with his sunset-themed beanie. "His cousin, the second-year, had a pet rooster that was chasing him!"

Hayati shook her head. "You mean his *stepbrother*. And it wasn't a rooster chasing him, but a shadow."

I clapped my cheeks. How didn't they get that I was an alchemist on the run from shadow monsters and, after being chased by robo-roosters, I discovered the kitchen had been a necromancer lab? Seemed easy enough.

The dust had finally settled on the kitchen explosion over two weeks ago. After a short investigation, Dean Saba had announced it was just a toaster malfunction. I figured it was time to let my friends in on the truth. After all, with all the hidden secrets we'd unearthed about the school, they could be trusted. Still, it was a lot harder to explain than I'd imagined.

"What's the deal with your math homework?" asked Rey, already wanting to change the subject. "You haven't been asking for my help lately."

"I finished it last night," I said, not mentioning that Sarah had been helping.

In my head, I continued searching for a way to better explain the necromancers. A way where they might believe me. Yet before I could say another word, Dean Saba skipped to the front of the dining hall.

"Students, quiet!" he said in an unusually harsh tone. "We have a real treat this afternoon, a *very* special guest."

One of the dining hall doors creaked open, and in came Dean Abdullah. I sank into my cushion. It had been weeks since I'd seen her wrinkly face and I nervously began to sip from my pineapple juice. Ever since I'd blown up the necromancers' alchemy setup, I'd worried that I'd left behind some piece of evidence, or that the robo-roosters had built-in cameras with footage of me running away like a chicken.

"Hello, first-years," she said with a smile. "First, I have sad news. Our beloved dean for the third-year students, Dean Ibrahim, has taken a teaching job in another school across the world."

I spat out the juice. Did that mean the necromancers were leaving? Had I sent their leader on the run? Maybe blowing up their experiment and recipe dashed their hopes of making a Revival Elixir that worked.

"And on to better news," she said. "I was going to sit out this year, but now I have no choice but to join the science fair panel as a judge in Dean Ibrahim's place. I hope you all have determined your projects now that your groups are finalized. It's in just under two months and will be a really special one, I can just feel it!"

As the announcement ended, I noticed that I'd been gripping the table and shaking in excitement. Not because of the science fair. No, that announcement caused a stir among the students, Rey and Hayati whispering plans for group meetings and the like.

But what I cared about was the news around Dean Ibrahim. I couldn't wait to tell Kahem that I'd taken on the necromancers and won. I'd not yet been able to finesse the Communication Alchemy, which would allow me to deliver the message to him, but that would come in time.

For now, my excitement had me eager to do something else. Another demonstration. After all, I could do whatever I wanted now that the necromancers were beaten. Who could stop me from showing my friends some alchemy?

"I know you don't remember the first trick I showed you," I said, reaching around the table for salt, some olive oil, and various other spices, "but how about the second one from a couple weeks back?"

"Nope."

"Nuh-uh."

"Are you serious?" I asked. "How could any of you forget about the Cooling Dust?"

"Shad, you never showed us anything," insisted Rey, his hands on his hips. "We are science geeks, and that sounds like some kind of made-up magic."

"It's *not* magic," I said through gritted teeth. "Alchemy is—"

Ding!

The bell interrupted our argument. While the other overachievers rushed the dining hall door to avoid being late to class, Hayati and Rey remained.

"So, we're going with a renewable heater," said Rey.

"It doesn't need gas or anything harmful to the

environment," explained Hayati as I stared at the ingredients I'd gathered. "It's going to be a whole lot of fun, Shad. We can't wait to explain it to the fourth team member once we find someone."

I nodded, only remembering once they'd left that I'd forgotten to mention Sarah joining our group. Yet my mind was on something else. A strange sense that not everything had been fixed here at the Academy.

Sure, it had been a few weeks since I'd done alchemy in the dining hall, but I wouldn't chalk up my friends' forgetting both the Green Eyes Mist *and* Cooling Dust to bad memory. Not a chance. Deep in my gut, an uneasy feeling had me wondering if the necromancers were still out here. If they were still lurking through the halls.

Or perhaps they'd left behind a Forgetting Charm that had been crafted to only affect certain people. It would explain why Sarah and I could remember everything. Kahem talked about being able to modify certain mixtures that way during our training, and I'd read about that charm in *The Alchemist's Hand*.

But combining the two was something only a master alchemist could pull off. Were the necromancers so powerful that they could manage it for the entire school?

Whatever the answer to that question, I needed to get to the bottom of it—and soon.

Chapter 24

While I *continued to* watch for necromancers and my science fair group worked on our project, the days turned into weeks. A month passed without a problem. No shadowy figures, no frightening bully attacks, and somehow no Yakoub.

Now listening to Mr. Mustafa's lecture during this advanced algebra class, I struggled to understand a single word he was saying. Seriously, it was like the teacher spoke an entirely different language. But I didn't mind because Rey, Hayati, and Sarah had all been helping me with homework and studying.

Our science fair project was all but finished. After a few close calls, the group really believed we had a heater that could start on its own and stay running without any electricity. Reusing the steam it made, the chimney-like device could continue to stay hot. I wished I'd had something like it all throughout those cold winters in Portland.

Speaking of Portland, I'd begun to wonder about the last promise Kahem had made there. Maybe he'd gotten busy, or he'd learned the necromancers were gone, but I needed to accept that my alchemy teacher might never show up.

I also needed to accept that I could teach myself. Here at the Academy, the lab where we'd practice for our science fair presentation had served as a perfect spot for practicing new alchemy. Away from robo-roosters and with the necromancers nowhere to be seen, I was free to experiment as much as I wanted.

But not only to experiment—also to *prepare*. Most of the elixirs I brewed, the mists I conjured . . . they were all kept hidden in case the necromancers returned. Just as the charms would remain around my door to protect Rey and me, these mixtures would protect the school if those persistent figs decided they wanted a fight.

That's exactly why I snuck into the lab following the end of advanced algebra. Lunchtime had arrived and, while I was hungry as ever, I reached into my pocket for *The Alchemist's Hand* and set it on an empty table.

"Destruction Dust," I muttered, trying to memorize a mixture I'd been eyeing for the longest time.

Kahem had warned me about the mixture, one of the best for alchemy battles. What better time to try my hand at it than when, according to the Academy's schedule, the room would be free for the next hour?

I maneuvered to the side of the room where, other than shelves of books, nothing but the ingredients awaited. All but two were listed in my guidebook. One by one, carefully, I brought them over to the table, where I set a glass boiling—vinegar, mercury, and magnesia.

But in the place of quicklime and silica, which were two less common ingredients, I let my hand hover over the cabinet for a few moments and closed my eyes. Same as all the times Teta and I'd baked and cooked and enjoyed each other's company, when she made me prepare the kousa without beef, I improvised now, choosing tin and farina.

I worked in complete silence, taking pinches and handfuls out of the ingredients. No measuring. No stressing over the amounts of each ingredient. Trusting my training, both from Kahem and Teta, I worked through this slightly advanced alchemy until the time came to shut off the flame and let it cool into a drying gray powder.

Pressing my hands together, I eased the contents into one of the discarded pouches from the ingredient cabinet. According to *The Alchemist's Hand*, Destruction Dust needed a trigger. Another ingredient that we mixed in to set it off.

But that would have to come later since I didn't want to blow up this room.

At least now if any necromancers showed up, they'd think twice about messing with me. I'd yet to battle anyone. No real alchemy duels to speak of. Though if the need to battle came, then I'd have several pouches of useful mixtures to choose from.

The Destruction Dust fit nicely behind several of the ingredients, which I returned to their rightful positions. After classes ended, I'd come back to bring it to my room.

I cleaned up my mess and hurried out to the dining hall, where I found Rey adjusting a Batman beanie beside a snoring Donny. My roommate waved to me as something on the table stole my breath away.

"Cake!" I gasped, pointing at the plate in front of every seat.

Dean Saba cleared his throat at the front of the dining hall. Hayati came to sit, while Sarah's brown hair stuck out among the other bullies where she ate. I didn't get why she still sat with those figs over her own science fair group, but it seemed old habits weren't as easy to shake as I would've hoped.

"You must have noticed today's surprise," said the dean. "In celebration of being twenty days away from the science fair, we arranged a tasty dessert this afternoon! The last few pieces are coming out, but I hope you all enjoy it!"

The students began to bang their tables and cheer.

Focusing on the dessert in front of me, I licked my lips. Baba's necklace tingled slightly, but it wasn't a strong sensation like when I'd run into necromancers before. It must have had to do with the lingering alchemy that remained once they left. Nothing serious. If it were, I should have felt it stronger.

Ziad, the kitchen's lead chef, rolled out a cart as they handed out the last remaining pieces. My stomach roared. Cake cravings had been a constant struggle ever since I hadn't gotten to try my birthday cake from Halwa Heaven. I raised a fork over my piece with a wide smile but noticed Hayati not trying hers.

"What's up?" I asked. "Don't you like cake?"

She averted her gaze. "Well, my parents always told me I could have sweets, but that cake was off-limits. Too much sugar."

My heart stopped beating for several moments, her words jolting me. "Too much sugar?"

Nodding, she pushed away the plate of cake, a sight that almost brought tears to my baker eyes. Sighing, I didn't just shove her plate back, but as hard as it was, I also nudged my plate in front of her.

"There's no such thing as too much sugar," I said, handing her a fork. "Have my piece too."

Hayati's eyes widened. Of course, watching her dig the fork into the frosting, seeing how it had a gooey chocolate center, my mouth began to salivate. But I didn't complain. Even without much money, Teta used to buy me baklava, maamoul, and tasty cake. Every kid deserved that same experience.

"Say, can you help me with my chemistry homework after class later?" I asked, gently rubbing my belly for the torture I was making it go through.

Hayati swallowed, chocolate covering her lips as she smiled. I had to look away as she scarfed down the dessert.

"Whatever you want," she said. "Now, time for my second piece!"

Chapter 25

History class followed lunch today. Trying to focus on both the lesson and the returning threat of the necromancers didn't work. Instead, Moussa's pet monkey stole my attention from high up on the stacks. It danced and slapped its butt. No matter how hard I tried, I just couldn't look away.

"Shad, are you paying attention, or should I just start smacking my butt so you'll listen too?" The old librarian was glaring with wide, angry eyes.

The entire class erupted into laughter. I wondered if there was an elixir that could make me grow a shell like a turtle and hide away in it.

"I'm paying attention," I said dryly.

"Deduct points from his grade," said Jad with a smug grin. I didn't talk to him much, though the necromancers had mentioned him during their gathering a month ago, which told me to stay away.

"You will all get points deducted if you keep blabbering!" snapped Moussa. "Let's end the class with a game, eh? I hid a flower from the courtyard in the place of a book in the library. Now, I will not tell you the author, but if you've been paying attention, you will understand my clue."

Everyone started murmuring about how unfair it was that, in a library this big, we would be expected to find a book without knowing the author. Moussa's monkey hissed at the pouting students and they all quieted.

"Here is the clue from my lectures," he began. "The book was written by a poet born in 1883 who grew up in an Arabic-speaking country like many of us."

Even before the teacher finished giving the clue, I nudged Rey and whispered, "Partner with me?"

"Yeah, whatever," said Rey. "Not like we have a shot of finding this book."

The entire class paired up and our classmates began to fight over who would partner with Hayati, my smart friend. Right as two students began to argue in front of her, another figure shoved them both aside. Jad.

The very same bully who scared Hayati during our first day now glanced down at her and said, "You're with me."

Hayati glanced at the floor, unable to meet his eyes, and said, "Fine, let's go."

My friend was probably smart enough to realize it wasn't worth arguing. Not with the boy who could toss us both across the library like a simulation dodgeball. As for me . . . well, it was a good thing that Rey yanked me away before I could say something I'd regret.

The two of us darted through the shelves and shelves of thick, dusty history books. Each stack we passed was sorted by category, and just one would take months to go through book by book. The key was the riddle. All the students were heading into one section: *Poetry of the East*.

"This whole section has ten thousand books!" he complained, pointing up at the digital sign at the side of the stack, right under the section name.

Sunlight came through several domes like the one in the dining hall, but smaller and more spread out. We used those to find our way. Yet, for some reason, Rey had slowed. The other students couldn't keep up with me either. Behind us, Donny was basically a zombie, as always, but Herman trudged like he had rocks in his expensive shoes. His partner did too.

"Are you all right?" I asked Rey, slowing down.

"It's just up ahead," he said, nudging me to keep going. "I'm just tired is all. Come on, two more stacks. We only have, like, twenty minutes left in class."

We made it to *Poetry of the East* and started searching through book after book. They were written by poets whose names ranged from Al-Mutanabbī to Valmiki, and I didn't recognize a single one.

In fact, the only poetry I knew came from Baba and Kahem. Both used to love this one guy, Khalil Gibran. I personally preferred Cardi B, but it was worth a shot. After all, if both my dad and teacher liked him, he must have been a big deal.

My finger traced the authors' last names, and soon I was climbing one of the ladders, up one step, two, until . . .

Wait, where was it? It should have been right here, wedged between all the other books. Instead, there was an empty space. I swallowed, disappointed in Baba and Kahem for steering me wrong with their boring tastes.

I climbed down the ladder, lowering my head to watch my steps. A strange smell wafted into my nostrils, stopped me. What was that? It smelled a bit fresher than a book. My eyes scanned through the thick texts, following my nose.

"Bingo!" I said, whispering the words so only Rey could hear. "Winner, winner, falafel dinner!"

He dragged another sliding ladder next to me. After he'd climbed a couple of steps up to my level, his eyes widened. "Whoa, Shad. You really did find it!"

A dandelion. It sat right there, wedged two shelves beneath the empty space where Gibran's book should have been. Around it sat a bunch of other Arab poet names like Darwish and Qabbani. I reached to grab the dandelion while the other students kept searching. At least, most of them were searching.

Hayati's partner, the bully, smiled up at the both of us. "What do you have there, um . . . what was your name again?"

"Shad," I said. "My name is Shad, and I don't have fig."

"I can see you don't have a fig," he said. "Hayati, does it look like a flower in his hands?"

Hayati stood silent beside her partner, who looked as tall and strong as the Persian Punisher next to my teeny tiny friend. To our surprise, she said, "Just leave him alone, would you?"

Both Jad and I gasped, and I prepared to dive onto the bully if he turned on my friend. Luckily for her, the boy's desire to get the dandelion outweighed his anger over being disrespected, which ended up not being so great for me as he reached up and grabbed my sneakers.

"Hand it over and I won't pull you off," he threatened.

"Leave me alone," I said, adding, "This is probably the wrong flower!"

I tried to kick away his hand, which was beginning to hurt my ankle as he squeezed harder and harder. "Say, your name sounds familiar. I think Yakoub mentioned that if we ran across a boy named Shad, we should . . ."

"Let go!" said Hayati, this time shoving Jad with enough force to knock him over. She glanced up and smiled at me, before frowning at her partner. "You better stay down."

And Jad did. The bully didn't move, and I gasped at Hayati's newfound courage. "That was amazing, right, Rey?"

I twisted around for my roommate's reaction just in time to see him slide off the ladder.

Thump!

Luckily, he wasn't too high up, as he fell onto the tiled floor and landed against the stack behind us. Weirdly, he was fast asleep.

"What the . . . Rey?"

Thump, thump, thump.

Other students began dropping to the floor. All along the stack, our classmates were falling asleep. Hayati yawned. "I don't know what's going on, but I feel like I'm . . . I'm going to . . . to . . ."

Her eyes fluttered and her legs began to shake. We were the only two students still standing. But then she staggered and fell over Jad, her snores the loudest I'd ever heard.

"What in the figs is happening?" I shouted.

Just then, a familiar tingle worked its way down my chest and settled in my belly. Baba's charm, all those cedarwood links, sent a warning through me as they'd done before. Necromancers! And, as I glanced through the stacks, my blood froze.

Literally every student was on the floor, either

facedown or leaning against one of the stacks.

Every student except me.

I climbed off the ladder, shoving the dandelion in my pocket. A chill swept across the back of my neck, and my throat went dry.

"Oh figs..."

"The cake," said a faint, ghostlike voice. "All you had to do was eat my cake, and we could have had you."

I spun, but nothing was around me. No shadow in sight. I rushed toward Moussa's desk, the dandelion in one hand and the other reaching for *The Alchemist's Hand*, shaking from fear.

As I crept closer to the center of the hall, the room darkened more and more. With it being barely an hour past lunchtime, sunlight should've been attacking my eyes. Instead, the hairs on the back of my neck stood up as the lamps began to dim.

When I reached Moussa, he was leaning over the tall librarian's counter. The monkey was also there. Only, like the others, Moussa lay asleep. His head was facedown in a plate, smushing a piece of the very same chocolate cake we'd been served earlier. His monkey lay on its back with a belly bulge—snoring.

"Hey, where'd you get that dessert?" I asked, stirring Moussa. "You can't be sleeping right now. You've got to get up!"

"Hello, Shad."

Casting glances in every direction, I couldn't find where the voice had come from.

"Pssst. Over here!"

A black ball came at me full force, hitting me square in the chest, hard enough to knock me off my feet. I fell onto my back, and the dandelion fell out of my hand and skidded away. I got up quickly and turned my head, left to right, up and down.

"Why are you looking there?" asked the voice. "I'm right here!"

Another ball came from the side. I leapt away, scrambling to my feet while the voice laughed.

"If you wanted to play simulation dodgeball," I said, "you could have just come to Ms. Najoom's class!"

My words came out spluttery and weak. It felt like I couldn't breathe. Like I'd tried to swallow a whole apple and it got stuck, not letting in any of the air. The necromancers were supposed to be gone. Sure, Kahem had mentioned they didn't give up so easily, but to attack so soon and while I was all alone . . .

I gulped, stepping back, as my worst fears became a reality.

Bumping into something behind me, I stiffened at the sight of Dean Ibrahim standing over me. As the charm rattled around my neck, he bent over and, like on my first day at the school, I saw my trembling reflection in his dark glasses.

Black smoke receded into an alchemy coat he wore. Grinning, he said, "I believe we have unfinished business, Mr. Hadid."

Chapter 26

"You were gone," I stammered, backing away. "I destroyed your lab!"

"Yes," he said, reaching an open hand toward me. "That was quite a setback, but I merely stepped away to regather our resources while my apprentices kept an eye on things. Speaking of apprentices . . ."

The necromancer extended his hand, but I backed away and shook my head. "Not a fig's chance I'd become one of you. I've already got an alchemy teacher."

"Do not be stubborn," he said. "Throughout the past decade, as long as our order has been active here, alchemists have found their way into the school. They were all either sent home to continue their studies elsewhere, or we dealt with them in other ways. But you . . . you are different from those alchemists. My apprentices warned me, but I didn't realize it until earlier today, when I witnessed you craft that mixture without taking a single measurement."

"Y-you saw that?"

"Oh indeed," he said, his sinister smile widening. "I'd considered killing you right then, as I had several times before, but some of my equals happen to believe you show promise. After giving it some thought, I'm also coming to see why Kahem took you in off the street."

I cautiously stepped back and asked, "Why put my classmates to sleep?"

"Well, my order required some peace and quiet so we could scour the library for clues to the ingredients we need," he said, drawing closer, setting my heart racing. "You wouldn't happen to have discovered anything while here, would you?"

I shook my head again, but his lips only curled into an even wider grin. One that sent a shiver down my spine and made me wish I'd kept the pouch full of Destruction Dust handy.

"Help us and anything you desire can be yours," he continued. "Our order will give you a shop like the one your father owned; my apprentices will become your friends, and even family. With our goals realized, we will be able to revive your grandmother *and* grant her the gift of immortality."

"I don't believe you," I said. "Nothing can bring my teta ba—"

The dean vanished in a cloud of smoke, only to reappear beside me.

"See for yourself," he said, and thrust a mist out from an uncorked vial. The world became hazy as he leaned in and whispered, "Join us, and this can be your future. . . ."

I wandered up a familiar hill. Grass rose ankle high and the clouds crowded the sky up above. It wasn't clear where I was, not until I neared the peak. The tombstones came into view then. Hundreds of them, all spread out behind a fence at the other side of the hill. Right beside it, a sign read *Portland Cemetery*.

My breath quickened as I descended the steep incline, nearly stumbling as I picked up speed. Momentum carried me through the front entrance, and I skidded to a stop right in front of a giant stone.

"No . . ."

My legs began to shake as my eyes sank to the name on the grave. I bent down and read it over and over. Tears brimmed just as the first of the raindrops hit the stone, building into a downpour.

"Shaddo, what are you doing here?"

The voice stopped my heart. Teta stood over me with a black umbrella held over both our heads. Her wrinkly smile shone so bright I swore the sun was out, even as rain continued falling around us. Without hesitating, I sprang up to wrap both arms around her.

"Oh, Teta, please tell me this is real."

She eased out of my grip, nodding, and said, "Give the

necromancers the Revival Elixir recipe from your guide-book, and then we can share as many dinners as you like."

Backing away from her, I said, "Teta . . . I can't."

The darkness from the umbrella spread around me like a shadow. It swallowed Teta, even as I reached for her. Everything went to dark until a glow dawned from my chest. It was Baba's charm resisting the illusion.

Only a whisper remained amid the fading darkness. *Join us, Shaddo. Save me. . . .*

My heart thudded against my chest as the vision faded, my eyes readjusting to the dim library, ancient, large, and radiating with invisible power.

Teta.

Even after knowing how evil the necromancers were, how little they really cared about ordinary people like me, the possibility of bringing back my grandma still forced me to pause. To consider the offer.

But I refused to let the necromancers hurt anyone at the Alexandria Academy because of me. And I wouldn't let their Shadow Alchemy harm my friends. The class-mates who accepted me, even if they couldn't remember my alchemy. The ones who were teaching me that I *could* find people who cared. Teta would never want me to abandon them. She taught me better than to fall for a dirty trick like the one Dean Ibrahim just used.

Slapping the man's large, outstretched hand away, I said, "I would rather swallow Diarrhea Dust."

"No such thing exists."

"Oh. Well, maybe I made that up. But if it *did* exist, I would rather swallow it than join your fig-faced group of necromancers."

Dean Ibrahim frowned. "Stubborn, stubborn boy. Don't you understand that we will get what we want, whether you join or not? We will wipe out the rest of the alchemists who oppose us. In fact, I shall start now by killing you!"

He lunged in and, before I could react, wrapped an arm around my neck. I couldn't shake free from his powerful grip. Slowly, his eyes turned green. His gray hair also changed, receding and growing lighter to become a patch of blond at the top of his scalp.

Just when this situation couldn't get worse, my guidebook slipped right out from under my waistband.

"It can't be," he gasped, releasing me so that he could snatch it from the floor as his disguise continued to melt away. "*The Alchemist's Hand*! This contains all that we've spent years searching for. All that we need to complete our plans."

I lunged for the book only to become tangled in something. Shadowy tendrils wrapped around my arms and legs. They lifted me to be eye level with the necromancer standing in front of me, his face completely changed.

Fear made my tongue twist. "Y-you are not Dean Ibra-him. . . ."

Dr. Salazar wiggled his creepy mustache. "No, I am not. You evaded me back at your apartment, but not this time. If only you had listened to my warning about that imagination of yours being trouble."

I fought the tendrils, punching and kicking, but nothing worked. The shadows wrapped around Salazar to become a black alchemy coat.

"Why are the necromancers doing this?" I asked. "Why are you all ruining the Academy by getting rid of alchemy?"

"We are doing no such thing," he said. "The alchemy is simply being kept from those who won't use it our way. The *right* way. And we are creating some wonderful technology here that will transform alchemy for everyone to enjoy!"

"You mean for your fig-faced followers to enjoy?"

"Enough of your nonsense!" Thrusting a hand out, the tendrils shoved me against the librarian's counter, where Moussa still lay fast asleep. Pinned, I watched while Salazar opened my guidebook. "I always knew you were hiding something, but *this* is truly remarkable. How unfortunate that this will be your last day at . . ."

But as he started to look at the pages, the tendrils

fell away from around me and the necromancer's voice trailed off, his eyes widening as I landed on the floor. Salazar gaped not from the shock of what he saw, but what he *couldn't* see.

"What is this trickery?" he said, bushy blond eyebrows rising. "These pages should hold all the secrets of the original alchemists!"

"I guess you just aren't good enough for those secrets," I snapped.

Dr. Salazar growled as he reached forward, a black tendril springing out of his arm. It curled around me, yanking me into his grip as he reached into his coat with his other hand, drawing out a vial. Lifting it to his teeth, he uncorked the cap and a dark green mist drifted out. I screamed. Leaning away as it came toward me, I needed to do something but couldn't break free.

"Tell me what the book says!" he demanded.

I shook my head, choking as I said, "Go eat some Sleeping Dust cake because I'd only ever do that in your dreams."

He brought the mist closer. "Our apprentices were given normal cake. They are helping the more experienced members of my order now. It is too bad they weren't here to witness what happens to someone who disobeys my commands."

As the wisps drew near my eyes and nose, I shouted,

"Help! Is there anyone in the stacks who can hear me? Anyone still awake?"

But no one answered. I closed my eyes and got ready to face my end, to go to the big bakery in the sky.

Baba's smile came to mind, the way he'd pick me up over his shoulders as a child in Lebanon. Then I remembered standing by Teta's side during his and Jiduh's funeral on a hot summer day. Teta held my hand and fanned herself, the tears streaming down our eyes. Now they were only streaming down mine.

Wait . . . the fan. I could use something like that now.

I quickly searched my pockets, the floor, anywhere nearby. There was a short stack of notebooks on the librarian's counter right by Moussa. I reached for it. The mist was inches away, nearly too close not to breathe in.

"Tell that grandmother of yours I said hello," Salazar sneered.

I stretched so far that I thought my arm might pop out of the socket. Only an inch away, it remained just out of reach. . . .

At least until Baba's charm kicked in. Salazar moved to lead the mist into my face when my necklace glowed bright, repelling the alchemy and sending a jolt out of me and into the necromancer. Quickly, I grabbed a notebook and twisted toward him, fanning the mist back into the large man's face.

Dr. Salazar began to reach into his coat for another

mixture. "You think such tricks work on ... work on ... me ..."

The creepy alchemist caught one sniff of the mist and his face went purple. He broke into a cough while I back-pedaled, stumbling away from both him and the mist so fast that I fell onto my butt.

Dr. Salazar staggered toward me as I crawled back. He reached out, his large hand nearly getting me, but then he stopped and grabbed his throat, gagging. Right before my eyes, the necromancer toppled onto a pile of books on the floor, the mist he'd inhaled now fading away around him.

Rising to walk over to the unconscious necroman-cer, I searched inside his black alchemy coat. Between pouches, I drew out a book from one of the largest pock-ets and breathed out a sigh of relief. *The Alchemist's Hand*'s old green cover and yellowing pages, my baba's guidebook in my hands once more. Now, to ...

"Ouch!"

I yelped as something leapt onto my head before bouncing off. I followed the figure to where it landed on the counter—it was Moussa's pet monkey. It pointed back at the old man, who was still snoring. At least until the monkey leapt up and landed right on the librarian's chest.

Moussa spat out a chunk of brown gunk, which, gag-ging, I realized was a piece of the dust-ridden cake. The librarian jerked awake and sat upright.

Taking his pet monkey into his arms, he said, "Nice

one! Now, what did we miss?"

Unsure of what to say as my history teacher spotted me, I pointed back to where Dr. Salazar should be. "You missed *everything.* The cake was laced with a Sleeping Dust because the necromancers were trying to get to me. Dean Ibrahim came back, only he was really *another* necromancer in disguise and—"

"Wait just a second there." The librarian halted me, raising his hand, and nodded to the space behind us. "What are you pointing at?"

"What do you mean?" I asked, twisting as my stomach sank.

Where Dr. Salazar had fallen after I'd knocked him unconscious, the tiled floor lay empty. But how could that be possible? He'd been there just a minute ago.

No, *seconds* ago.

As I wondered how anyone could have escaped so quietly, my eyes darted across the Great Library until I spotted something farther down through the stacks. Down where the lamps cast only a dim glow, several shadowy tendrils curled around a bookshelf.

There, vanishing into the darkness, another necromancer carried away Dr. Salazar in their arms. Two bright eyes peered out at me. Then they were gone.

Chapter 27

I *tightened my hands into* fists. It took everything not to shout.

Salazar had escaped. He'd been right in front of me, and I'd let him get away. Kahem would never forgive me if he found out.

Slowly, Herman and the other students all stepped out from behind the bookshelves where they'd fallen. Most limped like zombies, while others appeared to have wide eyes, fully awake. A mob of my classmates soon formed behind me, students telling our confused librarian about how they'd fallen asleep.

Rey's familiar voice caught my attention and I rushed to hug him as he approached, relief flooding my belly at the sight of him unhurt. My roommate pulled away and rubbed his droopy eyes while I searched the students who were staggering out from behind the bookshelves.

"Where's Hayati?" I asked.

He shrugged. "Not sure. Let's find her."

We shoved past several classmates and hurried through the stacks. Hayati lay where she'd first fallen at the *Poetry of the East* stack. She leaned against one of the ladders, still fast asleep, and she wasn't alone. Drowsy Donny napped by her side too, and I stirred him awake first since he was closer.

"Oh, hey, Shad," he said, smacking his lips. "Ahlan wa sahlan, buddy. Let me sleep some more, will ya?"

It sounded like Donny was okay, so I left him to sleep and moved on to Hayati. Only, she wasn't snoring like Donny. Even when I shook her silly, she still didn't wake up.

"Nap time's over!" I said, bending down and poking her head. "Hello, anyone in there?"

She didn't budge. I began to shake her harder, even yelling when that didn't work. My heart raced. My mind flashed back to the last person I couldn't wake up—Teta.

There was nothing I could do, the vials in my pocket useless for this situation. I stomped. Realizing I'd let down my friend made me so angry that I wanted to knock the entire bookshelf over.

"What's going on here?" asked Moussa, clutching his back as he walked up to us. His monkey tapped Hayati's cheek, but she didn't move. "The girl needs a nurse!"

Without giving us a chance to explain, Moussa bent and picked up my classmate, disappearing around the shelf with Hayati over his shoulder. The monkey poked my belly and hurried after him. Soon, the only noise around was Donny's snoring. I leaned against the stack and slid down to sit.

"Necromancers..."

Turning to Donny, who'd muttered the word as he slept, I asked, "What did you say?"

The boy only snored in response. I sighed, feeling more powerless than ever despite having knocked out a necromancer. Even if anyone had witnessed my battle against Dr. Salazar, they'd just forget it in an hour or two.

"Come on, Shad."

Rey nudged me up, and I followed him back through the library. All our classmates had already left, probably heading back to their rooms. We stood in what had once been the Library of Alexandria. Thousands of books, maps, and much more. Standing here, in the oldest library in the world, where all the smartest people came to hang out.

Despite its magnificence, my guilt weighed me down with each step. I couldn't think about anything right now. Not with my chest full of worry over Hayati. After all, *I* had encouraged her to eat the cake.

Not to mention, the necromancers had just launched their most daring attack yet. Now that they knew about *The Alchemist's Hand*, who could say what dangerous lengths they would go to for it.

But I would figure out a way to help Hayati, keep my

friends out of harm's way, and protect Baba's guidebook from the necromancers. Kahem had trusted me with its safety. And I couldn't let anything happen to my new friends. So, for these three weeks ahead of the solstice, I'd need to be *extra* careful.

After all, if Shad Hadid was anything, he was responsible.

When Dean Abdullah's voice came faintly over the Academy speakers, I'd just arrived at the bathroom. Rey had instantly passed out on his bed, snoring louder than a hibernating bear, but there was no way I'd be sleeping after my encounter with Salazar.

Whether or not you believe yourself to be one of the affected students, said the head dean, *proceed to your rooms for the remainder of the day. Again, classes for the rest of the day are canceled, all should report back to their—*

After flushing the toilet, I washed my hands and stepped out into the hallway, where a heavy stomping caused me to jolt. Spinning around, Sarah hurried toward me, her arms crossed.

"What's happening?" she asked in a loud whisper. "All the students fell asleep in my class. Even Dean Hayek passed out in the hallway outside our door!"

Instead of answering her question, I tilted my head and asked, "If that was the case, then how are you not asleep?"

"I felt a little tired," she said, "but it was no biggie."

"All right," I said, swallowing. "Remember the night I ran into you in Portland? I was running away from someone. Well, *something*. A necromancer. . . ."

Sarah's face went even paler than normal. "But you'd gotten away, right?"

"I did then," I said in a loud whisper. "But they are back, and *they* are behind this whole sleeping debacle. The necromancers put something in the cake."

Wait a second. . . .

"Did you eat the cake?" I asked.

Sarah rolled her eyes at me and shrugged. "Obviously. It tasted good, but I've had better."

My mind raced, pieces of a puzzle coming together in my head. I suddenly understood how Sarah remembered my alchemy while my other friends couldn't. Whatever kept her from forgetting was what kept her from succumbing to the cake's Sleeping Dust. It was what made her unique among all the Academy's students. . . .

"You aren't a descendent," I muttered, to which Sarah furrowed her brows.

She had no clue what I meant other than that Jad and some of the other bullies had teased her about it during her first few days. They made fun of how she wasn't Arab.

"Dean Abdullah said everyone here was a descendent," I explained. "The necromancers . . . because of what she said, they probably created their mixtures with the intent of going after only people who have blood ties to the original founders. That's why the Forgetting Charm, the Sleeping Dust, you're fine through all of it!"

Everything felt so much clearer now. I couldn't hold back my excitement about the discovery, though I couldn't necessarily prove it either.

Sarah didn't seem to care for how important this was because she turned and headed back to her room. Twisting back toward me briefly, she said, "Let's talk later. Maybe somewhere more . . . private."

I nodded and watched her trudge away, dozens of questions swirling around in my head. Discovering the reason behind why Sarah hadn't fallen asleep was only one mystery solved among many, like why Kahem hadn't come to the Academy, or how Dr. Salazar had been here this whole time.

The most pressing mystery now, though, was how I could stop the necromancer threat. After all, if they managed to resurrect their leader at the winter solstice, then neither teacher nor student would be safe.

Their success would dash any hope of the alchemists keeping balance in the world, and it would be all my fault.

Chapter 28

With just over two weeks to the science fair, I reached under my bed for my hidden mixtures.

Already, a few days had passed since the Salazar incident. No one else had attacked me yet and, after frantically gathering what I needed to craft some more protective charms, my fingers now brushed pouches, cups, glasses, bowls–

"What are you doing under there?"

I spun, gripping a pouch of Freezing Dust in case I'd need to stop a necromancer in their tracks. But it was only Sarah. She stood at my doorway, arms crossed and focus turning to the pouch in my hand.

Hiding the Freezing Dust behind my back, I said, "Don't sneak up on people like that!"

"But it's dinnertime, dude."

"Yeah, I must've lost track of time while studying," I lied, quickly changing the subject while shoving the pouch into my pocket. "Are you still sitting with *those* first-years?"

She nodded, probably getting that I'd referred to the bullies. "You mean Jad's table, or one of the others? I tend to switch."

"Yeah, well, you could try sitting with your science fair group. . . ."

Sarah glanced away. Ignoring my comment, she admitted, "One of the boys I sit with, Kareem, was making fun of Hayati and how she's still at the nurse's office. The things he and Jad were saying didn't rub me right, especially since I hear she's not waking up."

"Are you surprised?"

Sarah shook her head. "Over the last couple of months, that stepbrother of yours has turned some of our classmates into total demons. I mean, they joke about things I never would."

"Are you saying I was right about all those jerks?"

"Don't let it get to your head," she said with a half-hidden smile. "Though I heard something that might interest you, if you want to really get under their skin."

Leaning closer, I gestured her to go on. "I'm listening. . . ."

I couldn't tell if this was a trap, or if Sarah wanted to stick it to those figs, but I'd only recently sent Dr. Salazar fleeing. If I could deal with some of those mean bullies in the same week . . . well, that would just be the icing on the cake.

"A few of Yakoub's first-year followers are trying to make peace with Herman," she started. "Apparently, Herman's angry because of a girl who asked if his Gucci shoes were real."

"How are those two things related?"

Sarah leaned back into the hall. She looked in both directions, probably making sure none of our classmates could overhear us. "Apparently, the girl who angered Herman is a second cousin to Jad, one of Yakoub's first-year friends. What are the odds?"

I chuckled because Sarah clearly didn't understand how Arab families worked. "We all have, like, a hundred second cousins," I said. "It's not a coincidence at all."

"Whatever," she said. "Point is—"

"The bully can't go after their second cousin," I said, realizing exactly where Sarah was going with this. "You're saying that Herman and his friends could turn on my stepbrother and his friends if we gave them the right reason."

She nodded. "Exactly!"

A sudden rush of excitement had me wanting to jump up and hug her, but I quickly remembered who Sarah was. Who she *used* to be. I still hesitated to trust her, even if every instinct told me that she was an ally.

Maybe even a potential friend.

Whatever the case, a plan began to sprout in my head like a flower in Kahem's garden.

"Thanks for giving me the inside scoop on all this drama," I said. "It looks like the bullies are going to help do some good after all."

She snorted. "Why do you sound like you're planning something reckless? Wait, if it involves me, I don't want to know. At least not before dinnertime. You coming?"

I waved her away. "Get a head start, I'll catch up in a sec."

Nodding, she disappeared out the door while I teased the Freezing Dust out of my pocket. Imagine if I'd frozen her in place? That would've been awkward, though perhaps she'd have finally begun to believe in alchemy.

A loud growl escaped my stomach and I fought back the hunger for a few more moments while I touched up some of my charms. Once I felt confident that any necromancer who wandered in would be in a world of hurt, the time had come for a celebratory snack.

I tucked the leftover ingredients and *The Alchemist's Hand* under the bed. Trudging out of the room, my mind more at ease than before, I headed to a staircase that led me down a dim corridor. To keep away the older-years . . . well, Yakoub, I hurried through a back way that avoided the courtyards and gathering spaces.

A part of me wished I'd gone with Sarah. So much of the time at this school had been spent looking over my shoulder. I couldn't shake that feeling of being watched anymore, and it didn't help that Baba's charm shot a tingle down my spine. It wasn't one of the fainter feelings either, but a true shock. But when I twisted around to check my back, there was nothing.

Taking in a deep breath, I continued toward the dining hall, having forgotten what I'd just been thinking about.

I approached the corner that would take me into a courtyard walkway, where the sound of other students reached me. Older students who were probably lounging or experimenting with some cool new tech.

Necromancers didn't attack in front of others, I reminded myself. Just a few more steps and I'd be—

Another jolt from Baba's charm. This time it came stronger than the one previous, and I broke into a sprint toward the courtyard only to have a shadow hurry out of the classroom just in front of me.

No, not a shadow, but a student. Two of them.

Slowing to a stop, they blocked my way out. One I recognized to be Zara. She sometimes sat with Sarah in the dining hall. One of the bullies who, like Jad, the necromancers had mentioned during the meeting I'd listened in on.

Apparently, they'd made good on their decision to

turn her into a necromancer. Around both her waist and that of the older student standing beside her, black alchemy belts glinted under lamplight. My entire body trembled at the sight, the unexpected encounter setting my heartbeat racing.

"I'm not sure how someone like you could rough up Dr. Salazar," said Zara, snickering with her partner. "Look at him, he doesn't seem so tough at all right now."

"W-what do you want?" I asked, stepping back.

The other student reached for his belt. "Tell us what we need for the Revival Elixir. Either that or your little friend won't ever wake up. . . ."

My whole body stiffened at the mention of Hayati. To think the necromancers would be evil enough to use her against me. I gritted my teeth and said, "You can't have the recipe. Not when you'll use it to harm others like her."

The older student shook his head. "It seems we'll just force it out of you."

Together, they moved to attack with mixtures from their belt, but I beat them to it. My reflexes had sharpened during the weeks I'd spent practicing alone. I threw Freezing Dust at the older one, stopping him instantly.

Meanwhile, Zara dodged and continued toward me with a mist curling around her fingertips. "Come here!"

Out of mixtures, I hurried into the open doorway directly opposite where they'd both come in. Rushing through a small library-like collection of shelves, I hid among the dozens of books on what seemed to be world religions.

Zara's footsteps weren't quiet, and I ducked behind the Buddhism section as she passed by. Then I snuck back out the way I came.

The older boy remained still as a statue where I'd frozen him. I shivered at the one part of him he could move, his eyes, which followed me while I slipped away, unhurt and undetected by the other bully. I couldn't believe I'd escaped as I rounded the corner toward—

"*Oomf!*"

Thrown against the wall, I fell with a groan. Baba's charm tingled while I fought to stand up. The courtyard appeared less packed than I expected. Those who were gathered paid no attention to me, nor the girl who'd knocked me over.

"Now to put you to sleep like the cake should have," said Zara, reaching into her alchemy belt for a vial.

But her fingers never made it to the cork. Another figure rushed in, slamming into Zara and sending her soaring.

The bully landed feet away, the glass vial breaking and an ominous mist rising from the shards. It overtook her as she got up and I doubted she saw the person who'd thrown her as, her eyes rolling back, the bully fell into an alchemy-induced sleep.

Sarah dusted off her uniform, bending to lift me onto my feet. "What was that all about?"

I staggered to peer back around the corner I'd come from. The older student still stood there in the center of the hall, frozen as a fig Popsicle.

"I'm not quite sure," I said. "Thanks for that."

"You're lucky I had to use the bathroom on the way," she said, the both of us walking the rest of the distance toward the large dining hall doors.

All the while, my back aching, I considered all the things I hadn't told Sarah. Things like how Zara wasn't an ordinary bully. That she and the other student were necromancers, with alchemy belts and vials that could do serious damage.

But I pushed all that into the back of my head. Already, I'd been preparing for the necromancer threat, and I'd accepted that Kahem wasn't going to show up.

Now it was time to fight back, and I was just about to get started. . . .

Chapter 29

*D*ean *Hayek glared at me* from across the dining hall. Beside her, Dean Saba was being his weird self. She, on the other hand, always had a knack for sensing mischief.

She'd given the most punishments out of any dean for stuff like missing curfew or being late to class. A part of me wondered if she was a necromancer too, or if she just really liked seeing students in detention.

Dinner had been especially good since the cake debacle last week, and I had the full belly to prove it. Most of the students didn't dare to try the desserts. As for me, I trusted that Baba's charm would detect any alchemy in the food. Unlike with the cake, I wouldn't ignore the warnings next time.

I also trusted the charm would detect necromancers, who hadn't appeared since the bully attack three days ago. And if the attack hadn't left me spooked enough, Zara and that other student had vanished the next day.

It was as if the necromancers had sent them away and everyone at the Academy had just been all right with it.

But thanks to that incident, I didn't go anywhere without a few mixtures. I only parted from them in gym class, but I doubted necromancers would want to get in the middle of our sweaty games. Not when they were busy preparing for the solstice two weeks from now.

"So, I'm not really clear on the plan," said Donny, yawning. "You want Rey and me to do what?"

Sarah shot me a suspicious look but didn't say anything, especially since the plan came after the news she'd shared a few days ago. I smiled a thanks and she puffed her cheeks in a *whatever, dude* sort of look. I reached into my pocket and pulled out a recently crafted Disguise Mist.

Holding up the vial, I explained, "Give me a distraction. After that, leave the rest to me, and we'll be out of here and on our way to saving Hayati."

I stuck out my hand to show the glass vial shaped like a giant raindrop. In it, blue and white liquid swirled around, inviting the eyes of everyone at the table. Rey, also with us at the table, reached for it, and I quickly turned my hand around.

"No touching," I said. "Unless you're ready to break some rules so we can kick butt."

He puffed out a breath and gave Donny a look.

"Explain again why *we* need to save Hayati? I mean, I'm all for helping, but shouldn't we leave that to the nurse?"

"You just have to trust me," I said, not wanting to explain that Hayati was in an alchemy-induced coma. And I didn't mention the guilt over giving her my piece of cake, or how the necromancers were using her to threaten me. Even if they and their bully apprentices scared my socks off, I couldn't stand to have my friends in harm's way.

To my relief, Rey stuck out his hand to cover mine. "I'm in."

"Me too," said Donny, stretching out his hand.

That left only Sarah, but she was shaking her head. "I don't know about this. . . ."

I gave her a mischievous smile. Or at least I tried to, but it probably looked like I'd just farted on my cushion. "Come on," I said. "Let's show these figs how we do it in Portland."

She held out her arm so the four of us met hands over a table full of garlic hummus, spicy baba ghanoush, falafel drenched in tahini sauce, and more. Starlight sprinkled down from the glass dome and I just knew Teta was watching. These weren't only my science fair group members, after all. They were my friends.

And now I'd show this school just what an alchemist could do.

Dinnertime was nearing its end and, off to the distance, Dean Saba was showing the teachers' table the proper way to belly dance.

Meanwhile, at our table, Rey and Donny–who was taking another nap–sat across from me and waited. One minute ago, Sarah had just set in motion the first phase of my plan. She walked up to the bullies' table, shoved another girl off a seat cushion, and took the spot beside Jad.

"There they go!" said Rey.

Sarah whispered something into Jad's ear, and then stood up to go use the bathroom.

The bully stood up and followed Sarah toward the bathrooms. What she'd told him was that she had the answer key to our upcoming math test. Jad was expecting to find it hidden under one of the sinks, but that kabees had no clue it was just a trick.

"All right," I said, glancing at Rey. "Count to ten and then go ahead with phase two."

"Did someone say phase two?" asked Donny, waking up. "Oh, Shad, while I was dreaming, I remembered there was something I wanted to tell you!"

I furrowed my brows. "Really?"

"Just that I . . . I . . ." Yawning again, he shrugged. "Actually, I forgot again."

Grabbing a handful of carrots, I resisted the urge to fling them at my friend and instead stuffed them into my mouth for energy. Then I tried rolling like I'd seen in those spy movies but hit my head against the table. I opted to crawl toward the group of plants by the nearest shelf of cake-baking manuals instead.

A grouping of tall bamboo shoots gave me cover. I reached into my pocket and pulled out the Disguise Mist, popping the vial open. According to *The Alchemist's Hand*, the key to transforming into someone was a scrap from the clothes they wore, which we'd scored in the locker room.

Swallowing a deep breath, I said, "Here goes nothing."

I closed my eyes as the mist rose out, wafting it around me. It made my skin tingly. My necklace began to burn, which meant the alchemy was working. I pictured Jad in my mind and even whispered his name over and over until the tingle disappeared.

"I think he's choking!"

Rey's shouts were followed by the gasps of shocked students. I peeked out from behind the plants, and both my friends were where they should be, making a scene in front of Dean Saba. I stepped out from behind the plants, still seeing myself as the handsome shaytan I was but knowing that, to everyone else, I didn't look anything like Shad. To them, I'd be the taller and more buff Jad, and it was all thanks to the Disguise Mist.

Rey knelt over Donny, who grabbed his neck, pretending to choke. Everyone was looking over. The rest of the bullies were laughing as I passed them. No one noticed as I rounded the dining hall toward my target, a table on the other side.

"What's up," I said to Herman, smiling as I approached him and his friends.

"Oh, hey, Jad!" said Herman, brimming with hope. "Here to apologize for that rude cousin of yours?"

It felt slimy to pretend to be someone else. I never liked Halloween for that reason; costumes freaked me out. But I smiled to soften up Herman, trying to be brave and not have a panic attack mid-plan, especially now that everyone else had played their part so well.

"Actually," I said, "I'm here to say that your Prada socks are definitely fake."

Herman's grin quickly faded into confusion. Someone else at the table chuckled nervously, but Herman said, "Don't joke like that."

"I wish I *was* joking," I said. "Even Shad has better style. And Herman, you don't even have a belly. His belly is so big and round and awesome and . . ."

"Jad? What are you saying?"

I straightened, realizing I'd gotten a little carried away. "Yeah, Shad's cooler than you, and my second cousin was right to say you have a bad fashion sense."

Everyone at the table had gone silent. Herman had his teeth bared like a wolf getting ready to pounce and I knew I'd gotten him right where I wanted. He was mad, not expecting Jad to betray him, and now all I needed to do was grab this handful of hummus and . . .

Splat!

"What the Gucci?" Herman looked down at his uniform, where the hummus I'd thrown had splattered. "I don't care how big and popular you are," he said with a growl. "You are going to regret doing that."

"Oh yeah? Prove it, just like you should prove your necklace is actual gold and not a fake."

Herman shouted and grabbed the bowl of oily olives, starting to chuck them at me. I dove away and the olives hit a student behind me, who shouted, "Hey, what's your deal?"

Others started to look our way. I reached for another table and dumped a salad on another classmate's head. Their friends began to pick up food. Other students began to pick up food. I . . . well, *Jad*, grabbed a tray of baba ghanoush and started to dip my fingers and splatter everyone all around.

That got Deans Saba's and Hayek's attention off Donny. They gazed over at us, eyes wide at the angry students with food in their hands. This was the moment I was waiting for.

Sucking in a deep breath, I yelled, "Food fight!"

Chaos. The dining hall became a war zone. I ducked under a bunch of kibbe balls, which broke against a nearby table, making the veggies explode out, covering all who were seated. A few tables away, a student was launching pickles across the hall at the bullies, who were throwing pita chips in turn.

Older students rushed into the heart of the food fight as the deans handed out detentions left and right. Those who got in trouble stopped throwing food, and it seemed like everything was about to settle down, which couldn't happen. I shoved aside Herman and grabbed a handful of falafel that I dipped in olive oil.

"Get the older-years!" I shouted, chucking the falafel right at a last-year standing at the center of the tables.

He'd been facing backward. Yet when the falafel hit his head, he turned with wide eyes. "Who threw that?"

I pointed at another last-year, who was rushing toward our empty table. The girl put up her hands in confusion, but her classmate grabbed bits of the falafel and hurled them straight at her face.

The girl pulled out a device like what Dean Hayek had used on Yakoub our first day and said, "I've been dying to try this baby out!"

Seeing the older students going at it gave my classmates motivation to join back in. I placed my hands on my hips, watching the food fight unfold and smiling at my work. Selma was eating something off the ground,

Herman was screaming about his clothes being real, and Donny had gone back to sleep on a spinach pie.

But then the real Jad emerged from the bathroom. He looked around and, before he could spot me, I ducked and crawled across the tables toward the exit. Donny and Rey were already at the large double doors. Dean Saba was coming around and I waited for him to move past.

Whack!

A wet glob slapped my cheeks and my eyes began to burn. I wiped it off quickly, sniffing what was on my fingertips. "Garlic paste? Who would throw that?"

"In your face, Jad!" said one of the smaller girls. She had an Afro and a hearing aid, and I decided not to fight back. He'd probably deserved that by the way I'd seen him bullying Hayati.

I continued to crawl until a darkness hovered overhead. "Hey, what are you doing on the floor, loser?"

Recognizing the voice, the shape of the shadow above, my knees began wobbling. Yakoub grinned amid all the flying food. His hand formed a solid fist and he reached up to catch a tomato without looking, heaving it to pound another student right in the face.

"I asked you a question," said my stepbrother. "What are you doing, Jad?"

Swallowing, I said, "J-just looking for some food to throw."

Yakoub searched the cafeteria with his eyes and said,

"Makes sense. See my little stepbrother anywhere? This is a great chance for some quality bonding."

"Why do you hate your stepbrother so much, always talking about how you want to hurt him? But what did he do that you can't leave him alone?"

I blurted out the words before thinking. Yakoub glanced around and then back down, opening and then closing his mouth before he shrugged. For a moment, it seemed like the question got to him. Then he laughed, knocking me to the side with a kick.

"Why do I need a reason to beat up on a loser?" he asked. "My dad chased the Hadids out of Lebanon. And now I'm going to make him proud and chase Shad out of this school."

I shuddered, wondering if my stepfather was actually proud of ruining my life, and if he'd want his son to do the same. But I couldn't stick around the bully king for another moment. Before my disguise could fade, I pointed back behind him.

"Pretty sure Shad went into the bathroom. You can corner that *loser* there!"

Yakoub bent over and clapped my shoulder. "Thanks for the tip. This is going to be fun...."

While watching Yakoub stomp into the bathroom, I got up and hurried toward my friends. With everyone distracted, including the deans, we slid out into the hallway.

Only, not all of them were there. Not until Sarah showed up last, her hands shaking.

"Are you okay?" I asked.

She didn't say anything for a few seconds, hugging herself. "Do you understand how hard it is for me to leave a food fight? Being in one of those has been my dream forever."

Donny, Rey, and I rolled our eyes.

The clock above the dining hall door said we had only nine minutes before dinner would end. We needed to hurry, or we wouldn't finish in time. Every second mattered and this part was the most important.

"All right, team," I said, pointing down the hallway. "Lead the way to Ms. Wassouf's room. We have a mixture to brew."

Chapter 30

"One pinch," I said. "That was, like, five pinches!"

The mixture fizzed and died out, becoming a sad gloop resembling grape jelly. Standing in the middle of the lab space, distanced from the stacks and stacks of science books, I heard my stomach grumble. It both reminded me that grape jelly was quite delicious and yelled at me for leaving the dining hall early.

We had a chance at saving Hayati, thanks to my classmates. While they didn't know how to practice alchemy, they were the descendants of the Academy's original founders, some of the oldest alchemists who ever lived. Crafting charms and mixing elixirs were a deep part of their family histories, whether they believed in it or not.

And even if those original founders hadn't shared the secrets of this ancient art with outsiders, it didn't seem fair to leave Sarah out. After years of not being picked for gym teams or invited to sleepovers, the idea of excluding anyone made my gut twist. Sarah helped in ways the other students, the descendants of the so-called original alchemists, never could. I'd have let her help brew the mixture too. Only, she'd said that she preferred guarding the door instead.

Rey groaned. "How am I supposed to do anything with *this* going on?"

My roommate pointed at Donny, who'd somehow fallen into the deepest sleep yet. The second I mentioned alchemy, the guy was knocked out.

We were running out of time, so I stepped in to help, annoyed with myself because, knowing Donny, I should've planned for that. As for Rey, he and his Sultan of Slam beanie were the real deal when it came to mixing ingredients. Kahem said I had a gift for alchemy, but Rey was a *true* natural talent.

Even with all his skill, though, Rey had still messed up every mixture, and we were running low on ingredients. But then again, the alchemy we were brewing was advanced.

Removing the flask and replacing it with another one, Rey said, "All right, let's try this again."

"Well, make it snappy," said Sarah from outside the lab room.

Rey set the new flask to a boil and measured half a spoonful of crushed dandelion petals. I fiddled with ginger extract. My fingers shook while holding the flask that Rey began dumping key ingredients into. Stuff we'd found in Ms. Wassouf's supply closet.

"Hey, are you all right?"

Rey was looking at me intently. My hand wobbled, sending ingredients spilling out of the flask. Sucking in a deep breath, I said, "Sorry, let's just try again."

"You know you can tell me if something's wrong, right?" Rey said.

"Yeah, it's nothing," I said, "just that this brew isn't coming along, and there's Yakoub searching to pound me into a burrito back at the dining hall, and the necromancers . . ."

I sighed and Rey placed a hand on my shoulder. "Look, I get it. You have a lot going on."

"You have no idea."

"But I do," Rey insisted. "So, you have these necromancer baddies that want you gone. Well, I have lots of family back in Egypt who, well, I'm pretty sure they wouldn't mind if I poofed out of existence either. I–I'm different than the normal kids in my neighborhood, and I'm not talking about the beanies."

"Like, how the Persian Punisher eats bugs to scare the fans?"

Rey snorted. "No, it's a different kind of different. Let's just say it's about who I want to be around as, like, *more* than friends. The types of people I find cute. But my point isn't about that. It's about how I still trust myself, even when lots of family don't like that I'm a certain way. I know that I'm right because I'm being true to who I am."

I swallowed as the weight of Rey's message sank in. I could imagine just how he felt because I had a whole stepfamily who hated my butt. I'd never known about my roommate's struggles, but he was right.

The only way to handle Yakoub, save Hayati, and stop the necromancers was to believe in myself. To listen to the voice in my head—Teta's voice telling me to trust my friends. After all, my biggest fear was not having any, but here I was with three of the best buds anyone could ask for . . . even if one of them was snoring as loud as a monster truck and one of them wouldn't admit we were friends in the first place.

Donny's head shot up like a surprised kitty cat. "Hey, do any of you hear something?"

Rey said, "Yeah, the sound of you ruining another mixture."

"How could you even hear something if . . . *and* he's asleep again."

"*Shhh*," said Sarah, ear to the door. "Donny was right. Someone's coming."

She vanished out of the door and came back a few seconds later, her face going from pale to red, and then even redder. She closed the door. Locked it too.

"*She's* coming," she said in a loud whisper. "The head dean is on her way!"

Panic bubbled up in my chest and I realized this would be our last shot to get the mixture right. Besides, we used up nearly all the ginger extract, which was the Awakening Dust's key ingredient. There was only enough for one more try. Otherwise, we were out of luck.

Sarah nervously danced in place like she had to pee. Yet since Donny slept in a puddle of drool, I had to trust that Rey would get this right. Placing the vial of ginger extract in my roommate's hand, I carefully grabbed two more pinches of the sugar, another important ingredient I hoped I'd gotten right as it fell into the flask. Unlike the Green Eyes Mist, the very first alchemy I'd shown to my friends, I couldn't risk not using the exact right measurements here. Kahem's voice echoed in my ears, a reminder not to be careless.

I pointed toward the hallway. "The dust won't settle in time. I'll handle this while you and Sarah distract Dean Abdullah."

"Are you short on brain cells?" whispered Sarah from the doorway. "She's the head dean. We'll all get detentions for not being at the dining hall!"

She was right. Not to mention, Dean Abdullah could be one of the necromancers. She'd lied about the cake, after all.

The risk of being caught tinkering with Academy property was even worse than not being at dinner. A few detentions wouldn't matter if we got expelled, and that was the punishment we faced if the head dean of the school caught us.

"Rey," I said, handing him the vial, "I'm going out, so I'll need you to take over. Just one pinch, any more will spoil the mixture."

"A-are you sure?"

I nodded. "You're an alchemist, but even more importantly, you're a true friend. Thanks for helping me believe in myself again."

My roommate raised his hand to a salute. "Aye, aye, Captain."

It felt like a relief to put complete faith in my roommate. Like, finally, I didn't have to do everything alone.

"Wait here for me," I told Sarah.

But before I could leave, she grabbed my arm. "Can't let you have all the fun," she said. "I'm coming too."

Hearing that felt better than eating a double fudge chocolate cake all by myself. Together, we both slipped out into the hallways and hurried toward Dean Abdullah.

Chapter 31

Distracting a teacher was easy. Asking a question about homework, the next quiz, or even asking for directions to the bathroom was fair game as a first-year.

A dean was much harder to distract. Dean Saba maybe less so, since all I needed was to start humming my favorite Beyoncé song, or a Fayrouz classic. He'd break out into dance and wouldn't know how to stop. But Dean Abdullah might as well have been a brick wall; there was no getting past her.

I stopped Sarah right before we turned the hallway and asked, "What's our plan?"

She shrugged. "Who says we need a plan? Come on."

Grabbing my hand, Sarah jerked me forward, but we both skidded to an abrupt stop while turning the corner of the hallway. The head dean stood right in our faces. If Sarah had taken even one more step, we would've plowed through the wrinkly old lady.

"Oh my," she said in Arabic. One hand was on her chest, and if she was breathing, I couldn't hear it.

All three of us looked down, Sarah's left hand holding my right. Or was it my right hand holding her left? I couldn't even tell because of how shocked I was. Sarah must have had the same thought because we both pulled away.

"I remember my first crush," she said with a shake of her head.

"Crush!" we both repeated.

From back the way we'd come, someone made a rooster sound and I recognized Rey's nasally voice. Although confused by what the head dean had said, I was more concerned with the Awakening Dust. Hopefully our distraction worked.

"Who's there?" asked Dean Abdullah, looking over our shoulder.

I moved to block her way. "That's probably just a rooster!" I said as loud as I could for Rey to hear. "And if it really was a human and *not* a rooster, which it's totally not, then the human would know to go wait in their rooms!"

"Yes," shouted Sarah. "They should definitely go wait in their rooms if they are humans, which they are not!"

Dean Abdullah looked properly freaked. I took it to mean that she just thought we were full-on bananas, and not up to anything suspicious. But to make sure she kept thinking the same, we needed to keep up with the act.

"Come on," I said, this time being the one to grab Sarah's hand. "Let's go back to the dining hall. We can't keep doing homework forever, right?"

Dean Abdullah didn't look like she was buying it. She knotted her brows, probably about to sign our expulsion papers. We were so done. I should've known the plan would backfire. Disguise Mist and a food fight? It was messed up from the start. My self-doubt began to spiral out of control when something thudded against one of the courtyard pillars.

Sarah and I spun as an older student darted into the hallway. He bent over a robotic dragonfly. Two other students skidded to a stop after him.

"We put too much thrust in the wings this time, didn't we?" asked a girl who, twisting, froze upon seeing us. She tapped the shoulders of her classmates.

The boy controlling the dragonfly gasped. "Oh . . . we're as busted as a banadoora."

"That you are, my dear Aziz," said the head dean. "Experimenting with school property outside of class is strictly forbidden, and a high-level violation. You three are coming to my office. Now."

She gave Sarah and me both a *you better get going* stare, and we did. I couldn't have sprinted faster, and Sarah ran with twice the speed as we hightailed it back down the hallway. From behind, Dean Abdullah was dealing with Aziz and his classmates.

Once we were far enough away, Sarah stopped. I caught up to her, bending over my knees. We both needed a moment to recover our breaths.

She wiped the sweat off her forehead. "That was out of this world."

"Tell me about it," I said. "I can't believe the head dean of the Academy thought I'd be dating *you*."

I started to laugh, but Sarah didn't join me. She shook her head, arms crossed, and said, "Whatever. Let's get this over with already."

Sarah didn't look my way or say anything else as we hurried through the halls right before the last bell. I'd have felt guilty if I weren't shocked. After all, I'd just done the impossible, and I didn't mean the food fight or getting away from the head dean.

I'd hurt Sarah Decker's feelings.

"She looks so little when she sleeps," said Sarah, the both of us approaching Rey and Donny in the nurse's office. "Kind of like . . . a little brainiac baby, you know?"

"Focus on watching the doors," I told her, turning to Rey and saying, "Looks like you two actually mixed this right."

I held a flask covered at the top with tinfoil. Through

the clear glass, an orange mixture had settled and dried, forming the tiniest specks of dust.

Awakening Dust.

It was weird to hold an alchemy creation that wasn't mine or Kahem's. It almost didn't feel right. None of my friends had to practice all those hours in a dingy warehouse with the rudest ever teacher. None of them stayed up after cooking their Teta dinner just to memorize the names of mists and charms.

I did. I had to do all those things back in Portland.

"Dude, how much longer do you need?"

Rey was standing beside a still-snoring Donny, staring at me as I remembered that without him, we wouldn't even have the Awakening Dust. Now I hurried toward Hayati. Her eyes were closed, her hands cupped over her stomach. And, despite her size, her snores sounded like there was a jinni living inside her.

Nobody said a word as I removed the plastic covering and let some of the dust spill into my palm, explaining, "Only alchemy can overcome alchemy."

I leaned in next to Hayati, breathed in, and closed my eyes to add the final and most important ingredient—my wish. I pictured Hayati waking up, her eyes blinking open behind too-big glasses.

Holding on to that thought, I opened my eyes and blew the Awakening Dust right into her face. We all watched the dust settle and dissolve.

And we kept watching. A minute passed, then two. . . .

"Doesn't look like your little experiment worked," said Sarah.

"Maybe this alchemy stuff is a load of nonsense," Rey said. "We should—"

Achoo!

Hayati sneezed, leaning up in bed and looking around at all of us liked we'd just snuck into her room in the middle of the night. "Ugh . . . where am I?"

Donny lifted his head. "Heck if I know, sis. Want to switch places? That bed looks comfy. . . ."

"Holy cannoli," I said, and then louder, "Holy cannoli, I did it! *We* did it!" I rubbed my hands together, excited to get out of here before the nurse came back. "We don't really have time to explain, but you were in a coma, and now you're not. But if any of us are caught sneaking in here, we'll all be in detention until we graduate."

Hayati's eyes widened. "Well, don't just stand there," she said, pointing at us. "Help me out of this bed."

It was time to make like Vanishing Dust and . . . well, vanish.

Ding!

The bell sounded, and while Rey and I helped Hayati out of the bed, I said, "If only there was a charm that could block out that annoying ring, am I right?"

"A charm?" asked Rey, oddly confused for someone who'd just performed alchemy. "Not sure what you're talking about, dude."

I stomped in frustration. "Don't tell me you already forgot. Just before the bell we were ... *OH!*"

The key to all my friends' forgetting sat right under my nose the whole time. Well, technically, it was *over* my nose since it sat just beneath the clock tower. I meant the bell, of course. That thing went off *all the time*. What if that was the Forgetting Charm?

Before I could tell the others about my theory, Sarah pulled me out the door. We waved our friends over once we made sure the way was clear, all of us joining the shuffle of students heading back to our rooms from the dining hall. Food and sauces were splattered all over their clothes.

Behind us, Herman complained to a friend about what Jad had said. I smirked, patting my own back. That rich fig would never suspect Illusion Alchemy.

We all headed to our bedrooms. While Rey went to use the bathroom and other students took their showers to clean up from the food fight, I hurried into my room and shut the door behind me.

Flopping onto my bed, I reached under it to grab some ingredients, not expecting to find an orange ball of fur on the floor. A trail of similarly orange hairs that led all the way to—

"Meow."

"Holy cannoli!" I whispered, nearly tumbling onto the floor.

With my heart racing a hundred miles a second, I bit my lip to keep from screaming as I twisted to where two large white eyes peered straight at me.

Yolla sat on my pillow—alone.

Chapter 32

I checked under the beds, in each corner, and even opened the drawers looking for Kahem, in case my alchemy teacher knew some advanced recipe for shrinking himself.

A wave of relief had come from Yolla's presence. Kahem had finally arrived! I could tell him all about the necromancers and the coming solstice and how Salazar discovered I had *The Alchemist's Hand.* Yet something felt very wrong. Yolla was never far from my alchemy teacher's side.

As I reached, she darted away the second my fingers brushed her fur. I stretched out a hand to pick her up, but she leapt off my bed and onto Rey's.

The chase across my tight bedroom saw me stumbling on textbooks, reaching under beds, and grabbing for Yolla across every corner while the cat knocked over everything atop our shelves. Finally, I cornered her in my end of the room, coming closer and closer until . . .

"*Meow,*" she said in a low whine, a shiver running across her fur.

I hadn't ever seen Yolla scared, not like this. Sitting in front of her, I asked, "Did you come here all by yourself? Where's Kahem?"

Yolla cowered, her tiny paws covering her eyes. Carefully, I leaned in and brought her into my arms, my eyes widening at the sight of something bright blue and wrapped around the cat's neck.

"Kahem never gave you a collar. . . ."

Reaching for the strange band, my eyes widened at the sight of something attached to it—a paper note.

I unfolded the small piece of paper and began to read. . . .

> Shad, if you are reading this note, I have either suffered a terrible baking accident or our enemies have found me. I am sorry we never completed your training, my boy. Now the responsibility falls on you to prevent the necromancers from achieving their goals. The only help I can lend is this message: take this note and visit the gym storage room closet at midnight. Other than that, please care for Yolla and remember to be strong. I believe in you.

By the time I finished the note, tears were streaming down my face while my fingers trembled. I could hear my heart thumping. Yolla must have too because she glanced up, pawing at my chin.

If this was true, the necromancers had gotten to my alchemy teacher. I had to stop them alone.

The sense of being in over my head, that this situation was hopeless, had me hugging my legs while crying into my knees. With the best alchemist in the whole world unable to stand up to the necromancers, how could I? Sure, I'd turned Salazar's face purple with his own mist, but his buddies were ready to make me give up the final ingredient to the Revival Elixir. Who knew how long the Detecting Charms I'd set up along our bedroom doorway could stop them?

"Shad, are you crying?"

Rey trudged through the door, setting down his toothbrush and coming to sit on his bed.

"It's just seasonal allergies," I lied.

Sighing, Rey said, "The Academy has advanced air vents so no one can get seasonal allergies. Come on, dude, just tell me what's going on."

Meow.

Yolla's cry echoed from behind me, bright eyes peeking out in the darkness and startling my roommate.

Rey gasped, pointing to Kahem's pet. "Unless you're allergic to that cat, you've got some explaining to do."

"You wouldn't believe me if I told you," I said. "And even if you did, you'll forget in the morning!"

Ignoring me, Rey grabbed the palm-tree beanie on his nightstand and slid it over his head, squishing the messy curls underneath. I smiled at the familiar look.

"Do you want to know the truth of why I wear beanies?" he asked, coming to sit beside me. "Every single last one belonged to my older sister. She *loved* to wear different beanies and buy new ones from the street vendors in Cairo."

Yolla climbed onto Rey's lap and curled into his arms while I struggled to see what Rey's sister had to do with any of this. I asked, "So, why did you take her beanies?"

Rey smiled down at the cat, his fingers running through Yolla's thick orange fur. "I didn't take them. She left them to me when she died last year. She was only two years older than I am now."

Yolla and I both glanced up. "I . . . Rey, I'm so sorry."

He smiled. "It's okay. I hadn't told anyone since it happened, but I just wanted you to know that I recognize those tears. Not long ago, I cried just the same. But friends like you helped me move on, Shad, and maybe I can be that friend for you."

We didn't say anything for a few moments until I looked into Yolla's wide eyes and remembered Kahem's scowl. A giant lump formed in my throat, for both my alchemy teacher *and* Rey. But it was like Teta sat on my other side, encouraging me to open up.

Wiping my eyes, I asked, "What should I do?"

Rey placed an arm around my shoulders and squeezed. "Whoever you lost, I bet they'd want you to keep going, at least for them."

Lifting the note and studying my alchemy teacher's final message carefully, I didn't need anyone to tell me what Kahem wanted. He had made it clear I had to keep fighting. To overcome the necromancers and stop them from reviving their leader.

Tightening my resolve, I bent down under the bed to pick up *The Alchemist's Hand* along with some Darkening Dust and other premade mixtures, shoving them into my pocket. "This may sound odd," I said, "but are you up for a late-night adventure?"

Yolla crept through the halls, undeterred by the whooshing sounds of the windy nighttime desert or the creaks of old, forgotten bookshelves.

My heart was thudding. How couldn't it when, at every turn, we might run into a shadowy necromancer, a bully like Yakoub, or those red-eyed robo-roosters. The more I considered the dangers, the less confident I felt about bringing Rey.

We crept by the main courtyard now. A projector said it was ten minutes to midnight, so we had little time left.

Luckily, Baba's charm hadn't tingled yet. No necromancers were nearby and, with the bell not set to ring for hours, I wouldn't have to worry about Rey forgetting all that I'd whispered to him about alchemy so far.

"It looks like the coast is clear," said my roommate, pointing across the final hall between us and the gymnasium. "I'm crossing!"

As my friend hurried across, I considered how lucky I was that he'd come. That my roommate trusted me with the story behind his beanies . . . it meant more than all the Arabic sweets in the world.

Yolla charged forward alongside Rey. I followed close behind, passing through the final hallway across our school. The gym door lay open, and we tiptoed through. I cast one last glance over my shoulder at the main courtyard, and then we—

"Ah!"

Rey yelped at the same moment Yolla shrieked. I reached into my pocket for one of the premade alchemy mixtures. In front of us, a shadow slumped to the ground.

Moving closer, I stepped forward to stand between whatever that was and Rey. My roommate's scream continued echoing across the gym as I drew closer.

The shadow stirred and we all leapt back. Until we heard it say, "Sleepy time is the *best* time."

Shoving a Stiffening Charm back into my pocket, I

sighed. "Donny, what in the figs are you doing here?"

Rey shone a flashlight straight into Donny's face, the boy leaning up and wiping at his eyes. My classmate must have sleepwalked through the school. We'd seen it happen whenever he took naps during our meals, but why come to the school gym?

Suddenly, the beads along my necklace tingled. "Necromancers are nearby," I whispered. "We have to hurry!"

Picking Donny up off the gym floor, we scurried across the large space together. Rey's flashlight helped shine our way to the closet near the very end of the hall. What could be behind the doorway? Had Kahem left some secret alchemical weapon? Or maybe it was the baklava I always expected him to bring when he arrived?

Whatever it could be, our hopes were dashed at the sight of a glimmering metal lock on the double doors. I reached into my pockets, through decanters and Darkening Dusts, but had nothing for *that*. Meanwhile, the tingle from Baba's charm grew more urgent.

"Don't worry, I've got this!"

Unexpectedly, Donny staggered forward and began fiddling with the lock, rotating the dials back and forth through numbers. Rey and I glanced at each other. Did Donny think this was some kind of joke? I stepped forward to stop him until a *click* froze me.

Our sleepy friend pulled free the metal lock and held it up triumphantly. "Can I go back to napping now?"

"Dude, how did you know the combination?" asked Rey.

Donny paused, scratching his head. "Not sure. I might have noticed someone open it once or something."

Whatever the reason, I pressed forward and opened the door, a hand in my pocket just in case there was a necromancer in need of a stink bomb on the other side. Only, what we found wasn't anything special–a few brooms, trash bins, and a crate full of old sports balls that were replaced by the virtual ones we use now.

"Remind me why we came here?" asked Rey.

Meow.

Just then, Yolla leapt onto the crate of balls. Like they were the mice she'd chase through Kahem's old warehouse, she began pawing at them, eyes darting back and forth between us.

Kahem had taught her to sniff out alchemy, and the cat was quite good at it because a stream of light poked down through a perfect circle in the ceiling. We must be standing in an old chimney, or perhaps what had once been one of the burning spires.

I ran up to the crate and began pushing. "Come and help me out here."

Soon, all three of us stood with our backs against the crate, pushing with all our might. Around my neck, Baba's charm tingled more and more, but I ignored it while the container gave way to our combined efforts. Yolla leapt off and circled to stand in front of us once we'd moved it a few feet away.

Rey shone his flashlight down, where right under Yolla's feet lay the handle for a hidden doorway.

Chapter 33

Rey climbed down the stairs first. His flashlight brightened the descent while I fought spiderwebs, creaky steps, and a fear of heights I'd never told my friends about. One that had forced Teta to hold me all throughout the flight from Lebanon years ago.

While the two of us approached a room beneath the gym floor, Donny remained above in the closet, falling asleep the second we uncovered this hidden passage. I still couldn't figure out how he'd known the lock combination. Clearly, I didn't give my friends enough credit. Each one had helped me survive the necromancers in one way or another. I just hoped they hadn't made themselves targets in the process.

As we climbed down the last step, I vowed not to let that happen.

My shoe sank into the floor. By the sound of Rey's gasp, his did the same, and he dropped the flashlight.

Yolla's eyes were the only thing I could see in the almost-complete darkness. I reached to pick her up from the staircase when a strange tremble took hold of my body. One that reminded me of the night I accepted the invitation from Sarah.

"R-Rey, th-the l-light!" I gasped.

He managed. "C-can't f-find it!"

With no choice but to keep moving forward, I headed deeper into wherever we were. My sneakers kept sinking into the floor like it was muddy. Like the ground wanted to swallow us. I kept one hand out to avoid running into a wall, the other clutching *The Alchemist's Hand* safely in my pocket.

No sooner had I gotten deeper into this mysterious tunnel than the trembling subsided. Only, a tingle from Baba's charm soon replaced it. Could there be necromancers down here too?

"Rey, are you still with me?"

"Yeah, I'm right be–"

"Oomph!"

Rey ran into me as I stopped. Yolla slipped out of my arms, the both of us falling, my back sinking into the dirt as my friend lay on top of me. As I struggled to my feet, I didn't know where to begin cleaning off the gunk from my shirt and pants. Running my fingers through my hair, some of the stuff was there too. Definitely dirt. Only, it didn't smell like that, but like . . . roses.

If only we could see. Darkness enshrouded this basement, and I couldn't spot Rey, but heard him dusting off his clothes beside me.

Meow.

Something thumped on my foot. Bending, I brushed Yolla's furry side. She'd dropped something and I picked it up, accidentally clicking a switch that illuminated the path ahead.

"You found Rey's flashlight!"

Hoping this wasn't a cemetery, or even the location of the necromancer Dr. Salazar had been searching for, I picked up the device, and my jaw dropped at what lay ahead.

Roses, lavender, palm trees, and much more greenery I didn't even recognize. A lush, multicolored assortment of plants sprang to life before us. I pointed the flashlight across a vast enclosure that looked to be a garden, a forest, and a jungle all combined into one.

Rey placed a hand on my shoulder and asked, "Shad, did you ever wake me up or am I still dreaming?"

I shook my head. "Honestly, we might both be in a dream."

Yolla pawed at a bush of strawberries and one of my sneakers crushed a small bed of dandelions. Could this be why lots of neat flowers grew in the courtyards above? Vines ran up and down the walls, all the bushes appearing overgrown, untended the way Kahem's lush alley garden had once been. I doubted anyone had been in here recently.

My roommate hurried ahead. "Look, there's a table off to the side!"

I followed Rey, the both of us circling large trees and jumping over patches of flowers. We arrived at an old table covered in random junk. The chair underneath had been overtaken by vines and, as I hovered the light over the scene, a familiar assortment of vials, pouches, matches, and more was laid out before us.

Something caught my eye from the chair. Well, more like *in* the chair since moss had risen to cover most of it. But I dug away until a book was revealed underneath a mess of dust and roots.

"What's that?" asked Rey.

I blew some of the dust off and flipped the book open to find nothing but empty pages. "Not sure," I said. "Doesn't look like . . . wait a second."

Nearing the end of the book, I caught sight of words. A few paragraphs at first, then pages and pages of them. All written in Arabic and using pen ink. It struck me why there hadn't been any writing near the front–Arabic was written from right to left, whereas English went in the opposite direction.

Setting it down, I began to read quietly. . . .

*As one of the few at the Academy of
Alexandria still teaching our ancient
tradition of alchemy, I am afraid my days
here are limited.*

*The original deans are gone, replaced
with those who are clueless or necromancers
themselves. I suspect the same is occurring
with this school's teachers and yet my allies
are helpless to stop it.*

*I shake at the thought we were unaware
of the darkness forming within these walls.
It is too late to fight back. Soon no one will
stand in the way of those who would steal
the school's countless secrets. I have deduced
their order is after the ingredients to a recipe.
For it, they will scour the endless volumes
preserved over the centuries. No longer will
our school be a beacon of light, but a home
for shadows.*

My fingers were shaking by the time I finished reading. I checked the bottom of the page for some sort of
name, but found only the initials *M. S.*

If the necromancers had been here *that* long, what kind
of damage had they already done? Especially between
the workstation I'd destroyed in the dining hall kitchen

and all the apprentices they were training right under everyone's noses. Plus, there was definitely some kind of Forgetting Alchemy with the bell, messing with everyone's memories.

Still, even if the person who wrote the note gave up, I didn't believe the necromancers had won. Not after I thwarted Salazar in the Great Library and kept *The Alchemist's Hand* safe. If all hope was lost, none of that could've happened.

A tap on my back jolted me and I turned to shine the flashlight right into Rey's face. He threw up his arms, covering his eyes and batting away my hand.

"Dude, easy with my light," he said. "Did you find what you were looking for?"

That question was a tough one to answer since we could spend hours searching this huge garden and still miss something. If I were to guess, the journal had to be the prize. Besides the message, there must have been some hidden knowledge here, some secret that Kahem would know to decipher.

And the garden itself couldn't be overlooked. A hidden store of alchemy ingredients right here at the Academy. I could only imagine the mixtures that we could make....

"Wait, that was it!" I muttered, an idea sparking in my mind. One so brilliant that I bet it would put Hayati to shame. Pocketing the old journal opposite *The Alchemist's*

Hand, and handing Rey the flashlight, I continued, "Did I find what I was looking for? Yeah, I'm pretty sure we found that and more. But it's getting late, so lead the way."

Not wanting to worry him, I didn't mention that Baba's charm told me we could get unwanted visitors at any moment. Nor did I bring up my idea to come back tomorrow, when I'd locate the ancestral roots for each of my friends and craft them charms just like the one around my neck. The type of alchemy that could resist the necromancers.

Together, we retraced our steps through the garden, across a short but narrowing tunnel we must have wandered through when it was still dark. The snores I heard while climbing told me Donny hadn't left yet as we approached the steps.

Meow.

"Huh?" he said, jerking as Yolla stirred him awake. "Am I in trouble?"

"You will be if you don't move your butt," said Rey, adjusting his beanie.

Moonlight no longer peeked through the opening up above, another sign we'd overstayed our welcome.

Rey and Donny wouldn't remember tonight. As soon as the bell rang tomorrow after breakfast, they'd wake up and believe all this was a dream.

Next time I brought my friends back here, they'd be

wearing decanters. And one day, every student would experience the Alexandria Academy as the home for alchemy. That was, *if* we could stop the necromancers' meddling, ending that evil plan to resurrect their leader.

After all, they were quickly running out of time. . . .

Chapter 34

"**I** **can hardly believe the** science fair is next week," said Hayati.

She ducked beneath a simulation dodgeball as if she hadn't been bedridden just days ago. We were two weeks into December, and in the time that she'd been back, we'd been able to gather all the materials for us to finish building our heater for the upcoming fair.

"But something in my calculations might be off, I–"

Another dodgeball flew by. It made a fizzing noise as it hit the gym wall and vanished. A new one spawned at the gym's half-court line.

Watching for any more incoming dodgeballs, Hayati said, "Our heater should work, but it's been giving us some trouble when it comes to starting."

"Well, I might have an idea," I announced.

Rey pointed at all the strands of Yolla's orange hair along my shirt. "Does it have anything to do with cleaning cat hair? Where did that even come from?"

"Oh, this?" I said, fumbling for an answer. "It's nothing, the wind must have blown it in from Alexandria Town."

Rey had already forgotten about the wondrous underground garden. Even with all that we'd done, all that time spent together, the bell still charmed away his memory. It hurt almost as much as the bad news about Kahem. I suddenly felt sick but doubted Ms. Najoom would let me go to the bathroom now that class was almost through.

I needed to keep it together. If not for me, then for my friends. For Yolla. After cleaning my room and hiding that cat in a fort built from textbooks and bedsheets, I'd decided not to remind Rey about the garden. Not until I went back down to find everyone's ancestral roots. Soon, they'd finally be free of the bell's effect.

Donny sleepwalked over from down the court and asked, "Did I hear you say *cat*? Moussa has a pet monkey."

Normally, we wouldn't all be in the same gym class. But a stack of books had fallen on Moussa in the library, so Ms. Najoom volunteered to teach both gym *and* history while he recovered in the nurse's office. And, although she was much kinder than Moussa, she was pretty bad at it. I didn't know much about World War I, but I didn't think it involved the Egyptian Empire.

"Are we still on to work on the project in the Great Library tonight?" asked Rey, ducking a simulation dodgeball as his unicorn beanie bobbed up and down.

"Definitely," I said. "Meet you all after cla–"

"Hey, they aren't even playing!" cut in Herman, who'd been in a bad mood ever since he'd gotten a week of detention for starting the food fight.

Ms. Najoom whistled at us to get back in the game. I rolled my eyes while both Hayati and Rey rushed to grab their dodgeballs. Sarah, meanwhile, hurried to hit as many classmates as she could. She appeared more than a little excited, especially with several of her former bullies on the other team.

Just then, the class bell dinged. Everyone bolted toward the locker rooms.

"Mr. Hadid, a word?"

Ms. Najoom held her arm up, waving me over. I had to shove my way back through everyone, covering myself in other people's sweat. By the time I reached my gym teacher near the center of the court, my classmates had disappeared into the locker room, leaving us all alone.

"All right, before you say anything," I started, "I know my participation hasn't been the greatest. It's just, my leg is all cramped up, and—"

She cut me off with a whistle. "Enough with the excuses," she said, her voice sounding different now, no longer soft-spoken. "There's something I want to show you."

Ms. Najoom reached into her pocket and drew out two things that weren't hers. The two items I most treasured—Baba's charmed necklace and *The Alchemist's Hand*.

"Those are mine!"

My gym teacher shouldered me back before I could snatch either, but my fingers brushed one of the cedarwood beads. Just the quick touch sent an undeniable tingling from head to toe. Swallowing, I saw nothing other than an empty court. Wait... was Ms. Najoom, one of the most loved teachers at the Academy, one of them?

"I took these from your gym locker," she said, pocketing *The Alchemist's Hand* while raising the necklace. "All this time, I'd been asking you to take this off. Not until recently did we realize it was a charm, and a powerful one at that. Now you will hide nothing else from us. We may not be able to read your little guidebook, but you *will* give me the final ingredient to the Revival Elixir."

Ms. Najoom snatched my arm in her strong grip. She pulled out a cuff from her back pocket and wrapped it around my wrist. The techy bracelet was *beep-boop*ing and, no matter how hard I tried, I couldn't get it off.

"What did you put on me?" I asked.

Ms. Najoom stepped closer, blocking the light so all I could see was her brown hair and muscular shoulders. "This is so that we may track your every step from now until the science fair. And *this* is so that nothing can protect you!"

My gym teacher dropped the necklace and it clanked against the gym floor. I bent over to pick up Baba's charm, but Ms. Najoom stomped on it over and over until pieces began to fly out in all directions. The world stopped for a second as my heart broke with each of the smashed wooden beads. Quickly, I reached behind my back, grabbing one of the beads rolling by and shoving it into my pocket.

"Oh no," I said, pretending to be worried. "What will I do without my necklace?"

She laughed evilly. "Do you really think that I'd fall for that?"

I shrugged. "Did you?"

"No," she snapped, grabbing the bead right out of my pocket. "Years have led up to this. We planned for possible alchemist *heroes* like you. That bracelet also holds an Exhaustion Charm that will deplete your energy, putting you to sleep should you even think about alchemy. Meanwhile, our Forgetting Charm will ensure you remember none of this. That is, until we force you to give us the final ingredient during the science fair."

"Forgetting Charm?" I asked, my eyelids already drooping. "You mean the school bell. It's just as . . . as I suspected."

"Smart boy," said Ms. Najoom. "If it were up to me, we would have dispatched you by now, but I have been given orders not to hurt any students. No, that would bring unwanted attention this close to the solstice, and we took a big enough risk getting rid of that librarian for a day or two. . . ."

"You're the reason Moussa is in the nurse's office?" I asked.

She cackled. "Oh yes, our order wanted me to keep as much an eye on you as I could. There is no escape from my watch, Shad, and you will no longer be a thorn in our side without your precious necklace. We will restore your memory the day of the fair and you will provide that last ingredient to the Revival Alchemy."

"Go eat figs," I said. "I know what you're using that for, and I'd *never* help you!"

"Did you think we were giving you a choice?" she asked, turning to walk over to the bleachers. She picked up a large navy-blue cloth. "Give us the final ingredient and we will spare the life of your friends and Kahem. If not, well . . . their fate lies in your hands."

The cloth unfolded into Kahem's alchemy coat. Large and filled with pockets, exactly how I remembered it from all our time spent together, the sight made my stomach churn like a bad case of food poisoning. Still, a glimmer of hope came through the darkness at hearing her threat.

"Kahem is alive?"

Ms. Najoom chuckled. "Oh yes, and so is the cat we snatched from your room while you were in my class. We took her *and* that little journal you'd hidden beneath the bed. The students we assigned the job weren't happy. A Vomit Charm by the door sent a couple of your classmates to the nurse's office, but apprentices are dispensable."

I gritted my teeth, realizing how little she cared about her *own* students, let alone my friends, Kahem, or the school. "Okay, I'll do whatever you ask so long as you don't hurt anyone else."

"Excellent," she said, backing away. "Be ready just before the science fair kicks off. That is when I will be wanting that final ingredient. And remember . . . no one will save you here at the Academy, and you can't leave. You're trapped here like all the other students."

With an evil grin, Ms. Najoom threw down a powder and vanished in a burst of black smoke.

Instead of heading to history, I hurried toward my room. At each hallway, I stopped to check if there was another alchemist in disguise, or Yakoub, or even another robot-animal guard. When I got to the stairs, I felt more and more tired with each step I climbed.

"Ms. Najoom thinks she's so smart," I said, barely able to keep my eyes open. "She never even noticed my other bead."

Ms. Najoom had grabbed the bead from my pocket, but she hadn't caught the other one that I'd hidden between my fingers. Now I kept it in the one place more secure than my pockets—my sock. All grossness aside, this little bead was the last bit of alchemy that kept the brace-let from putting me to sleep.

In my room, Yolla's orange hairs were all over my bed,

but the cat was indeed gone. Taken. I got to work tinkering with the tracking bracelet on my wrist. It must have been weeks, months . . . well, it was just an hour or two, but it felt like forever as I heard the chime of the one class bell, then another.

They didn't just signal the end of each class that I'd skipped but also reminded me of the Forgetting Charm. It made me work even more to get the bracelet off. I tried everything: banging it on my bedpost, running it under water in the bathroom, and even biting into it (talk about a jawbreaker). Nothing worked.

I began searching under my bed, behind my pillow, and even through my drawers, finding the ingredients I'd stashed over the past few weeks. Oregano that Rey had gotten from a last-year who went into Alexandria Town. Crushed dandelion, roses, and lavender from the courtyards. Copper wire that Sarah snuck out of the chemistry lab, and, last of all, the salt I'd been taking from the dining hall since our first day of school. They were useless by themselves.

Together, they were alchemy.

Going through the recipes I'd memorized, I gathered the ingredients for a decanter that might work on this kind of charm. "Three pinches of salt, one cup of water, two pinches of flower and another two of turmeric . . ."

As I was repeating the last ingredient for the elixir, someone stomped into the room. Several someones.

Hayati and Sarah came to stand by the doorway, and neither of them looked happy. Hayati stepped in first and pushed her glasses up her little nose.

"We need to talk," she said with her arms crossed, and I realized that something had gone terribly wrong.

Chapter 35

You know that feeling when someone is saying something that you really *should* be paying attention to, but you're just too beat to care?

That was me, sitting on my bed, listening to Hayati while I just nodded and said *uh-huh* and *yeah, so true.* I saw her lips moving. Heck, I even heard her saying the words. But instead of paying attention, I leaned back in the bed. My eyelids were heavy. Dozing off would've been so easy. . . .

Of course, I didn't really want to sleep. Well, I did, but it was because of my bracelet. The way everything seemed to send Donny into a slumber, each thought of alchemy only made me more tired.

Sarah didn't know that, though. And as I tried to explain between breaths, she grabbed the water bottle from Rey's nightstand and began to unscrew the cap. I held up my hands to stop her. She pushed them away and, without giving me a chance to speak, splashed me with the water.

My moppy hair fell over my forehead in clumps. Water got in my eyes, went up my nose, in my mouth and, strangely, it worked.

I perked up on the bed as Hayati asked, "Did you hear a single thing I just said? I'm trying to explain how, thanks to you, Ms. Najoom gave us all detentions for the next three days. My first detentions ever!"

"Why would *you* get detentions?" I asked, fighting the sleep.

Sarah shrugged, stuffing her hands in the pockets of the wool jacket she wore. A jacket meant to protect against the sun instead of keeping warm. "Probably because we're in the same science fair group, but all Ms. Najoom would tell us was that it was your fault."

Just then, Rey stormed through our doorway. His curls danced from side to side with no beanie to restrict them, and he didn't look over at me or anyone else. Then I noticed the strips of rainbow cloth in his hands.

My gut clenched and I reached for his sleeve, but he snatched his hand away. Wiping his eyes, he fished a tie-dye beanie from his drawer.

"When you didn't show up to the library after classes," he said, "that stepbrother of yours and a bunch of first-year bullies ambushed me. He asked if I was your friend, and then he . . . he grabbed my beanie and shoved me onto the floor. He made me watch while he cut it up with scissors!"

Rey put on a new beanie and stormed out. My worst fears were coming true. I wiped away the wet hair from my forehead and felt my hands grabbing my sheets, squeezing. Somehow, some way, Yakoub would pay for that.

Hayati stormed out after Rey, leaving me feeling even guiltier. There was only a week left before the science fair. How could I stop the necromancers, save Kahem, *and* protect my friends from all the bullies?

The truth was that I had no choice but to give the necromancers the final ingredient. They would get to keep control of the Academy and, without anyone to stop them, they'd be free to brew their Revival Elixir. To recruit other students into their ranks. To hurt anyone who stood against them. I couldn't let them hurt my friends any further.

Strangely, Sarah still sat on the bed next to me. I tried to fake a smile but was too tired.

"Are you here to yell at me too?"

She shook her head. "I know you want to pass your classes just like everyone else. So, if you skipped class, there must have been a good reason."

"You actually believe that?" I asked. "No one else does."

"Sure," she said. "You aren't a bad person. Not like how I used to be."

I scratched the back of my head. "I don't think you're a bad person. You risked your butt to save Hayati, and you've helped with my homework. I'm glad you're in our science fair group."

Sarah nodded, her cheeks visibly red. She got up from the bed and began to pace back and forth. "So . . . Rey's beanie and our detentions, that can't be a coincidence, right?"

I sighed. "You have no idea."

She laughed at that. "Then what are we going to do about it?"

I breathed in deep because what I was about to say might not make sense, even to me. *Especially* to me.

"There's nothing we can do," I said. "Yakoub is using Rey to get to me. He's smarter, stronger. He can squeeze me into a ball and kick me into outer space. And the detentions . . . same story, but a whole different level of bully."

Sarah snorted. "The Shad I knew back at Portland Middle always stood up to his bullies."

"I don't know what Shad you're remembering," I said, lying back on the bed. "I was always scared stiff. I used to avoid an entire part of the school if I knew you were there."

"Fair point," she said. "The thing is, all the other kids at school were always changing so their friends would like them more. But you never changed. No matter what anyone said, you kept on walking right up to that bakery after school. It always made me so angry because . . ."

Sarah quieted, and I sat back up. "Because what?"

"Because I wanted to be more like you," she admitted. "Not caring what anyone thinks about loving desserts and Arabic food and popularity. There, I said it."

I almost fell off my bed in shock. Had I just heard Sarah Decker say she wanted to be more like *me*?

"When the kids at my dining hall table found out I had something to do with the food fight, they said I should go back to America, and that I wasn't welcome to sit with them anymore."

"I thought they stopped picking on you."

"Nope, some never really did," she admitted, "but I thought if I hung around them enough then, maybe, they'd start to like me more. I can't believe I was ever friends with those jerks."

"Well, if you think the bullies are bad now," I said, "wait until you hear this . . ."

Starting with the day I first met Kahem, I told her everything, all the way up to Kahem's kidnapping and Ms. Najoom's threat. The bracelet exhausted me. Luckily, the bead from Baba's charm helped to keep me up. That and the several times Sarah shoved me awake whenever I mentioned alchemy and dozed off. But once I'd finished, my former bully looked scared for the first time since I'd met her in the third grade. No snarky insults. No calling me a liar. She barely moved for a long while.

"They kidnapped your alchemy teacher and his pet?" she asked. "What are they going to do to them? What are they going to do to everyone at the school?"

I fought back tears. "Nothing good, but I don't think I'm strong enough to stop them. . . ."

"Shad Hadid, you will *not* give up!" Sarah shouted, startling me. "Sure, the students who bullied me need to get what they deserve, but we can't let necromancers bring back the dead. I don't want to have to deal with zombies!"

Trying my best to stay awake, I raised my hand and showed her my bracelet. "Well, if you want to do something about it, you can start by helping me get rid of *this.*"

Chapter 36

"*This isn't quite an alchemy* lab," I said, "but it will have to do."

The door to the bathroom was closed, locked shut so no one else could walk in on us. We'd assembled all the ingredients for the decanter. Turmeric, salt, water from the sink, and two pieces of bread Sarah had taken from the cafeteria. For the actual goo-making, we had a mug and a lighter she'd snuck into the Academy.

"How'd you manage to get this thing in?" I asked, picking up the small lighter carefully.

She snatched it away and flicked on a flame, holding it under the cup filled with water. "My mom and dad always liked going glamping," she said, stuffing it back into her jacket pocket. "They never took me with them, of course, but I taught myself all the survival basics growing up in hopes they one day might. For example, boiling water kills germs. That's why you should always have a lighter handy."

I took Sarah's advice and instructed her to toss in two pinches of turmeric, followed by the pita bread. I hoped enough flour would leech into the brew.

She hadn't wanted to be the one mixing the ingredients, but Baba's charm had its limits. Well, what was left of it, that was. . . .

"Nothing's happening," she said.

I closed my eyes trying to remember the recipe without my guidebook, and then said, "Try tossing in three pinches of salt."

She did, and the ingredients just sat there like a wet shawarma, which wasn't supposed to be wet in the first place. Sarah flashed me an impatient look, and I reached out and tried the one thing that only I could. The part Teta had trained me all my life to do.

Observing the current condition of the mixture, I carefully added another pinch of turmeric. Concentrating, fighting the fatigue of the necromancer charm, I then pictured the ingredients dissolving into a goo. The liquid began to soften. It melted into an orange glob, Sarah's jaw dropping.

"Just like baking," I said.

"Baking?" she asked. "No, this is chemistry, Shad."

As the mixture settled into its final, gooey form, I said, "Chemistry is boring and full of weird-sounding ingredients. Baking is an art."

"Alchemy is *literally* science," she argued, and suddenly

I had flashbacks to Kahem yelling at me. "Al-*chemy*," she said, emphasizing the last part. "Notice the similarity with *chem*-istry? It's obvious, isn't it?"

Oh crud. I'd never realized that before.

In another life, Sarah would've been Kahem's dream apprentice. Not only was she tougher, but *way* smarter. She helped me see things in a way I couldn't on my own. Maybe that was why Teta had wanted me to make friends.

The goo now settled. I lifted the mug and turned it over on top of my hand, covering the metal bracelet with orange slime. Sarah gagged. I felt a little churning in my stomach too. As the goo hardened over my bracelet, the bead from my necklace charm burned. I considered tossing the bead into the toilet, but then the pain eased up.

The goo made a shell around the bracelet, a clear orange crystal covering the metal all around. Although I still couldn't take the thing off, my fatigue had begun to clear, the alchemy crafted into the Exhaustion Charm fading away.

"The tracker looks like it still works," said Sarah. She sounded disappointed, the both of us noticing the lights still beeping red on my bracelet.

Whether the tracker worked or not didn't bother me. I chipped away at the hardened goo crystal, smiling. "It's actually a good thing that they can track me."

She frowned. "What do you mean?"

"Since they can still track me," I began, "they'll think that the Exhaustion Charm is doing its job. Now, no one will suspect I'm practicing alchemy as long as I don't get caught, and what's left of Baba's charm will protect me from the bell. It's like . . . like when the Persian Punisher thought he'd won the last WrestleFest main event, except the Sultan of Slam had only pretended to be knocked out. So when the Persian Punisher was celebrating, the Sultan of Slam hit him in the head with a rubber chicken and pinned him for real!"

Sarah frowned. "I don't watch pro wrestling, but why a rubber chicken?"

Bang, bang, bang!

"I really have to go," said someone from outside the bathroom. "Like, number two!"

With one hard slam against the sink, I broke the hardened goo into pieces and washed the evidence down the drain. Sarah undid the lock and told whoever was out there that it smelled like a stink bomb.

Turning back to me, she pointed to my wrist. "I don't really get what we just did, but now that it's over, I'm heading back to study for a—"

I lunged in and hugged her. She froze like I'd turned her into ice. And although she didn't hug back, her shoulders began to soften. Melting like I would whenever Teta hugged me before bedtime.

We'd worked together rather than pranking one another. Not only that, but she'd even apologized for her parents. Her friendship didn't just motivate me to save the Alexandria Academy for the classmates who were nice, but for the Hermans and Jads too. Sarah made me realize that I should try to see things from the perspectives of other people, even if they were jerks. After all, if she could change, so could anyone else.

Quickly, I reached into my pocket for the last bead from Baba's charm and without her noticing, I snuck it into her jacket pocket. If I couldn't stop the necromancers during the winter solstice, I wanted Sarah to be safe, even if it risked my being affected by the Forgetting Charm. The bead might offer her some extra protection against Shadow Alchemy.

After parting with my last piece of Baba's charm, I eased out of our hug. Sarah didn't say anything. She only stood in place with a face redder than strawberries.

Swallowing a lump in my throat, I asked, "So, um, are we actually friends *now*?"

Sarah's eyes met mine and she quickly glanced away. "I guess we are . . . yeah."

"You think the others might forgive me too?" I asked. "It seems like they never want to talk to me again."

Sarah bit her lip. "Well, we recently discovered Hayati's idea for the science fair project might not follow the guidelines. Her heater needed an ingredient the school didn't have. If you could come up with something using, you know, *alchemy*, it could really help get them on your side."

While she explained our science fair group's dilemma, I started to smile. There was a mixture that would solve the group's problem. One that I had waiting to be used right under my bed–Destruction Dust.

"This sounds like a problem alchemy can solve," I said once she'd finished explaining everything. "You know, you're a great friend."

Sarah nodded, but her smile dropped a little. "Yeah, just friends..."

I almost asked what she meant, but instead I thought back to Baba's charm. Well, what little was left of it. Hoping she wouldn't check her pockets for the bead, I added, "Make sure you wear this jacket the day of the science fair. It, uh, seems like good luck."

"Uh, okay?" she said. "Well, I got a book quiz tomorrow, so I'm heading to my room to study."

Sarah hurried out and left me alone, my mind teeming with ideas on how to make things right. There was a lot of work to be done to make sure my Destruction Dust would be a success with the science fair project. Even more work to figure out just how I could stop the necromancers. They may have thought they had me in a corner, that I'd give up as soon as they took my mentor.

But now I was free to do alchemy again, and they could bet their necromancer butts that Shad Hadid would *not* give up.

In fact, I was just getting started.

Chapter 37

Two minutes to midnight.

The time was projected over one of the classroom doors and I tightened the straps on the Sultan of Slam backpack, continuing down the halls.

Getting out of my bedroom proved hard enough. I caught a lucky break when the necromancer guarding our hallway had to use the bathroom. With the science fair and the winter solstice tomorrow, more of them were sure to be lurking. Preparing for the moment the burial site of their order's founder would be revealed.

I couldn't move *too* quickly with my remaining alchemy ingredients jingling in the backpack borrowed from Rey. Any noise could alert the many necromancers guarding the halls. But I couldn't move slowly either. Sarah showed me how to transfer the tracking chip from my bracelet into her smartwatch using a couple of tools she'd borrowed from a janitor's closet. The catch was that she couldn't sneak out of her room with the necromancers around, and her watch battery would die in an hour. So I had to get back and return the tracker chip to this bracelet before the necromancers figured out what we'd done. Of course, there was a chance they'd catch on to our tinkering sooner.

But even more pressing than the tracker was that the decanter I'd crafted earlier was dissolving in my pocket. It had protected me from the bell's Forgetting Charm all evening, but I needed a replacement and didn't have enough ingredients. If I couldn't craft a new one tonight, my memory would be fried before the science fair.

Nearing one of the smaller courtyards, I bent down and muttered a silent prayer that none of those figs might be around while I attempted one of the riskiest alchemies in a space like this.

"Please don't make me regret this," I said to the Ember Elixir that I drew out of my pocket.

Uncorking the vial, I glanced both ways before swinging my arm and dousing the grass. Flames sprang up. Real and hot and glowing, they spread through the courtyard. I didn't stick around for the show, but before I twisted to hurry toward the gym, I first sprinkled dust from a pouch along the edge of the courtyard. It was a decanter I hoped would stop the spread of fire from crossing into the halls and threatening the bookshelves.

With the distraction set, I turned and hurried away. Everything hinged on reaching the garden that Rey, Donny, and I discovered. The ingredients it housed would be the key to not only a newer, better decanter for me, but for my friends and other classmates. One that relied on their families' ancestral roots. I needed all my friends to resist the bell's effects. Maybe then we'd have a fighting chance.

"What's that smell?"

I dipped into a classroom as someone's footsteps swept past, heading toward the burning courtyard. My heartbeat raced while I crept out into the hallway and headed toward the gym entrance.

Shouts sprang out from behind. Not loud enough to be heard from the student bedrooms upstairs, but enough to alert nearby necromancers wandering the halls. Shadows that swept across the hallway ahead as I closed in on the gym.

"I still don't get why they let him stick around the Academy. . . ."

"Are you talking about that first-year we tried to recruit? Overheard Ms. Najoom saying he won't be alive much longer, much less a student."

"Oh geez. Good thing we joined up with this crew."

Voices stopped me right in my tracks. Just before rounding a hallway, I paused, listening to what sounded like two older students who hadn't gone to follow the others toward my fire. They stood just in front of the gym entrance. I gripped the backpack straps so tight that my knuckles turned white. That the necromancers were guarding the gym door meant they must've discovered the garden. How would I get in there now? I reached into my pocket, beginning to yank out an Odor Charm when a new voice stopped me. One from a classroom a few doors down from me.

"Are we clear for the ritual tomorrow?" asked a deep voice.

"We are," answered Ms. Najoom.

She and whoever she was speaking to were hurrying out of a room and, by the dim glow cast from the courtyard, I spotted both their shadows drawing closer. Again, I ducked into the classroom and waited until their footsteps grew distant.

"What is all the commotion about?" she asked the guards. They stammered, slow to respond, and she groaned. "Whatever, just be quiet and guard the door. If either of you leave, I'll send you both down into the garden next. It's rumored the ghosts of dead students haunt it."

As Ms. Najoom threatened her apprentices and my distraction drew everyone's attention away, I left the classroom and sneaked down the hall.

I wouldn't get into the garden tonight, and without another way to get the proper ingredients for decanters for me and my friends, my only choice was plan B. One that I'd hoped it wouldn't come to, mostly thanks to my fear of heights. But that fear couldn't compare to the thought of letting the necromancers get their way, so I hurried toward the bell tower at the other end of the school, trembling with each step.

It was time to get rid of that annoying Forgetting Charm.

Well, I'd arrived, but I sure as figs didn't want to be here.

Neither, apparently, did the necromancer stationed in front of the tower door. She kept muttering, telling herself to stay awake.

From this part of the Academy, we couldn't hear any of the shouts coming from my distraction in the courtyard; none of the panic of necromancers hoping to extinguish flames that only grew stronger with water. Slipping off my backpack, I didn't have the ingredients for a decanter, but I managed to find olive oil, salt, tahini, and ground-up chalk from Ms. Wassouf's science class—everything needed to make the necromancer's wishes come true.

I stirred all the ingredients and imagined the desired mixture, the resulting blue mist curling out of my palm. I whirled it around with my finger for a few moments before quietly, carefully, easing it toward the girl until it came right up under her nose and . . .

Thud!

She collapsed and I didn't waste a beat, hurrying up to the newly napping necromancer with my open backpack in hand. The deans typically closed off the bell tower during the school day. Nobody ever thought to come here anyways. Coming too close while it rang would rattle one's eardrums. But zipping up Rey's bag and throwing it over my shoulder, I took my chances, standing at the base of the tower and whimpering.

"Holy. Cannoli."

The Alexandria Academy had several towers, one at each corner of the school and a few in between. This tower stood the tallest, but also the thinnest. What made me want to curl up and cry wasn't just the height, but also that there was just one way to get up—by rope.

The first rope that hung down was meant to be for ringing the bell. A second rope came down next to it, the one I'd use. Too bad I'd never climbed anything more than a couple of flights of stairs. But the fate of alchemy rested on me getting my butt up to that bell before the necromancer could wake up.

Gripping the rope with shaky fingers, I pressed one foot up onto the flat wall, followed by the other. The rope didn't snap, so I began to climb.

"Brimstone, mercury, lead, sugar . . ."

Listing out ingredients helped take my mind off the height. Still, each inch I climbed was a battle, each tug of the rope as terrifying as though I were tugging on my very heartstrings. I didn't look back. I couldn't. After a minute of climbing, a fall from this height would—

Twisting my neck, I saw I'd only gotten a few feet off the ground.

Now I focused. Without glancing back, the ascent took less time than expected. I must have listed out every ingredient in *The Alchemist's Hand* by the time the bell hovered just above my head. Reaching out, my hand caught one of the tower windows, which helped maneuver me onto a small ledge.

There I stood, setting down my backpack full of alchemy ingredients, none of which could help me now. While I did have the beginnings of a Destruction Dust formed, an explosion right now would do more harm than good. Especially with the bright orange glow of my Ember Elixir coming from across the Academy.

The bell hung golden and shiny and bright, even as darkness touched every other part of the Alexandria Academy. I owed a thanks to the especially starry night for illuminating the charm stuck on the underside of the bell. All it took to disable the most powerful Forgetting Charm I'd ever seen, maybe one of the strongest to ever be crafted, was me squeezing my fingers around it and yanking the grayish glob right off.

As soon as I did, the bell began to shake. I quickly wrapped my arms around it, steadying the massive thing before it woke the entire school.

Sweat beaded on my forehead, droplets running down my cheeks. My arms and legs ached to the point I wasn't sure I could stand. And, to top it all off, a small army of necromancers who wanted me dead were spread out across the halls below.

But by all the fig trees in Lebanon, I'd done it.

Holding the Forgetting Charm in my hand, I stuffed it in my backpack and set my butt down on the tower ledge. If I didn't live through the science fair tomorrow, I could at least say I'd thrown a pretty big wrench into the necromancers' plans.

Now, letting my legs dangle off the giant tower, the wind nipping at my cheeks, I gazed out at the desert beyond the Alexandria Town walls. I didn't sweat the staggering drop.

"You worried about me since the day I was born," I said, staring right up at stars like they were Teta's eyes. "No more worrying. Tomorrow, I'm going to make you proud and keep our family tradition alive. Either that or I'll be joining you sooner than we expected."

Chapter 38

All around the main courtyard, first-years practiced their science fair presentations, running
last-minute tests. The deans and teachers gathered at the
center of the field, waiting to start handing out grades.
Ms. Najoom stood with the rest of them, quietly watching me.

Did she know that I had something to do with the fire
last night? None of my classmates mentioned it, which
must mean the necromancers found a way to cover up
the mess before daybreak. Either way, that whole evil crew
expected that I'd have forgotten I was even an alchemist
by now. That, come time for them to get their final ingredient, they could force me to read it out of *The Alchemist's
Hand* and complete their elixir.

I fought back my nerves as our science fair group hud-
dled in one of the courtyard's corners. It wasn't far from
the entrance to the gym just beyond the pillars, where the
doorway remained blocked off just like it had last night.

And, approaching my friends, I expected to find them practicing the presentation. Instead, Hayati and Sarah were arguing.

"But *your* idea might cause the heater core to explode," said Sarah, wearing the smartwatch that I'd slipped back under her bedroom door this morning. "Trust me, I should be the one to do the demonstration."

"In your dreams," said Hayati. "This project was *my* idea."

Sarah narrowed her eyes. "Remind me, how old are you?"

Hayati didn't shy away from the stare, answering, "Old enough to be smarter than you."

"Whoa," said Rey, adjusting an exploding-volcano beanie. "That was cold!"

I nearly asked if Sarah needed some ice for that burn but kept quiet since Hayati had yet to forgive me. Over the last week, neither the science whiz nor Rey had let me help on our project. They didn't even sit with me during lunch.

But in their place, Sarah spent more time with me. I'd gotten to tell her all about Kahem and my alchemy training, and even taught her some of the recipes.

This was my first time seeing our science fair project in its finished form. It looked like a chimney made of clay and stones, only wheeled on a cart since it must've weighed a ton. My fingers nervously dug holes in my pockets as I approached my friends.

"Nice . . . uh, heater you got there," I said.

Rey averted his gaze, the way my roommate ignored me stinging like a fresh paper cut. Meanwhile, my cheeks grew hot under Hayati's glare. I was ready to turn back, but one look at Sarah reminded me that if I could make a friend out of my bully, I could do it with anyone.

"Listen," I said, taking off my backpack. "These past few days have been really hard. If you still don't want to talk to me after the science fair, fine. But I just want you all to know that I've learned a lot since I came to the Academy. About being a good friend, and trusting others, and believing in the good in people.

"Hayati, you showed me that science and math can be fun whenever we worked together on homework. Rey, well, you're my best bud, no matter what color beanie you wear. I learned to be myself thanks to you. . . ."

Unexpectedly, Rey wrapped his arms around me, and I stiffened. Tears brimmed and I hugged him back. Out of the corner of my eye, Hayati still stood apart from us with her arms crossed. One step at a time, she came forward and then leapt onto Rey and me, bringing it in for a group hug that knocked us all onto the grass, laughing.

Sarah bent to lift me up. We helped Rey and Hayati to their feet, the four of us coming to face one another now that the hardest part of the day was through.

"I learned to stick up for myself thanks to you," said Hayati, glancing away nervously. "No amount of math equations could have taught me that."

"Same here," said Rey.

I would've wanted this moment to last much longer, but there was a whole group of figs that needed smushing, so I eased my backpack off. Setting it on the ground between us, I pulled out a sandwich bag full of stinky brown Destruction Dust. It turned out I hadn't needed the stuff to earn Rey's and Hayati's forgiveness, but that didn't mean we couldn't still use it.

"Okay, so I heard you were having trouble with getting the heater warm enough to start. . . ."

"That's just powder; how can it help with starting the heater?" asked Hayati.

"It's not just powder," I said, handing it to her. "It's alchemy. This dust contains a powerful mix of gold, ammonia, and oxide powder. Those last two ingredients, I got from the chemistry lab."

Rey leaned in closer and whispered, "Where did you get the gold?"

I grinned, but before I could answer, someone screamed my name. We all turned as Herman marched toward us. "I'm missing one of my chains," he said, getting right up in my face. "Someone told me they saw you snooping around my room."

I shrugged. "Don't know what you're talking–"

My back hit the ground before I could tell what was happening. Herman towered over me. Some of his friends formed a wall behind him, hiding us from the sight of any teachers. Yakoub must have taught them that move. A smart one since no one could save me from them now.

Like in so many of my bad dreams, my rich classmate raised his fist. "I hope you're hungry, Shad, because I got a knuckle sandwich I've been wanting to give you."

I tensed up, ready for a serious pounding when, out of nowhere, Sarah rushed in and headbutted Herman straight in the face. He fell like a tree, and I almost yelled *timber.*

Herman's friends all looked at each other, and then at Sarah. She gave them a *bring it on* look, and they didn't know what to do, so they just grabbed the boy and started dragging him back toward their project.

"That's right," said Rey. "Make like eggs and scramble!"

Just as they were leaving, one of the bullies gave Sarah the meanest stare I'd ever seen and said, "Go back home, you're not even one of us!"

Sarah stepped back. She was rubbing her forehead, which was sure to bruise, but it looked like the bully's words had hurt much more than that.

"You know what?" I shouted back. "A true Arab sticks

up for their friends, so she's more like us than any of you figs!"

"Yeah, you *fig-brain*," said Rey.

Even Hayati added, "Get out of here, you peanut-head!"

My friends joined in to defend Sarah, although they were getting my insults all mixed up. Rey helped me to my feet as I said, "Yeah, so that's where I got my gold."

At first, they all just stared at me, jaws nearly down to the ground. Then came the giggles. Sarah and Hayati, hands over each other's shoulders, broke out in laughter. Rey next, whose beanie nearly fell off as we re-huddled.

"I know we're all caught up with this science fair," said Sarah, "but there are really bad people who are going to try and not just ruin our project, but our school. Like, listen to this . . ."

Sarah explained the necromancers better than I ever could. How they were responsible for putting most of the school to sleep, how they got some of the bullies to work with them, how I was being blackmailed, and how everyone at the Alexandria Academy was in grave danger if we didn't stop them. We'd both agreed yesterday that it was better coming from her, since my friends had blamed me for their bad luck over the past few weeks.

But while Sarah talked, the deans were drawing closer. Time was running out, and we had to pull off a much riskier plan than the dining hall food fight. Luckily, we had the element of surprise.

"Come on," I said to my friends. "Let's blow the roof off this science fair and show the necromancers why they shouldn't mess with us. Are you all with me?"

Chapter 39

"*A floating table using magnets?* Eight out of ten!"

"A small turbine? Oh, and it makes enough electricity to power a fan. How refreshing. Eight out of ten!"

Dean Saba went around from project to project, carefully poking, testing, and playing with each team's creation before giving them a final score. The other deans followed behind. Dean Hayek scowled at every project as if she would give each one a zero, and Dean Abdullah kept a good distance from the others, staying a minute longer at each of the projects.

"Oh, a solar-powered . . . earthquake simulator?" asked Dean Saba, placing a hand on a mushy carpet with solar panels at the end.

Donny's eyes drooped less today as he stuck up a finger. "Actually, this is a solar-powered *massage bed*, the comfiest kind of bed. Sleep is the most important activity there is, after all."

The deans each took turns sitting on a bed that was barely large enough for a cat to sleep on. Then each one oohed and aahed as Donny thumbed different settings. My group looked impressed too.

"Eight out of ten!" declared Dean Saba, coming one project closer to ours.

Several of the past science fair winners had been invited to attend. Now, they strutted into the courtyard. One of them was Aziz, who'd won a couple of years ago with his remote-controlled dragonfly drone. It weaved around one group's robotic flytrap, which wasn't quick enough to catch Aziz's bot. I hadn't seen him since his crash saved Sarah and me from Dean Abdullah.

But next to Aziz stood the only other older student I recognized.

"Yakoub," I growled.

For now, my stepbrother wasn't anywhere near our project. If he did come, I hoped that Sarah was ready to knock him out like she'd done to Herman. Even if I'd faced necromancers, I still wasn't sure I had the courage to confront my stepbrother.

"Oh, and what is this?" Dean Saba did a ballerina hop from the last project to ours, taking my attention off Yakoub. He leaned in close and poked the heater with his finger.

As Hayati and Rey explained our project, Sarah hoisted some Destruction Dust into an opening, replacing the chemical mix my group had prepared. It felt good to at least help with a small part of the science project. The deans watched Hayati hand Sarah the vial. Sarah tipped it, letting only a drop or two mix into the powder below.

Whoosh!

The deans all clapped when they felt the warmth of the chimney-like heater. Only Dean Hayek backed away, clearly too hot in her favorite red suit.

Dean Saba pointed to us all and said, "For such a warm heater, you all get an eight out of ten!"

The deans moved on to the next project and Sarah turned to us. "Is Dean Saba giving everyone the same score?" she said. "Something weird is going on."

Sure enough, right when Sarah mentioned that, Ms. Najoom began her approach. Her glare felt like it gave me third-degree burns.

Hayati tried pulling the charm out of her pocket, but I stopped her. "Stick to the plan," I said. "Just like Sarah told you."

I swallowed, wondering for a second whether maybe it might be better for everyone if I just gave the necromancers what they wanted. What if our plan didn't work? What if they hurt my friends and it was my fault?

No, we could do this. The necromancers at the Alexandria Academy could go eat figs, because we were going to stop them. Together.

Since the teachers weren't supposed to ask about the experiments until *after* the deans were done, Mr. Fares tried to stop Ms. Najoom. He hurried after the gym teacher, but she turned and shoved him out of the courtyard with just one hand. Ms. Wassouf rushed to help Mr. Fares, but no one dared to get in Ms. Najoom's way after that.

The deans were too busy to notice our approaching gym teacher. Only when Ms. Najoom was a couple of feet away did some of our classmates see her muscular shadow drawing near.

Selma waved. "Hi, Ms. Naj—"

"Be quiet," she snapped, and the girl cowered.

Dean Abdullah was listening to the next group describe their robo-chicken, which they named Chick-Bot 1.0. It was meant to be a kinder, less evil version of the robo-rooster, and the presentation had been going on for a few minutes. All the deans were close, but still too far away to notice Ms. Najoom grab me without warning and shove me away from their sight.

I gasped, suddenly breathless, like I'd been hit by a bus. Hayati raised her fists while Sarah growled, but they didn't move. I didn't want them getting involved in this part. If I went down, I went down alone.

Ms. Najoom gritted her teeth. "Okay, time to read the last ingredient for our recipe."

Slowly, I raised my wrist to show her the bracelet, still

beeping. "Sorry, it's just this thing has me feeling so tired, I can barely talk."

"You *will* talk," she said.

"Wait, I must have forgotten your directions," I said, shrugging. "Could you remind me what I'm supposed to do? Does it involve you and your necromancer friends, the ones who have been secretly running the Academy for years?"

Ms. Najoom brought out a toothpick-shaped key and unhinged the bracelet on my wrist, letting the charm fall to the ground. She held up *The Alchemist's Hand* and said, "If I don't hear an ingredient in the next ten seconds, I'm going to tie you to an Instant Oasis and see how long you last underwater."

"Just like you put all those students asleep with the cake?" I asked.

"Of course, you little—"

"Serena Najoom!" snapped Dean Abdullah, interrupting us.

She and the other deans had gathered right behind us. My friends, the rest of our classmates, and all the other teachers and students were standing still. Everyone had gone silent. You could have heard a fart from across the courtyard.

"You wouldn't believe it," I said, grinning. "Those voice amplifiers are sneaky."

Rey hurried out from the audio room, where he had

snuck in and turned the amplifiers on for us. He came to stand by Sarah's side. It felt nice to have so many in the Alexandria Academy finally realizing that I wasn't faking. At least I thought that, until our gym teacher started laughing.

"You think you can outsmart me?" she asked, slowly walking forward. "Look at the final project, the one *my* own apprentice is standing by."

The gym teacher's hand stretched back to the last table across the courtyard, where Jad waved back at us. With a sinister smile, he slowly drew back a tarp. What he unveiled made me gasp. Giant vials simmered over a fire; pouches as large as my head, and measuring tools, were all laid out neatly. All the advanced tech and digital measuring devices looked like the setup I'd found in the dining hall kitchen, only this one had so much more.

Smoke billowed out of pipes that extended out of the sides of the vials. Ten years of planning, hard work, and research all leading to this moment. They had everything in order for tonight, when the moon shone bright and the winter solstice would reveal the original necromancer.

My heart stopping, I asked, "An alchemy lab?"

"Indeed," said Ms. Najoom. "You see, we had planned for this from the very moment we learned of your presence, Shad. We never really needed *The Alchemist's Hand*. Sure, it would have made our search *much* easier, but we always knew that if we left you to explore, you would help us discover it all on our own. And indeed, you did."

"B-but you attacked me!" I said, unable to believe they'd planned this for so long. That I let myself get fooled this way.

"Oh yes," she said. "But each time you thwarted our plans only assured us that you were the key to this whole operation. And after years of searching, the journal in your room finally revealed zaffer was what we needed. I will not deny that we are still searching for the exact measurements, but through trial and error, we have been able to get the mixture close enough. A smaller batch revived a mouse just this morning. And in mere minutes, a much larger elixir will be complete, ready to bring back our founder when their location is revealed tonight!"

My stomach flipped as Ms. Najoom threw her head back, laughing at my confusion. The charms in my room hadn't protected that old alchemist's journal I'd found in the underground garden, and now not only had I failed to keep the Revival Elixir recipe from the necromancers, but I'd led them to its last ingredient. The realization that the necromancers outsmarted me had me feeling sick.

Pointing at the clock tower, Ms. Najoom said, "Oh, and the best part is coming now."

Everyone, including me, glanced up. The giant clock read *12:58*.

"In two minutes, none of you will remember any of what Shad or I said," announced Ms. Najoom. She laughed again as the time changed. "Make that *one* minute."

All hope seemed lost, just as when she'd first threatened me in the gym. Only, this time I wasn't left to face Ms. Najoom alone. Turning to my friends, I remembered the *old* Shad. The one who never asked for help and always stood up to bullies. But now I knew to trust my friends, and I raised a hand to give them the signal.

Taking in a deep breath, I said, "Here goes nothing."

As soon as the bell chimed, my friends sprinted to different science fair teams, ready to protect our classmates with the alchemy charms and dusts that Sarah and I had been making ever since we reversed the effects of the Exhaustion Charm. Those decanters wouldn't be as powerful as the ones I could've crafted had I been able to access the underground garden, but they'd have do the trick. Meanwhile, I lunged and grabbed *The Alchemist's Hand* back from Ms. Najoom before she could react.

The bell stopped chiming with the deans—and everyone else around us—unaffected by any Forgetting Alchemy. After all, I'd flushed that charm down a toilet last night.

Dean Hayek pointed at Ms. Najoom and asked, "What's the meaning of this? You better have a good explanation, or I'll personally toss you out of the front gate myself."

Ms. Najoom ground her teeth and turned to me. "So, Shad, you've somehow gotten rid of our hidden secret? No matter—let us show you all just who holds the power in this school!"

The gym teacher reached into her pocket and uncapped a vial, releasing a dark mist that swallowed her. Black wisps reached out in all directions as she revealed her necromancer form. All around us, teachers in the crowd began to do the same. Mr. Boutros from Arabic class, Mrs. Mustafa, the advanced algebra teacher, and even Ziad, the school chef. So many faces I'd seen almost each day during my time here. And more necromancers continued to sprout out as darkness descended on the courtyard.

"Is that the gardener?" asked Sarah beside me. "*And* Ms. Warda, my biology teacher . . . are they all necromancers?"

Our classmates screamed and dispersed. My friends moved to help several first-years to safety, but another group of students circled the courtyard, blocking the exits. Some had just arrived on the scene wearing black robes rather than the Academy uniform. Others were fellow first-years like Jad and even Zara.

Ms. Wassouf tried grabbing one of the shadows, but she got a face full of green dust. All the teachers and students did, dropping unconscious from whatever the mixture was. With the science fair over, the courtyard in chaos, my friends and I prepared for a fight.

The school's shadowy alchemists had revealed their true forms.

Chapter 40

Ms. Najoom flung a fistful of green powder at me and Dean Abdullah as the battle for the Alexandria Academy erupted.

I pushed the dean away, believing we'd be safe, but another necromancer hit the woman with a mist that put her right to sleep.

As I stared in horror, Ms. Najoom yanked me back toward her. There was nothing I could do as the teacher's black tendrils wrapped around my waist, ankles, and neck. Long and powerful, Ms. Najoom's shadowy fingers pressed tight against me.

A sudden gust flung her off, the tendrils releasing me as I fell onto the ground. My hands sank into the dirt, Dean Abdullah still lying asleep beside me. Across the courtyard, necromancers were chasing students and teachers. Sarah wrestled with several bullies off to the side and I began to wonder if I'd doomed everyone.

"Come on," said a familiar voice that steadied my heartbeat. "Let's get you up...."

Hayati and Rey helped me onto my feet, both with dirt-stained faces. I smiled, glad to have them with me.

"Some of these alchemy things you made for us are really strong," said Rey, gripping a small jar of Wind Mist in a way that had me wanting to yell for him to be careful. "Feels like I just got payback for all the simulation dodgeballs to the face in Ms. Najoom's class."

Hayati snorted. "Yeah, you should have seen how she—"

Waves of black slammed into all of us, knocking me and my friends onto our backs. Necromancers surrounded us and I quickly rolled away from the dusts they threw. Rey and Hayati weren't so lucky, being knocked asleep before they realized Ms. Najoom was to blame. She hovered in the air now, the bottom half of her body a shadow. I backed away, reaching into my pocket as she darted in closer.

"No!" shouted a familiar voice. "Complete the mixture. He is mine to finish!"

A shadow emerged from out of the Academy wall, and it formed into the shape of a person. Tall, muscly, mustache-y...

Gasping, I stumbled away. "Dr. Salazar?"

"You thought you could so easily defeat me?" he asked, taking a giant step closer. "I ran this school before *you* showed up. I am the darkness, the shadow that all alchemists fear!"

The sight of our former dean made my heart beat a million miles a second. I stumbled back from both necromancers.

"You were not to reveal yourself until tonight," said Mr. Boutros, approaching Dr. Salazar.

Ms. Najoom drifted across the courtyard, lifting the steaming Revival Elixir, the orange mixture deeper and richer than the improvised version of the mixture I'd made for Teta. It carried a glow as though radioactive and she lifted it to her nose to inhale, grinning and setting it back down. "Lighten up, Boutros. We have completed our mission!"

"Yes, forget the plan," snapped Dr. Salazar. "The moon will soon rise and our ritual will begin right here where I stand, but we will *not* have the alchemist boy escape the Academy after humiliating us. Grab his book and kill him!"

"We need to get out of here," said Sarah, appearing by my side. "I can carry Rey if you take Hayati."

The voice amplifiers made it impossible for the necromancers not to overhear. Ms. Najoom charged at my friends and yelled, "Seize them!"

All the necromancers and their apprentices surrounded us. We couldn't go anywhere, couldn't fight them all, but we didn't have to. A sudden explosion shook the ground, stopping everyone in their tracks.

"No!"

Ms. Najoom screamed. The entire alchemy workstation was in flames. Stumbling away, the necromancers all stared in silence as the Revival Elixir vanished in the wreckage. They didn't have time to react because another burst sent them scattering, an explosion of dirt and grass from the opposite side of the courtyard.

Donny stepped out from behind his science experiment. He no longer appeared his same drowsy self. Instead, he wore a blue alchemy coat and held another Blast Charm, an alchemy more powerful than even my Destruction Dust.

He held up a busted bracelet like the one Ms. Najoom placed on me, and we both grinned at Ms. Najoom's surprise. He tossed the hunk of metal on the ground and said, "Thanks for spotting the Exhaustion Charm, Shad. Feels better to have it off my ankle. Now, let's see if I can still remember my mixtures after a few months out of practice."

I waved to my friend. For the longest time, I'd wondered what it was Donny had always been trying to say, and why he never stopped being so drowsy. After experiencing how Ms. Najoom's bracelet zapped me of my energy, I cornered my friend and caught a glimpse of the

Exhaustion Charm along his ankle. Once I removed it, he told me about being approached to be a necromancer apprentice. How when he refused to join, the necromancers placed the charm on him, just to be sure he wouldn't get in their way.

"You ruined everything," snapped Ms. Najoom. "Leave Shad. Kill the other boy!"

The necromancers hesitated. Donny's interruption didn't just save my friends and me, but completely turned the tide of this battle. I could feel their spirit sapped at seeing their Revival Elixir destroyed. Unless they had another lab, no one would be brought back to life today.

To make matters better, Dean Hayek swooped in. She didn't have an alchemy coat, or any charm to use, instead holding up the pointy end of one of her heels.

"I may not be whatever you all are," she said, snarling at the necromancer teachers, "but nobody lays a finger on my students!"

"We will see about that," said the gym teacher, lifting a vial full of green mist.

Before she could uncork it, something small and furry flew across the air. A monkey that kicked the vial right out of Ms. Najoom's hands, a burst of red filling the center of the courtyard.

"It's been too long since I've worn a belt like this," Moussa said as he picked up his monkey. Our librarian, donning a faded brown alchemy coat, beamed a smile and pointed at Ms. Najoom. "You, my dear, are about to be *history!*"

I could hardly contain my excitement as Moussa lunged at several alchemists. He vanished in a cloud of red before reappearing to sprinkle dust over the heads of Jad, Zara, and several of the bully apprentices, who stiffened up like statues and fell, unable to move.

"You kids fail my class!" he announced.

Moussa, the old and slightly cranky librarian, was in fact an old and slightly cranky *alchemist.* It all made sense after I'd found that journal in the underground garden. It had mentioned the teachers losing their alchemy, but that didn't mean they'd been replaced. No, they must have been here the whole time, stuck under the grasp of the bell's Forgetting Charm just like my classmates.

Not to mention, the initials of the teacher who'd written the journal entry were M. S. . . . Moussa Saud.

But the librarian wasn't the only alchemist to appear. More cherry-colored bursts of smoke sprang into existence all over as other teachers appeared, alchemists who'd forgotten who they were just like Donny. Necromancers leapt away from the familiar faces.

To the side, one of the teachers who'd appeared with Moussa sprinkled something over Mr. Fares. Our science fair coordinator rose and accepted an alchemy belt the teacher held out, glancing down to study it.

"I ... I remember now. I'm an alchemist!"

Hope welled in my chest. I patted Sarah's back and she turned to me, smiling. With the Revival Elixir destroyed and backup arriving, what once seemed like a desperate situation was coming around.

At least until Dr. Salazar curled into a cloud of black smoke, knocking into a group of teacher alchemists and sending them crashing into the hallway.

"Enough of this madness," he snapped. "We will not be defeated!"

Multicolored bursts filled the courtyard as the battle between necromancers and alchemists raged on. Moussa against Mr. Boutros, Donny against Ms. Najoom. I used the distraction to pull out a crumpled piece of paper from my backpack. A paper that held my secret weapon—an old-fashioned Hadid family stink bomb.

Sarah's eyes widened as I brought my arm up. "What are you planning to ... *oh.*"

Ms. Najoom sent Donny flying back with a fiery mist and stomped in our direction. The gym teacher held up her hands, alight with burning black flames. I grinned at my friend, placing it in Sarah's hand.

"I still remember the first time you used one of these on me," she said.

"Good, then you know what it can do. Just don't miss."

Sarah pulled back her arm, and she leaned forward and heaved my stink bomb, just as Ms. Najoom lunged.

Splat.

The charm smacked our gym teacher's forehead. All it took was a moment to work its alchemy as her face, and those of several necromancers by her side, went purple.

That stink bomb was stronger than anything I'd ever made. Anyone standing within feet of us, alchemists and necromancers alike, panicked as the worst smell in the world drifted into their nostrils. Ms. Najoom took two more steps toward us before thudding onto the grass. Even her bulging muscles couldn't beat that stench.

All around us, decanters flew to block dusts, charms warded off other charms, and black smoke clashed with the red as teachers who'd been friends just an hour ago now fought for the fate of our school.

I bent to check on Rey and Hayati. They sounded fine, aside from the loud snoring. Of my science fair group, only Sarah remained, holding an arm over her nose from the recent stink bomb. She shoved Dean Saba, who'd been standing in stunned silence toward the nearest hallway, and watched him run away. Not everyone on the teaching staff had been an alchemist or necromancer. Some were just normal people, caught in the middle of an ancient struggle.

Scrunching her forehead, Sarah pointed behind me. "What's going on over there?"

I turned my gaze and froze. A new cloud of black smoke appeared, slowly transforming back into its true mustached self, which, to me, looked far more terrifying than its shadow form.

"Salazar!" I screamed.

Dr. Salazar laughed before turning back into a shadow that headed straight for us. I took Sarah's hand and we darted out of the courtyard, through shelves and shelves of dusty books, toward the dining hall.

Dr. Salazar returned to his physical form, stomping after us with ground-shaking force. The flap of his black alchemy coat drifted behind like a lingering part of his shadow. My breathing grew heavy after only a few steps.

"You somehow managed to sabotage our plans," he shouted. "But even if we are not fated to revive our order's founder, I *will* have my revenge. Should I turn you into a little mouse and feed you to my pet snakes, or maybe tie you to the bell and watch as you melt in the sun?"

Any remaining students, teachers, or other Academy workers who hadn't been at the science fair now leapt out of our way. Several thudding noises jolted me. When I turned, Salazar was hurling Sleeping Dust into the faces of each person we passed. Then he reached into another pocket and hurled a charm at us.

It missed, but splattered on the dining hall door ahead, which suddenly transformed into a flat wall.

"What's going on?" asked Sarah, pounding the space where the door had been.

Dr. Salazar closed in on us, his smile curling wider

and wider. I had no time to explain the Walling Charm to Sarah. Pressing my hands against the barrier, I felt around for where the door should be.

"Here!"

My fingers closed around a handle hidden by Illusion Alchemy. I swung open the large doors, and Sarah and I hurried into the dining hall and shut it, turning the lock, and–

The door burst open and threw us each into one of the tables. Luckily, I landed on a pile of butt cushions, though I'd busted my knee in the impact. While getting up, Salazar stormed in, wisps of black smoke circling around to give him a half-human and half-shadow look. He reached into his coat and yanked out a pouch.

"Finally," he said. "Now I can finish what I started back in Portland."

Chapter 41

"*Before I turn you both* into dust," he said, "I have a gift for *you*, Mr. Hadid."

Dr. Salazar threw down the contents of the pouch and vanished in a cloud of black smoke, reappearing by the kitchen door. A sudden screeching noise caused my ears to ache. Salazar dragged out a chair that seated none other than Kahem. My alchemy teacher's hands and feet were bound with rope so he couldn't move, and the tape around his mouth prevented him from speaking. Then Salazar reached back into the kitchen, drawing out a caged Yolla.

My heart stopped. Kahem glared at me behind furrowed brows, struggling against the rope. Meanwhile, Salazar turned to Sarah.

"I like you," he told her. "It's such a shame that Shad snuck you into the Academy. I might have taken you on as an apprentice in Portland."

Sarah suddenly tensed up. "Snuck me in?"

Dr. Salazar laughed. "Oh, Shad did not tell you? You were only brought here by accident. Never in a million years would the snotty alchemists invite *you* to come study at their school."

Sarah's legs began to shake. "Shad, is this guy telling the truth?"

In the split second that Sarah turned to look at me, Dr. Salazar sprang forward, quicker than a cheetah with rockets for feet.

I dove away, but Sarah didn't move. She was one of the biggest kids in our class, but he easily wrapped her in his arms. Even as she kicked and squeezed, it was hopeless. He only smiled wider as she fought.

"Yes, the boy lied to you," said Dr. Salazar, "but I can show you the truth. You see, other students here will never accept you, but you are welcome with me. Shad has been keeping his alchemy to himself. I will teach you to be a true alchemist, and you will help us restore glory to this fine institution."

Sarah stopped fighting. She was really listening to Dr. Salazar and his lies. It was all my fault. I should have told her about the invitation. Deep down, all she wanted was to fit in, and now I'd broken her trust.

"I'm sorry," I said. "But you can't believe him. Salazar will pin the blame on you to whoever he's working for, or worse!"

The necromancer laughed. "See how scared Shad is?

He doesn't want anyone else to learn the truth."

"You lied to me," said Sarah. "I thought we were friends, Shad, but you lied."

I shook my head, tears welling in my eyes. "No, I might have kept some of my secrets from you, but never alchemy. I tried to share that with everyone!"

"You kept the biggest secret of them all," said Sarah, straining to pull something out of both her pockets. "When you told me about necromancers, you never said they were so stupid!"

My friend held what was left of the Destruction Dust, and she let it fall onto the floor beneath her. I hadn't realized she'd kept it, and I lunged to stop her as she leaned her head back and spat into the dust, triggering an explosion that sent me flying into a bookshelf of thick cookbooks across the dining hall.

I started coughing, and I rolled onto my belly to get up. The smoke slowly cleared. All the tables near the explosion were blown to smithereens. Dr. Salazar was back against the dining hall door. Ash and soot covered his face, and his mustache had been burned away.

"Forgive me," he groaned, eyes rolling back in his head. "I have failed you, my teacher . . ."

He tipped sideways, cheeks thudding against the floor, unconscious. It all didn't seem real. Sarah had done it. She'd beaten Dr. Salazar. We'd stopped the necromancers, but . . . she was gone.

Tears rolling down my face, I crawled back to where she'd been, searching for my friend. "Sarah," I said between coughs. "Sarah, where are you?"

There was no sign of her. She'd sacrificed herself to save me, and now she was dead. I slammed my fists on my knees and buried my head on one of the carpets, letting out a scream. Even if we'd beaten the necromancers, none of it was worth losing my friend.

"Alchemists do not give up!" snapped a familiar voice.

I twisted toward Kahem. His hands and feet were still bound, but he'd chewed through the rope around his mouth. Beside him, Sarah crawled toward Yolla's cage, the cat licking at my friend's soot-covered face through the bars.

"Sarah, you're alive!" I shouted. "Are you hurt?"

She lifted her arm to inspect a few scratches. "I could use a Band-Aid or two, but I think I'll be all right."

"I'll take care of it with a simple Healing Mist," said Kahem. "Now, someone please untie me."

I stood up, wincing at the pain in one of my legs as I limped back to my teacher and wrapped him in a tight hug. While I began to work on the rope, I had a hundred questions. Maybe more. But when I started asking them, he shushed me.

"Quick, turn around," he said sharply, though I hadn't finished untying him. "Take Dr. Salazar's alchemist's belt and adjust it to fit you. We have company."

The dining hall door creaked open and in came the last person I expected to see right then—Yakoub.

Dean Saba followed my stepbrother. They marched in, both wearing black alchemy coats like Dr. Salazar. Of course Yakoub was one of the necromancer apprentices. It only made sense. How had I not figured it out earlier?

"So, we finally meet the evil mind behind this conspiracy," said Kahem, struggling against the rope bindings.

"I'm afraid our meeting will not last long," answered Dean Saba. His high-pitched squeal changed as his voice grew deeper and strangely familiar. He sounded like the person Ms. Najoom was talking to in the halls last night. "Ten years have passed since I have revealed my true self to the outside world. I cannot deny that I am surprised our plan was foiled by your apprentice, Kahem, but now I will brew the Revival Elixir myself. Once I witness both of your deaths, that is."

Kahem twisted his neck to glare at me. It seemed like he was trying to get me to hurry while I undid Salazar's alchemy belt and wrapped it around my waist. I could tell this belt had the same standard layout as Kahem's, grouped by vials to one side and pouches on the other.

"So," Kahem finally said, "are you going to keep rambling, or should my apprentice and I finish you off?"

Dean Saba chuckled, and he pulled out a pouch from

his black coat, sprinkling dust over himself as his face and body transformed. Holding both hands to my mouth, I could hardly believe that Dean Saba had been acting this whole time. I gasped as his Disguise Alchemy melted away, revealing his true identity: a tall and thin frame, big round glasses, and a beard trimmed neatly to show the sharp edges of his face.

My heart skipped a beat. I couldn't move. Couldn't think straight.

"Are you happy?" asked my stepfather. "For years, my alchemists and I have worked tirelessly to combine our ancient traditions with modern technologies using some of the world's brightest minds. All while searching around the clock in pursuit of a Revival Alchemy that truly works. Yet you, Kahem, have sent your apprentice to ruin our plans!"

"If only you used that new technology for good rather than to advance your own selfish goals," said Kahem. "Besides, the kids discovered your secret scheme on their own. I couldn't be prouder of my apprentice."

"What could be a more noble purpose for alchemy than curing death?" questioned my stepfather. "An immortality elixir would change the world!"

"No, it would ruin it," Kahem said. "Humans, like all other living creatures, are meant to die. It is a natural part of life. Tipping that balance threatens *everything*, and for that reason, we will stop you from unleashing the original necromancer, whether I'm tied up or not."

"Quiet!" snapped my stepfather. Turning to me with a chilling stare, he said, "For your mother's sake, I sent that worthless Salazar to offer you a chance to join us, but now both of you will die. It will be a pleasure watching my apprentice dispose of you right in front of your alchemy teacher. A shame you will not be here when we finally open the door to eternal life."

Yakoub stood in place. He didn't appear as excited to attack me now as he normally did until my stepfather nodded him forward.

"Go on, son. Do not disappoint me. . . ."

Yakoub bowed his head and when he glanced up, he eyed me with a hateful stare that caught me by surprise. My stepfather was a real jerk, sure, but I never expected that he'd really want me hurt. That made me angry at Mama, who'd fallen for someone so unlike my loving baba.

Kahem shook his head. "No, this is between us. You and I will battle, Elias, and we will—"

"Let's do this," I said, wrapping the alchemy belt around my waist.

My stepfather had already begun to draw ingredients out of his alchemy belt, setting them along one of the dining tables. My eyes widened as I counted off a total of five pouches and vials, the exact number of ingredients necessary for the elixir. He must've prepared for having to brew it himself.

Meanwhile, Yakoub stepped forward. I locked eyes with my stepbrother as we moved to the center of the dining hall. I wasn't going to back down. Not this time. Sarah and all my friends had put themselves in harm's way for me; Kahem remained a hostage; the fate of the Alexandria Academy hung in the balance. Not to mention, my stepfather would soon have the Revival Elixir in time for the solstice if I didn't stop him.

Reaching into my alchemist's belt, I said, "Bring it on, you figs."

Chapter 42

Yakoub attacked first. Combining spices and oils, he flung the mixture at my face from across the hall. "How about Nightmare Dust!"

"The only one having nightmares will be you!" I said, countering with a decanter made of sulfur and zinc.

I could barely keep track of the ingredients across Dr. Salazar's belt, but my recipes were working. I grabbed two pinches of salt, a vial of garlic extract, and copper powder. Mixing them together in my palm, I flung a potent Coughing Dust.

Yakoub gagged as it entered his throat, but no coughing. The thing about doing alchemy on the fly, without flasks and lab equipment, is that it's hard to mix the ingredients just right. Only the best alchemists could do it and, since I wasn't one of them, my mixtures wouldn't always work.

Up above, the sun was beginning to set, inviting darkness into the hall as my stepfather continued to brew the forbidden elixir while Yakoub came closer and closer. Soon the moon would be up, and if I didn't stop them, the necromancers would be back on track to find their founder's tomb and revive them.

"You can try to run," Yakoub said, shining his devilish grin. "No matter where you go, I'll always catch you, little brother. *Always.*"

"I am not your brother!" I shouted with all the breath I had. "Sarah is more like family to me than you. At least she tries to be better. All you care about is looking good in front of your fig-headed dad. You ruined everything in Lebanon, and you've tried to ruin everything here, but I'm going to stop you."

Yakoub shouted in anger, closing in on me. He was quicker and had more ingredients in his belt. Mixing the last of what I had, I pretended to hurl something and faked him out. He threw up a decanter and I waited until his Protective Alchemy faded. That was when I *really* hurled the Blinding Dust in my hand.

"My eyes!" screamed Yakoub, the dust finding its mark. "That was a dirty move!"

My stepbrother lunged, barely able to see. I flung my body out of the way, narrowly escaping while he clawed at the air. Kahem shouted at me to run while my stepfather urged Yakoub to grab me. I scrambled into the kitchen, where, right away, I felt at home. Nothing remained in the pouches of my belt, but here I had ovens, cutting boards, and, oh yeah baby, all the baking ingredients I could ask for.

Yakoub stumbled through the doors a few seconds later. His eyes were now red and teary, but he was still smiling confidently. I shivered but didn't back off.

"Nice move," he said. "You really are a trickster."

"You always bullied me," I said, stalling as I stuffed my alchemy belt with spices, salts, and oils. "Now I'll show you why you should be nice to your siblings. Why you shouldn't be such a kabees all the time."

Yakoub laughed, moving toward me, but when he was just steps away, I unleashed a Confusion Charm I'd quickly put together.

Or at least I tried. Yakoub lunged and grabbed my arm. I couldn't move my hands and the charm plopped to the ground. He twisted my arm around my back and wrapped his other one around my neck to choke me.

He leaned into my ear and said, "You see, brother, I can do whatever I want because I'm stronger, faster, *and* smarter, like my baba. That's why Mama chose him over your pathetic dad."

Having Yakoub literally squeezing me to death made it hard to concentrate, especially with his awful words. Yakoub was too strong for me to break free. I was about to let Kahem, my friends, and my classmates down.

"Even if you are one of the weakest alchemists on the planet," he said, "I will give you one more chance to join us, Shad."

Resisting his grip, I gasped, "Never!"

"Why don't you ask your teta to save you now?" he laughed.

I could feel my body weakening, but I wasn't scared. Kahem always said the right ingredients were what mattered and that I couldn't break his first rule of alchemy.

But Teta taught me to be *different*. She trained me not to rely on the ingredients like Yakoub and his stepfather did. *The Alchemist's Hand* wasn't her most important gift. No, it was the lesson that a recipe sometimes called for new ingredients and a bit of imagination. The kind of creativity that could combine baking and alchemy together.

With my one free hand, I quietly mixed a few pinches of vinegar, flour, and, substituting for sugar, I squirted some honey into the concoction. As soon as the first drop of sticky bee sugar touched the mixture, the entire table started to rise into a mist, and not just any ordinary one—Diarrhea Mist.

Yakoub dug an elbow into my back. "What, nothing to say?"

I twisted around as far as I could and tried to look him in his eyes. "Maybe Mama really did choose your family," I said, waving the mist around with my free hand, bringing it up higher and higher. "But alchemy chose mine!"

I brought my palm up and threw the mist right up Yakoub's nostrils. I heard his belly grumbling as the alchemy worked into my stepbrother's body. His arm loosened, and then he let go completely.

My entire body had gone numb. Although I didn't feel the floor shake, I heard Yakoub crash onto pots and pans. He was trying to get up, gripping his cramping stomach. I climbed up onto the kitchen table. Suddenly, I wasn't an alchemist, or even the baker, but a wrestler.

"Hadid Head Crusher!" I shouted, and belly-flopped right over Yakoub.

My stepbrother gasped and then slumped back. Easing off him, I couldn't tell whether it was the alchemy or my wrestling move, but Yakoub's eyes had closed. I'd knocked the boy out cold.

I limped to the kitchen door.

My stepfather stood over a new bubbling orange mixture. The Revival Elixir appeared all but complete. I wondered how many tries it had taken him without knowing the right measurements, but that didn't matter anymore. Soon, we wouldn't be able to stop him or the person he'd meant to revive—the keeper of the Elixir of Immortality.

Meanwhile, Kahem remained in his bindings and Sarah lay against Yolla's cage. Both widened their eyes as I approached.

"Where's Yakoub?" demanded my stepfather. "Could you truly have beaten my apprentice?"

"Check for yourself," I gasped, still a bit out of breath.

He didn't seem worried by the news, only sighing as he said, "No matter. I will deal with him once I've finished my—*no!*"

The sight of me drawing my arm back must have worried him. Clenching a vial taken from Yakoub, I readied to throw as the necromancer's hands went up.

But my stepfather had gotten my intentions wrong. There was no way I'd stop him like this. Not alone. Instead, I twisted and heaved a vial across the dining hall toward Sarah, who managed to reach up and snatch the glass vial out of the air.

"Use it for the rope," I shouted. "That and the cage!"

My friend uncorked the Melting Mist, wafting it toward Kahem's bindings and the iron bars entrapping Yolla, both burning away like paper over a fire. Now I didn't have to face my stepfather alone.

"It's over, Elias."

Kahem rose to full height, towering with a seriousness that had me shaking. Only, my stepfather stepped forward to meet us, unnerved. I locked eyes with my alchemy teacher. Then we both charged.

Everything happened in an instant. A wave of power sent me flying back into a table, pain lancing up my spine, but not before I tossed my belt to Kahem. My alchemy teacher didn't fall quite so easily, dueling my stepfather as the floor shook, the lights rattling. I wondered if their battle might cause the entire school to collapse, but Kahem didn't have the ingredients to keep up. My stepfather sent him soaring into a bookshelf, and then did the same to Yolla when she tried to attack, laughing until he realized we were just a distraction.

"Spill the mixture, Sarah!"

At my order, she rose to stand over the table, having crawled across the dining hall. It was like watching Donny blow up the alchemy lab in the courtyard all over again. This time, Elias Monsour watched all his work tip over onto the floor as Sarah used whatever bit of strength she had left to knock the vial off its support, glass shattering everywhere. She quickly backed away toward a fallen Kahem.

My stepfather's eyes were wide with rage while he stood over the failed mixture. "You have ruined everything!"

The way the true leader of the necromancers looked at me now, the anger in his eyes, had me trembling. He stomped straight for me as I rose to meet him. With nothing to defend myself, I raised my fists, at which fire sprang from his fingertips.

"I did not kill your father," he said. "Yet letting your mother convince me to spare him was a decision I regret, and I will not make the same mistake twice!"

Nothing I could do would stop the attack. I winced, ready for the end, but Kahem burst from a cloud of red just before my stepfather could finish me off. Standing just behind the most powerful necromancer I'd met, my alchemy teacher curled a mist around both of his fingertips.

"Make one move and it will be *me* finishing *you* off," said Kahem.

Elias Monsour sneered. "Perhaps your mother would like to hear from you," he said. "If only she weren't under the effects of my Forgetting Charm."

I gasped. "What do you mean?"

My stepfather barreled through the kitchen door and I went to follow, but Kahem grabbed my shoulder, stopping me before I could dart after him. "It is a trap. He means to draw you in!"

Just then, a loud and thundering noise jolted us. Light flashed through the kitchen window. Hurrying toward it, I found both Yakoub and my stepfather gone.

My chest ached from the questions swimming through my head. Most were about Mama and what the necromancers had done to her. Elias Monsour was big wad of pure evil, but using a Forgetting Charm on the person you love sounded so wrong.

But it made me realize that I'd abandoned her. A part of me had resented her all these years, and it made my heart heavy with guilt as I buried my head in my hands, new tears streaming down.

Kahem dispelled the mist and hurried to a nearby table to grab his gear. When he reached into one of the pouches of his coat, I expected some Healing Mist for Sarah or a Recovery Charm for me, but instead he tossed some cat food onto the floor for Yolla.

I limped toward him and the fluffy orange cat. Kahem began tending to the burn on Sarah's shoulder, and I smiled to see them both doing okay.

"How did you survive that explosion?"

Sarah slowly reached into her pocket and drew something out. My heartbeat stilled and I saw the last bead from Baba's charm, the very one I'd stashed in her jacket. As she held it up for us, the wood began to wither and fade away, vanishing before our eyes.

"Thank you," she said, her voice hoarse.

Kahem placed a hand on my shoulder. "Well done, my young apprentice. For protecting your friend, but also for how you handled the duel. I saw you through the door. You used honey in the place of sugar . . . it was brilliant."

"Yeah, sorry about that," I said.

Kahem knelt to face me. "You have a gift, Shad. Being able to create an actual mixture without the set ingredients means you have a special grasp of alchemy. I have never met someone who can do what you do, not even myself. That is why your Revival Alchemy worked all those months ago. Why you were able to beat an advanced necromancer like Yakoub all on your own."

"Too bad he and my stepfather escaped," I said, sulking.

Looking around, I saw that Yakoub and I had basically destroyed anything that wasn't already blown up from the Destruction Dust. Dr. Salazar was still lying by the dining hall door, his chest rising and sinking, but the guy was as unconscious as my stepbrother had been.

After Kahem made sure Sarah was healing okay, he went over to stand by the fallen necromancer.

"They are indeed still out there," said Kahem. "While I doubt they will wait another ten years to attempt this revival once more, the school will remain safe for now. You have restored the alchemists of Alexandria to their rightful place."

"And what about—"

"Your mother?" he said, reading my thoughts. "We *will* get her back. For now, go have a well-deserved nap and don't worry about any punishments. I have a hunch that the deans will be quite forgiving, especially to the Academy's heroes."

"Wait, what about *The Alchemist's Hand*?" I asked, drawing out the guidebook and offering it up. "Both Ms. Najoom and my stepfather mentioned not yet having the right measurements for the Revival Elixir, so the necromancers are going to need it now more than ever. Maybe it's best you took it for safekeeping."

Leaning his head back, Kahem laughed, his thundering voice bouncing off the walls of the vast dining hall. He shoved *The Alchemist's Hand* at me and I nearly fumbled Baba's book. Grasping it tight, I could see his eyes were glossy.

"A-are you okay?"

Kahem smiled. "This book is safer in your hands, boy. Besides, what am I going to do with a book I can't read? You make me a proud teacher, and I'll be seeing you again as soon as Yolla and I make sure this necromancer is brought to a prison fit for his crimes."

"Like, a normal prison?" I asked, unsure if that could contain someone as crafty as Salazar.

My alchemy teacher shook his head. "There are a few hidden spaces in the alchemy world that are still maintained by those who respect the old ways, charmed to keep necromancers and other evil alchemists from breaking free. They are run by volunteers like me. When I have the time, that is."

Before I could react to news about these secret alchemy jails, Kahem reached for his belt and tossed dust onto the ground. One last explosion shook the floor as I waved off the red smoke. Once the air in the hall had cleared, Kahem, Yolla, and Salazar were gone.

After a quick side-to-side glance, I pumped a fist in the air and shook my butt. "He said I made him proud. That's right, Shad's the best alchemist ever."

But my victory dance didn't last long as something else crossed my mind. Well, not something, but some*one*—Mama. Just thinking of her being trapped with my stepfamily, a Forgetting Charm making her my step-father's prisoner . . . it turned my stomach.

What if I couldn't save her? Worse, what if she didn't want to be saved? After being around my stepfather for so long, maybe she'd become a necromancer too.

Sarah limped over to my side. "We beat them, Shad."

I wrapped an arm around her shoulder and said, "For now. My stepfather won't give up, so he'll be back to try to finish what the necromancers started. But today, we kicked their cannolis right out of the Alexandria Academy!"

She coughed, whispering, "Serves them right. Never mess with the bully and the baker."

"You mean the *brains* and the baker," I corrected her as she broke into the widest smile.

Chapter 43

*H*urrying *down the hall to* the science department, I wondered if I'd ever get the hang of my schedule. Almost a week had gone by since expelling the necromancers from the Alexandria Academy, and I still couldn't remember what classes I had this morning.

Passing shelves and shelves of books, I slowed to a stride as I entered through an open door where Ms. Wassouf and the rest of my classmates sat waiting.

"Late on the last day before winter break," said my teacher, shaking her head, although one side of her lips had notched up in a smile. "Why am I not surprised, Shad? We're on page twenty-two of the new textbook."

I maneuvered through the classroom, waving at students like Selma as I passed. Students I could now call friends.

In the seat next to mine, Donny reached out for a fist bump. Normally, he'd be snoring up a storm by now, but my new alchemist friend saved his sleep for nighttime these days. It turned out his family ran an alchemy shop back in Chicago, and his aunt was a friend of Kahem's. Even though Donny wasn't affected by the Exhaustion Charm anymore, he tended to practice mostly sleep-focused alchemy, stuff like Calming Elixirs and Dream Charms.

While Ms. Wassouf taught us about photo-sentences, or whatever they call it when plants eat sunlight, my alchemy-loving brain told me to go for my guidebook. Still, it was hard to think about *The Alchemist's Hand* and not consider the lengths I'd gone to to protect it. How it had almost cost me everything.

Luckily, although the necromancers still needed it to get the Revival Elixir's exact measurements, they were no longer a threat at this school. Kahem and the other alchemist teachers made sure that Dr. Salazar, Ms. Najoom, and all their accomplices were brought to that hidden jail.

I still wondered about the winter solstice, and how I'd never noticed a sign that hinted at where the original necromancer was buried. Maybe I'd looked for the wrong thing, but no one I asked seemed to have noticed anything out of the ordinary either.

Yet as much as I wanted to continue thinking about alchemy or to run my fingers across the green cover of my family's old guidebook, I held off. Seeing how well our science fair project worked with my Destruction Dust made me realize that maybe this science stuff could be as fun as all my friends thought. After all, the Academy wasn't going to stop being a school for math and science, so why not beat the necromancers at their own game and use all the bright ideas my classmates had to make the world better?

Ding, ding, ding!

At the chime of the *new* bell, all the students hurried past me. I got up from my desk to follow when Ms. Wassouf's hand stopped me on the way out.

"Hold on, Shad." She started tapping on her tablet to erase the notes from the wall display. "I wanted to ask you something."

I swallowed, expecting a scolding for being late, and a punishment to come after. Instead, she just smiled. "Moussa and many of the other teachers were talking about restoring the Academy to the way it was . . . you know, *before* the necromancers. Our problem is that, after ten years without practice, they are a bit rusty when it comes to alchemy. We're working on hiring some new alchemists to come help with that. In the meantime, would you like to design a lab session or two? Something that can combine alchemy with science lessons."

I scratched my head. "You want *me* to help with a science lab? I don't even know the scientific method."

Ms. Wassouf laughed, smiling as she said, "I can lend a hand with that part."

"Then it would be an honor," I said, smiling back.

The thought of helping to truly restore alchemy to the Alexandria Academy felt like a dream. When I'd first come here, no one even knew what alchemy was. Now all the students at the school were eager to practice.

I waved goodbye to Ms. Wassouf and hurried to the dining hall, where I passed a group of older students reprogramming the robo-roosters in one of the courtyards. The deans, both the old ones and Saba's and Ibrahim's replacements, had decided the roosters should be less mean, like the Chickbots from the science fair. Still, those red eyes would always give me the creeps.

The dining hall doors slid open automatically as I stepped into a large, remodeled room. Butterflies fluttered in my stomach as all the eyes in the hall seemed to look directly at me.

The baking and cooking bookshelves on either side had remained, and everyone still ate on the floor, only now there were several long tables at the center of the hall instead of many smaller ones. Bringing more students together was one of Dean Abdullah's new goals. And, as one of the few non-alchemist administrators, she also vowed to keep out necromancers so that *everyone* could feel safe, alchemist or not.

Teachers crowded a table on the outskirts. Moussa sat there in his brown alchemy coat, the monkey taking the space beside him. As I passed by the first of the student tables, some of my former bullies were setting their food down. At least they weren't the ones who'd worked with the necromancers. Those ones were expelled.

Still, these classmates didn't hide their mean stares as I lifted a hand, waved, and said, "Wonderful day we're having, right, friends?"

One of them made a growling noise, while the others ignored me. Meanwhile, at another table, Herman tried to convince a classmate that his parents really did own a yacht, and I tuned that conversation out too.

My friends were sitting at the last table, passing plates around and stuffing their faces silly. I found an open seat right in front of a glorious bowl of tabbouleh salad and two trays packed with falafel. Walnut baklava lingered within arm's reach. The sight was so beautiful, my eyes wanted to water almost as bad as my mouth did.

"Did you hear about the latest WrestleFest?" asked Rey as I adjusted my seat closer to the table. "Ms. Laham, the new gym teacher, was telling me all about it. She's a fan too!"

I filled my plate with hummus and carrots before moving on to the tabbouleh. "Didn't that new wrestler beat the Sultan? What was her name . . ."

"Cairo Caterina," he said proudly, adjusting a brand-new beanie. On it, Rey's new favorite wrestler flexed with an Egyptian flag outfit.

I didn't say that I hoped the Sultan would win back his championship belt. Enough fights had taken place in the dining hall lately, and I preferred the peace, when I could stuff my face like everyone else. Meanwhile, Hayati and Donny were arguing from several seats away about a group project. She flicked his nose, making him turn red in anger. While Donny called her several not-so-nice things in Arabic, Hayati interrupted to correct his grammar.

A pea hit my face and I grabbed the bowl of falafel, ready for another food fight, but then I saw it was Sarah. She had a full plate herself, though her focus was clearly more on me than the food.

"Know what you're doing for winter break?" she asked. "Dean Abdullah let me call my parents, and they're fine with you staying over."

I threw the pea back. "Don't know yet, but I'll ask Kahem. He's still sorting stuff with his old bakery, but I remember he said that he'd be at Alexandria Town to collect some supplies tomorrow."

"Sweet," she said. "I'm itching for another lesson. I'm working on this new prank and need a way to make someone vomit."

I dropped my fork. After everything, I'd thought we were past this. Yet Sarah looked down at the fork and exploded into laughter. My other friends joined in too,

Rey slapping his knee, telling Sarah she'd got me good.

"I'm kidding! Dude, you should've seen your face!" said Sarah.

"Oh, put a fig in it," I said, but couldn't help but laugh too.

While we stuffed our bellies and got ready for school break, my gaze lifted toward the glass dome. Stars peeked back down, bright as ever. But the brightest one sat right in the middle, just where it was every night when I tilted my head to the sky.

"You were right," I whispered to the stars, to Teta. "Friends are pretty great. And you can tell Baba and everyone else up there not to worry. I'm going to free Mama of that Forgetting Charm and stop the necromancers from getting immortality. You'll see—Shad Hadid is going to be the best alchemist there ever was."

Acknowledgments

Like Teta tells Shad at the beginning of this story, we cannot face the world alone. Similarly, I couldn't have written this book by myself. Please bear with me while I sing the praises of all the talented alchemists who crafted charms and mists to help me get this book into your hands...

First and foremost, I must credit Jennifer Azantian and Megan Ilnitzki, my agent and editor, respectively. Book publishing is a business and you wouldn't believe how complex and political it can be. These two are about as good as it gets in this industry, and I'm blessed with their infinite wisdom and patience. Not to mention, they are unbelievable editors. Similarly, the rest of the team at HarperCollins deserves a round of applause. Thank you to Erin Hamling, Molly Fehr, Anabelle Sinoff, Parrish Turner, Delaney Heisterkamp, Robby Imfeld, and Anna Ravanelle. We did this together and I would shower you all in Arabic sweets if I could.

If you were as awestricken by the cover as I was, please give Khadijah Khatib all the love. As far as cover artists go, she is in a league of her own.

A big shout out to Adrianna Cuevas and Sarah Kapit. These two mentors are everything a young, budding writer could ever want. We bonded over fart jokes, heartfelt moments, and our mutual love of writing books that can make readers believe in themselves. I'm truly thankful for you two.

Of course, when any writer sets off to write a novel, it is important that they are surrounded by like-minded dreamers. These are individuals who have read my work, and who have given my characters and me room to grow and blossom. I will surely miss many, but thank you to Long Quan Nguyen, Peter Lopez, Kate Robertson, Sami Ellis, Sabrina Prestes, Stuart White, Jess Creaden, Bethany Hensel, and Naz Kutub. Thank you to Ben Baxter for awesome edits on my work alongside Jen. And, of course, thank you to Boston-based friends Rob Vlock, Susan Tan, and Tui T. Sutherland.

Chelsea Abdullah, it is an honor to be counted among your friends. I can't wait to see the wondrous things you do, both within the pages of a book and outside of them.

Jamar J. Perry, your friendship and encouragement will always be appreciated. You write with purpose and your words are a blessing to children everywhere. Long live Cameron Battle!

Carlton Galligan, if you ever read this, thank you for showing a young, overconfident high schooler what it meant to live by their values. I count myself extremely lucky to have you as a teacher and friend. Srini Sitaraman, you helped me get through college, and for that you also have my endless gratitude. I only ever took one creative writing course, and I'm glad I took it with Vicki Stiefel.

To all those who have called me a mentor and trusted me with their words, it has been a tremendous honor. I will continue to serve the writing community so long as I can string sentences together.

Hannah Vilas, you're my muse. You are also clearly an excellent photographer, as evidenced by my author photo. I'm so excited to be on this journey called life with you by my side.

My family is everything, I give them all my heart for they have given me that and more. When anyone asks where the character of Shad came from, I tell them that he is a snapshot of who I was at twelve. But that isn't fair. In truth, he is the sum of my father's tenderness and my mother's fearlessness, as am I. Yolla and Toufic, you are the best mom and dad I could've ever asked for.

Catherine, Anthony, Eliana . . . you put up with me and my many shortcomings, which makes you the real heroes. I couldn't have asked for better siblings, even if we argue sometimes (usually, it's my fault). I love you three unconditionally.

To my real life and Tetas and Jiduhs and the rest of my supportive extended family, you all have a special place in my heart. Storytelling is a rich tradition in our culture, and one that may have been lost to me without you.

Sushi, you are the goodest mini-labradoodle in the whole world.

And, of course, to *you*, my reader. Whether you purchased my book, checked it out from the library, or bartered for it in one of the hidden alchemy markets, I owe you everything.